Praise for the Low Country Dog Walker Series

"Low Country Dog Walker series offers a protagonist with substance, heart and personality."

—Cynthia Smith, Netgalley Reviewer

"Heartwarming."

—Janet Graham, Goodreads

"An excellent and engrossing cozy mystery."

—Annarella, Goodreads

"Brimming with Southern charm."

—Breda Arnold, NetGalley Reviewer

Books by Jackie Layton

The Low Country Dog Walker Series

Bite the Dust

Dog-Gone Dead

Dog-Gone Dead

A Low Country Dog Walker Mystery: Book Two

by

Jackie Layton

Gillian,
I hope you
enjoy this book. I
look forward to one
day reading your books.
Feel free to reach out
to me anytime.
Love,
Jackie Layton

Bell Bridge Books

Bell Bridge Books
PO BOX 300921
Memphis, TN 38130
Print ISBN: 978-1-61194-988-9

Bell Bridge Books is an Imprint of BelleBooks, Inc.

We at BelleBooks enjoy hearing from readers.
Visit our websites
BelleBooks.com
BellBridgeBooks.com
ImaJinnBooks.com

10 9 8 7 6 5 4 3 2 1

Cover design: Debra Dixon
Interior design: Hank Smith
Photo/Art credits:
VW Bug (manipulated) - © Zobeedy | Dreamstime.com
Shovel (manipulated) - © Dmytro Nedvyga | Dreamstime.com

:Lgdd:01:

Dedication

Dedicated to Nancy and Dick Lutz, who raised me to stand strong and not give up.

I love you both!

Chapter One

A YELLOW VOLKSWAGEN Beetle with white daisy decals barreled toward us, racing at a ridiculous speed on the narrow entrance road of Richard Rice Plantation. The car never slowed or swerved back to the other side of the lane. With my heart pounding, I jerked the steering wheel then slammed on the brakes.

My best friend Juliet Reed screamed from the passenger seat of the landscaping pickup truck I drove. Her hands flew forward as if to clutch the dashboard and brace her body, but the seat belt had her pinned.

From the back seat, my German shepherd barked.

"It's okay, Sunny." I fought for control, but we slid off the road and into the sandy grass under an ancient oak, missing the massive trunk by inches.

The VW whizzed past us.

White-knuckling the steering wheel, I glanced at Julia. "Are you okay?"

Her face was pale. "I'm fine, I think."

"Did you see the driver?" I loosened my grip one finger at a time then reached back and rubbed Sunny's head. "Good girl."

"I think it was Wendy Conn." Juliet pushed the button to release her seat belt, twisted around, and looked out the back window. "I didn't actually see the driver, but it was her Bug. Had to be. Nobody else around here drives one with all those daisies."

Perspiration broke out on the back of my neck. *Un, deux, trois…*I counted to ten in French then edged back onto the plantation's entry road. "Next time I see Wendy, I'm going to give her a piece of my mind. I don't care how close you two are."

"I wouldn't go so far as to say we're close. Old co-workers, but nothing more." Juliet glanced behind us. "Wonder why she's in such a hurry?"

I didn't care. "There's no excuse for reckless driving."

"She's probably running late for an appointment at the salon. I was always getting on her to be on time when I owned Lovely Locks, but I didn't fire her because she's a good stylist. Tuesdays are senior discount day, so she'll have a full schedule." Juliet dropped her head back onto the headrest. "Let's discuss your brother. It was nice of Nate to leave us some mulch for the bed and breakfast."

I couldn't help but smile, which lessened my tension. Juliet thought my brother was more than *nice*. "Don't try to change the subject." I turned right.

"Take a deep breath. We were having a good day until Wendy almost killed us. We should count our blessings. Starting with the fact we didn't crash into that humongous oak."

I sighed. "You're right. We're blessed with good family and friends. Not to mention our morning jaunt to Daily Java for coffee and blueberry muffins. Wendy's not going to spoil our day."

Except for Sunny's panting, we crossed the large parking lot in silence. It was surrounded by oak trees and magnolias. Good shade trees for large groups of visitors during tourist season.

I thanked God for keeping us safe and for providing me with an amazing brother. Even though Nate was younger, he'd always looked out for my best interest, like now. He'd brought over some mulch for us to use on the grounds of my B&B. "His landscaping truck should be toward the back of the lot."

Juliet pointed. "I see his trailer."

"But where's his truck?" Odd. I stopped in the middle of the near-empty lot and reached for my phone. I punched in my brother's number and waited for him to answer, but it rolled to voice mail. "Nate, we're here. We'll meet you at the trailer."

A dark color SUV appeared from a blacktop drive leading from the river and the plantation chapel or school house. At least that's what the green and white sign said. Richard Rice Plantation had transformed from a thriving rice plantation on the river to a historical site where visitors came to learn more about South Carolina history.

The SUV's driver barely tapped his brakes before taking off in the opposite direction from us. He sped away toward the entry lane.

Juliet said, "How weird. Where's everybody going, and where's your brother? This early in the morning, it seems like employees should be arriving. Not leaving."

"We know Wendy doesn't work here. The other driver probably doesn't either. Too bad the dark windows concealed their identity." The plantation wasn't open for guests this early in the morning, in fact it'd be a couple of hours before patrons could enter. So what were Wendy and the mystery person doing here? It wasn't even eight o'clock. The parking lot was empty except for Nate's trailer at the back. He'd parked parallel to the edge, giving us easy access to what we needed.

A random car sat on the opposite side of the lot. The driver had parked in two spaces as if he didn't want anybody to hit his vehicle. "I know. The only other vehicle in the lot is that blue sports car."

"It's a brand new Audi. See the four circles on the hood?" She whipped out her phone and snapped a picture. "For my dream board."

I laughed. My friend had a weakness for fancy sports cars, and I had a need for big dependable vehicles for my dog walking business. "If I ever wanted a cool car, it'd be the red one on Magnum."

"It's a Ferrari 488 Spider in the new series."

I laughed. "Of course you'd know that, but I'll never splurge on one. I'm still saving up to visit France." I backed up to the trailer so we could load mulch into it easier. "Let's get to work. Nate keeps shovels attached to his trailer."

Juliet pulled her hair into a bun and checked her reflection in the truck's side mirror. "It's warm for January, and we're going to sweat like pigs if we do all the work ourselves. I don't mind waiting a little longer."

"You look fine. Come on." I hopped out of the truck, and Sunny followed me to where the trailer had been parked parallel to the edge of the blacktopped area. A few months earlier, I'd suspected Juliet cared for my brother, and this was one more clue to add to my list. I called to her over my shoulder. "I don't want to wait all day. Nate will help when he gets here."

Juliet glanced around before she joined Sunny and me at the landscaping trailer.

Mulch lay scattered on the ground, and I frowned. "Nate always cleans his work space before leaving at the end of the day. He must be around here somewhere."

"Should I get a rake and a broom off the rack in back?"

"Not yet. Something's off." My scalp prickled. Nate had scrimped and saved to buy the side dump landscaping trailer. With the front section he could pour out mulch or grass clippings with ease, saving him time and energy to focus on creating beautiful outdoor settings. I patted the ledge. "Our mulch is in here."

Juliet inspected the deck space at the back of the trailer. "There's no wheelbarrow." Juliet planted her hands on her hips.

I hurried to check it out. "I wonder why there are still shovels here. Today the men are scheduled to plant shrubs around the building where you pay to take tours of the plantation."

"It makes me think his crew is late or working at other sites. Call him again." She ran the zipper of her jacket up and down.

I hit redial, but still no answer. After leaving another message, I turned to my friend. "Let's stay calm. Do you see Nate's truck? He would've pulled the trailer here this morning, because the bin is full of mulch. I just can't figure out where he went with his truck."

Juliet snapped her fingers. "Maybe he drove to town to get us coffee."

"No, once he starts working, he only drinks water and stuff with electrolytes." My stomach tightened. Big time. "He might've driven to another area of the plantation. Maybe he had trees or concrete pots in the back of the truck and drove to the exact area where he's working. Let's see if we can find him."

Juliet nodded. "Should we split up?"

"No. We stick together." Nate had promised to meet us here, and he was a man of his word. "It's not like him to stand us up."

"I know." She stuck to me like glue. "He could've run into a snake or alligator or fallen into a hole. Anything could've happened."

My heart thundered. In June, I'd found Peter Roth's dead body. Bad things happened to good people. I shook my head, stopping the negative thoughts beginning to form. "It could be as simple as he lost track of the time."

"You said Nate was supposed to landscape around the welcome center. Let's go to see if he's there."

"Good idea." I patted my leg. "Sunny, come."

My brother was going to be fine, and we'd laugh about the mix-up later. My dog sniffed around a pine tree, paused, then bounded toward me.

"Good girl." The three of us traversed the parking lot and took the path to the entry gate. Birds sang their morning songs as the sun continued rising. A normal morning, except it didn't feel normal. A shiver stole up my back, and it wasn't due to the brisk January breeze.

Nate's truck sat in the grass near the gate. The tailgate was lowered, and the bed was empty except traces of dirt.

The flower bed around the gate held camellias and winter daphne. Buckets of liriope at the side waited to be planted, and a half-full wheelbarrow of chunky brown mulch needed to be spread in due time. There were also artistic pots of bright colored pansies. Yes, it all looked like a typical day for a landscaper, apart from a pair of men's running shoes poking out of the mulch. I did a double take. Yep, it was definitely a pair of shoes. My gaze traveled from one shoe to a black sock, a flash of skin and blue jeans. I gasped. Was it my brother? Nate almost always wore work boots on a job site. Not Adidas. It didn't make sense he'd change his work habits.

Juliet screamed. "No!"

"Call 911." I raced to the body. It couldn't be Nate buried in the flower bed.

Juliet's voice wobbled as she spoke to the person on the phone.

I fell to my knees and crawled toward the top of the body. Wood chips covered the person. A wadded-up handkerchief lay in the mulch with a slash of lipstick on it. A shade of scarlet with a slight orange tinge. Small slivers of wood clung to the material.

Pushing aside the man's hanky, I dug through the mulch to uncover the head of the body. Bits of pine bark adhered to my sleeves and jabbed under my fingernails. I didn't stop scooping away mulch until I uncovered a hand. My breathing hitched.

"No! It can't be Nate." Juliet's high-pitched voice turned hysterical. She held the phone in one hand and collapsed at the border of the garden and grass.

I cleared away more of the ground covering. A wedding band on the left ring finger and a fancy watch at the wrist sent waves of relief rippling through me. My single brother didn't own an expensive watch. "It's not Nate."

"Then who is it?"

Who indeed? I moved to the head. Dirt and grime covered Corey Lane's handsome face. I lifted my eyes and met Juliet's gaze. "It's Corey Lane." The words left me panting. My head swam. The man in the mulch wasn't my brother.

"Is he alive?" Juliet's voice trembled. "The operator wants to know if he's breathing."

Sunny stood at attention next to my friend.

"Give me a minute." I'd assumed Corey was dead, but I hadn't checked his pulse. Gritting my teeth, I reached forward and felt his neck. Nothing. I moved my fingers to the inside of his wrist area. No pulsing sensation. No chest movement and cool skin. Not cold, like dead cold. Gathering my courage, I leaned my face close to Corey and listened for sounds of breathing. Zilch. I held my position, trying to feel Corey's breath against my skin. Zilch. "I can't feel anything." Hysteria rose. This couldn't be happening again.

Juliet moaned then spoke to the emergency operator. "No, he's not."

"Corey, can you hear me? Open your eyes." Tense seconds ticked by. Corey's wife was a friend of mine. They'd met while attending Clemson University and had fallen in love. When Erin returned to Heyward Beach, Corey had followed, and despite family objections, they soon married. Corey was a businessman involved in many different ventures. Some legit, and some shady. Borderline illegal. I'd even considered him capable of murder the year before. Yet, despite his bad traits, on the surface he was a likable guy in the prime of his life.

With one hand on his forehead, I tilted his head back and lifted his chin, in case there was something obstructing his airway. Nothing visible in his mouth, and his tongue appeared free, but the cool body depleted my hope. "Should I try CPR?" I glanced at Juliet.

"Probably." My friend gripped the phone with both hands and spoke to the person on the other end. Juliet's gaze drifted back to me. "She says yes."

With the heel of my left hand on the lower part of his breastbone and my right hand on top, I began compressions. "What's the song? You know the one that helps you keep a good rhythm."

"'Staying—'"

"'Alive.' Yes." I hummed the tune softly and pressed. Soon I had to quit humming and only focus on compressions. My arms burned. "I'm not doing it right." I tried to put more of my body into the motions.

"Yes, you are."

"Can you do the rescue breaths?" How'd I forgotten them? I paused my motions and gathered my strength.

Juliet told the operator what she planned to do then dropped the phone and crawled closer. She pinched Corey's nose and delivered two breaths. "Your turn. I can't believe we're doing this."

I returned to compressions. "Juliet, ask the operator what's the ratio of compressions to breathing." The Bee Gees tune played in my mind.

She scrambled for the phone and pushed the speaker button. "Ma'am, what's the compression-ventilation ratio?"

The dispatcher said, "Thirty compressions to two breaths. Unless you get exhausted or feel like you're in danger, don't stop until the ambulance arrives." Her voice was calm and matter-of-fact.

I counted twenty more chest compressions, figuring I'd at least done ten already. "Your turn. Man, I need to get in better shape."

Juliet gave him two breaths then stopped and looked at me with wide eyes. "Do you hear that?"

Not a soul was visible. The sound came from around the bend in one of the walking trails. One, two, three limping footsteps followed by a thud and a scraping against the sidewalk.

Had Corey fought his attacker before he died? Could the killer be returning to the scene? Would the killer off us, too?

"Juliet, somebody's coming."

Her face grew paler, and she snatched her phone. "Tell the cops to rush. Somebody else is here."

"Find yourself a safe place and get out of there." The woman's voice lost its soothing tone.

Juliet sucked in a breath and grabbed her phone. "Yes, ma'am."

I might not have remembered how to perform CPR perfectly, but I knew a good idea when I heard one. I grabbed my friend's hand, and we raced into the shadows under a clump of pine trees. Sunny stayed at my side.

"Oh, no." Juliet stopped and tugged on my arm. "I dropped my phone."

"Leave it. We've got to take cover." A man's image appeared in my peripheral vision. "Get down so he doesn't spot us."

Sunny barked, circled around us, and ran toward the other person.

"No, Sunny. Stop." I sputtered as I looked around the narrow tree trunk. Of all the times for her to disobey.

Juliet shrieked then ran from our hiding place. "Nate." Juliet raced after Sunny toward my brother with me on her heels. I took off after Juliet and only paused to snatch her phone out of the faded winter grass. My dog beat both of us to my brother.

Nate's wavy red hair was messier than ever. There was no sign of his ever-present ball cap advertising his business, Nate's Landscaping and Designs. His long-sleeve gray T-shirt was ripped at the shoulder. Grass stains covered his shirt and jeans. One of his work boots was untied, and dirt smudged his face. To top it off, one eye was swollen and turning dark purple. Yet, he'd never looked so good to me. My legs quaked as I hurried to him, and tears leaked from my eyes.

Who'd beat up my brother? Why was Corey dead? Had the same thug attacked both men? Or had they fought each other? If Nate had killed Corey by accident in a fight, there was no way he would've tried to hide the man with mulch. Somebody else had to be involved, but who?

Juliet touched my brother's arms then held his hands. "Oh, Nate. What happened to you?"

His good eye widened, and he opened his mouth but no words came out.

I swallowed hard and swiped at a stray tear. I had to get my emotions under control. For over a decade, I'd taken care of my siblings. I was entitled to a tear or two of relief, but Nate looked in no shape to deal with two emotional women.

I gave him a gentle hug. "Oh, baby brother. Let's find a bench where you can sit before you collapse. Juliet, we'll be his human crutches." I slid under one arm and supported him on his right side, and Juliet did the same to his left. Sunny walked beside me, her head swinging back and forth as if watching for trouble.

Majestic oak trees appeared ominous. Tractors hitched to trailers with bench seats stood ready for tours. The little building where visitors bought admission tickets didn't look cheerful or inviting. The killer could hide anywhere.

Nate groaned. His eyes opened and closed in slow motion, almost like he was drunk, but my brother had never been a heavy drinker, and he didn't smell like alcohol. Did he have a concussion?

I spotted a horizontal wooden slat bench on the other side of the walking path and pointed with my free hand. "Let's go over there."

Sirens wailed in the distance.

We helped him sit on the bench, and Juliet plopped down beside him. She took his hand and faced him. "Nate, I'm so glad you're safe. What happened?"

"Not sure." He stared at the ground and shook his head.

I paced, and Sunny matched my steps. "Nate, what's going on? You're hurt, and Corey is dead. Who did this?"

His eyebrows drew together. "I don't know."

"What do you mean, 'you don't know?' How can you not know?" I paced in front of him—if I stood still, my knees might lock and cause me to faint.

"I remember driving over this morning, but everything else is like a thick fog." He fisted his hands on his thighs.

Sunny whined. I stopped walking back and forth and bent to rub her head.

"I hope the fog clears before the cops get here." The sheriff would expect a better answer when he learned Corey Lane was dead and partially buried under a pile of mulch that most likely came from Nate's business.

Chapter Two

NATE SQUINTED, even though the trees surrounding us filtered the winter sunlight. He ran a hand over his face. "All of my men called in sick, so I decided not to waste time waiting for you. My plan was to start planting on my own then help you."

"Keep going." I made a circular motion with my hand.

"I never saw the attack coming. A twig cracked, and I turned to see if it was you. That's when I got clobbered in the back of my head." He winced. "Do you have ibuprofen or anything?"

I kept some in my Suburban's first aid kit, but I'd driven his old truck. "No, I'm sorry."

"It's okay." He ran his hands up the sides of his face before speaking again. "I turned to defend myself, but my ankle twisted. Next thing I knew, the goon hit me in the face with a shovel. I don't remember anything after that until I woke up on the ground."

"Where did this happen?"

"Near the cotton gin past the entrance gate where you buy tickets for plantation tours. I was sprucing up the area."

Sunny propped her head on Nate's thigh.

"Who attacked you?"

Nate shrugged. "I, um, it was fuzzy because of the black spots in front of my eyes. I never got a solid look at the man, but I feel like he was shorter than me." My brother's words slurred.

A siren whooped-whooped and tires squealed. A sporty patrol car angled to an abrupt stop. Another followed close behind the first one.

Nate stood and swayed.

Juliet slipped her arm behind his back and braced him with a hand on his abdomen. "Whoa, there."

Two deputies jumped out of their vehicles and raced to us with guns drawn as another patrol car slid to a stop near them.

At the sight of weapons from the first two deputies, Nate and I raised our hands. Juliet didn't release her hold on my brother.

My brother emitted another groan but remained vertical.

"Nate, are you okay?" Juliet's voice rose with each word.

"I'm fine. You can let go of me."

She stepped away and lifted her hands.

"You again, Andi Grace?" Deputy Hanks barked deeper than my dog.

"We're the ones who called for help."

The second deputy kept his gun trained on us but didn't say a word. I'd lost track of the third officer.

"Hmm." Deputy Hanks frisked each of us, starting with me then Juliet. After patting down Nate, he stepped back and eyed my brother. "What's the matter with you? Get in a tussle with the victim?"

"No, sir." He cleared his throat. "I was attacked."

The younger deputy holstered his weapon but remained vigilant in keeping his eyes on us.

Deputy Hanks leaned closer to Nate. "Some shiner you got there."

Nate fingertipped his black eye and winced. "Ow. Somebody snuck up on me."

Deputy Sawyer jogged to us. "I've established the perimeter."

"Good job. We're shutting down the place to tourists until we wrap this up. Find out who to notify then do it."

"Yes, sir." He glanced toward Corey's body then hurried away.

An ambulance and the coroner's van arrived and parked on a wide sidewalk near the butterfly pavilion, some distance away.

I raised my hand. "Can we get an EMT to look at my brother?"

"It can wait." Deputy Hanks frowned and looked right and left. "Let's head to the plantation café. I've got a few questions for you while this morning is fresh on your mind."

"No. Nate's hurt. He got hit on the head, and it knocked him out. He needs some kind of treatment."

His nostrils flared. "Seems fine to me."

"Where's the sheriff?"

The plantation café was near the building to buy admission tickets, and Nate pulled us in that direction. "Andi Grace, don't antagonize the man. Let's go with him and get this over with."

More law enforcement vehicles appeared. Some deputies walked around the property, no doubt searching for evidence. Others took notes and conferred with each other. Was the sheriff in one of the vehicles, or was he on the way? Once he arrived, I'd feel a lot better about the situation.

Juliet and I supported Nate between us until we entered the building.

We walked across the no-frills café, putting some distance between us and Deputy Hanks. The three of us sat in sturdy chairs at an old maple table.

Deputy David Wayne arrived and spoke to Deputy Hanks.

Sheriff Wade Stone appeared and shot a glance in our direction. He shook his head, then crossed the room without first speaking to his men. "Andi Grace, why am I not surprised to find you here?"

I ignored his taunt. "Wade, Nate's in bad shape. He needs to go to the emergency room. Please, can you let us go?"

A growl formed in his throat. "Andi Grace—"

"Please, Wade." We'd forged a friendship of sorts, seven months earlier when Peter Roth was murdered. "I'm really worried about him."

The sheriff sighed. "Keep your seat, and I'll assess the situation with Nate."

Nate, walking unassisted, and Wade stepped outside on the porch, where I'd left Sunny. Wade was a reasonable man and wouldn't make somebody suffer unnecessarily.

Deputy David Wayne stood in front of Juliet. "Come with me where we can speak in private."

Juliet's eyes widened. "Okay." She trudged behind him to a table in the opposite corner of the room and answered his questions. David had graduated from high school with Nate and seemed to be a decent guy. He was on Heyward Beach's unofficial most eligible bachelor list.

A few minutes later, Wade re-entered the room and sat across from me.

"How's Nate?"

"The EMTs are looking him over as we speak." Wade pulled out his Toughbook, his special laptop for taking notes on investigations. "Tell me what you saw this morning."

I relaxed a smidgen, knowing somebody was concerned about my brother. Wade had done me a favor, so I gave him my full attention. At least as close to full as possible. "Juliet and I came here to get mulch for my place."

"You get your mulch from Richard Rice Plantation?"

I straightened in the chair. "Like steal it? Never. Nate brought extra over on his truck for me. His trailer is divided into sections, and I'd paid him for mulch for the B&B."

"Continue."

"As we drove in this morning, a Volkswagen ran me off the entry road. It was bright yellow with daisies, like the one Wendy Conn owns.

When we got to the parking lot, an SUV pulled out from a private drive and hurried away. It was dark gray. Maybe black. Those are the people you need to question."

His thick dark eyebrows rose. "Did you see the driver of the SUV?"

"No. The windows were tinted."

"What next? And please slow down. I don't want to miss any details."

I took a deep breath and launched into the rest of the events. When I finished, I studied the man in hopes of reading his expression, not that I'd ever been able to before.

He picked up his computer and stood. "Stay here."

I sat and prayed we'd be released soon. Through the window, Sunny paced on the building's front porch. I longed to comfort her, and yeah, she'd comfort me as well.

Finally, Wade returned to my table. "We're releasing you. For now. Your brother is being taken to the hospital, but this isn't over."

I nodded. "I can leave? As in right this minute?"

"Yes."

Relief swelled over me, and my knees buckled. Juliet had crossed the room and she caught me before I collapsed. After I steadied myself, I grabbed her hand and rushed outside to rub Sunny's head. "Let's go, girl." The back door of the ambulance was still open, and we hurried over. If my brother had a head injury, he might not be out of the woods. "Nate, we'll be right behind you."

His eyes were closed, but he lifted a hand and pointed a finger at me. His typical sign for agreement.

The medic said, "Ma'am, I'm going to close the doors now. We'll meet you at County Memorial Hospital."

I glanced over the man's shoulder. "I love you, Nate."

"Love you, too." His words lacked strength.

I backed away, and the door slammed.

Gray was the only color to describe my brother's face. He was big and strong at six-two and didn't carry an ounce of fat on his frame. His job kept him fit. I rubbed my chest, willing the tightness away. Memories of Nate as a red-headed toddler hit me. His sense of humor often made me laugh, and his sweetness sometimes moved me to tears. The stereotypical hot-tempered redhead didn't describe my brother.

Juliet latched onto my arm. "Why are we standing here? Let's go."

"Right." Juliet, Sunny, and I jogged all the way to the old work truck, my thoughts jumbled. After we settled with my dog between us, I drove as fast as I dared, gripping the steering wheel, holding back my tears. Crying now would only slow us down.

Juliet said, "I don't like the way Nate slurred his words. That stinking deputy made me so mad when he insinuated Nate might be hungover instead of hurt. I bet the knock on his head gave him a concussion. His eyes didn't look good."

Everything she said was true. I felt ill and my stomach rolled. Once again, a friend had been murdered, although *friend* might be a stretch. "Acquaintance" fit my relationship with Corey better. His death meant a killer was on the loose—again. At least this time the sheriff wouldn't suspect me. This time, I had a witness.

But Nate did not.

Chapter Three

FORCED TO COOL my heels in the hospital waiting room, antici-pating word on Nate's condition, was about to drive me nuts. I leaned forward and placed my elbows on my knees, allowing my face to fall into my hands. On a TV situated in the corner of the light blue room, a national weatherman droned on about a blizzard in the northeast United States.

Lord, please watch over Nate. Amen. No more words came.

Juliet had taken Sunny outside, but I wasn't alone. A middle-aged couple sat on orange vinyl chairs in one corner, holding hands. The wo-man's splotchy red face and puffy eyes spoke of her pain . . . her fear. Was she praying for her loved one like I was? I added them to my prayers for Nate. The only other occupant of the waiting room, a young Hispanic woman, held a sleeping toddler in her lap and stared at the floor. Who was she concerned about? I also included her in my prayer. We all needed strength, and our loved ones needed healing.

A shadow drifted across the floor in front of me. I looked up and met Wade's gaze. The sheriff hadn't wasted time following us to the hospital. "Hey."

"You by yourself?" Wade held his broad-brimmed hat in his large hands in front of him like a shield.

"Juliet's outside waiting for Marc to pick up Sunny and take care of her until I get home." Not only was Marc Williams my friend, he was also my attorney. We'd even gone on a couple of dates.

"Gotcha."

Marc planned to drive Sunny home to my cottage on Heyward Beach. Juliet would be back inside to wait with me as soon as Marc came.

Wade stepped closer. "Andi Grace."

"Why are you here? Didn't you get enough information at the café?" The words slipped out before I could stop them. Wade probably had expected my verbal assault. No wonder he held his hat like a defensive shield. "Sorry. I didn't mean to be rude."

"I understand you're worried."

"Today I had a witness. You've got no reason to suspect me." The only other time I'd found a dead body, I'd ended up helping the sheriff solve the crime to make sure he didn't arrest *me*. As long as Wade didn't suspect Nate of murdering Corey, I'd stay out of his way.

One side of his mouth lifted. "You're not on my suspect list."

The tightness in my shoulders eased. "Good. This time I won't help with your investigation." I didn't ask if Nate was a suspect, because I didn't want to plant any ideas in Wade's mind.

"Interfere." This time he didn't crack a smile.

It became hard to swallow. Of all the nerve. "We caught the killer, didn't we?"

His face reddened. "Yep. Any updates on Nate's condition?"

"They're scanning him for a concussion. I can't imagine why it's taking so long."

"He stated somebody hit the back of his head then punched him in the face."

The hairs along my arms stood at attention. "It's obvious somebody attacked Nate."

Wade avoided my gaze and glanced around the room with a grimace. "Not obvious, but it's clear he participated in some kind of altercation."

"What are you insinuating?" My heartbeat increased.

Before Wade answered my question, Juliet entered the room. Her eyebrows lifted. "What's going on? Is Nate okay?"

Wade shot a glance at her but didn't answer.

"Yeah, Wade. Why don't you tell us what's on your mind?"

His fingers tightened on the hat. "Nate appears to have been in a fight. Plain and simple."

Juliet's eyes widened. "He was attacked. From behind."

Wade's nostrils flared. "Did you see it happen?"

"No, but I believe Nate." She clenched her hands.

The situation was getting worse by the second, and my chest hurt. I reached for my phone and texted Marc before uttering another word. **Please come to waiting room ASAP. Wade is asking more questions. Sunny will be okay in your truck for a while.**

Juliet planted her fists on her hips. "Nate never lies. If he says he was attacked, then he was attacked."

Three sets of eyes watched us, and the toddler whined in his mother's arms.

Our voices had gotten too loud. I touched Juliet's arm. "Shh. You'll upset the child."

Wade surveyed the area. "Why don't we continue our conversation in the hall?"

Juliet nodded. "Fine by me. As long as we're available when Nate gets back."

The tightness in my chest lessened. If Juliet and Nate ever got together, she'd make a great girlfriend. Maybe this incident would propel them to take the leap from friendship to dating. Nate needed somebody he could laugh with, and Juliet helped him relax and enjoy life.

I dismissed matchmaking thoughts, and we followed Wade to the end of the hall and stood by a window. "What are you trying to say, Wade?"

"It appears Corey may have suffered a deadly blow to the head. My guess would be a shovel was the weapon, since there's a landscaping truck and equipment. Keep in mind, the obvious answer isn't always the correct one. In time, the coroner will give us the official cause of death."

"How gruesome." Heat infused my body, and I shrugged out of my jacket. If I could cool down, I wouldn't faint. "Why was there blood on Corey's body? If he'd been attacked with a shovel, there'd be bruising. Not blood. He may have been clobbered with a baseball bat, a golf club, or even a lacrosse stick. How about a fire poker? Oh, a fire poker could cause bruising and bleeding. Right?"

"Whoever attacked Corey was seriously angry." He shifted his hat in his hands.

"Well? What kind of weapon caused the bloody wounds?"

He hesitated, clearly debating his answer. "This stays between us, because I know you won't give me any peace until you know more. We found blood on a pair of hedge shears not too far from the body." Wade spread his feet shoulder length apart. "In addition, there's blood on the shovel. Once we confirm the shovel and hedge trimmers are the murder weapons, and because they belong to your brother, we'll possibly have our killer."

My palms grew damp. "Just because they belong to Nate doesn't mean—"

Juliet interrupted. "What makes you think the tools belong to Nate?"

I touched her arm. "It's his landscaping business, so it's a safe assumption."

Wade shook his head. "It's more than an assumption. His initials are carved into the handles. NWS."

Nathan Ward Scott was indeed my brother's name. The implycations chilled me to the bone. "Only Nate can say for sure if they are his personal tools. Lots of men mark their belongings so they don't accidently lose them when working on big projects, but it doesn't mean somebody else didn't use it. Anybody could've picked up Nate's shovel and clobbered Corey."

Familiar footsteps sounded on the tile floor behind me. I turned, expecting to see Marc and wasn't disappointed. The man had a special walk making it easy to identify him by sight or sound. Not a clip-clop or tapping. He had a light step, but his Cole Haans made a gentle click on the tile floor.

Marc met my gaze and smiled. "Andi Grace, you okay?"

"Better—" *Now that you're here.* The words almost slipped out of my mouth. I smiled back. To reach us so fast, he probably never left the parking lot. Knowing Marc, a phone conversation with a client delayed his departure.

Wade cleared his throat. "You trying to lawyer up?"

I turned my attention to the sheriff. "Should I? You said I wasn't a suspect."

"You're not."

Marc touched my shoulder, but his gaze was trained on Wade. "I'm here as a friend unless you're about to arrest somebody for Corey's murder? Are you?"

Juliet looked from Marc to Wade. "Andi Grace and I've been together all morning. The only one left to arrest here is Nate."

"I'm not planning to arrest anybody. Yet. Once the lab goes through the forensic evidence and tests for fingerprints and blood, we'll know more. Deputy Wayne will take lead on this case."

Doors at the end of the hall opened. A nurse walked briskly toward us. "Your brother is back in his exam room. One of you may go with me." She glanced at Wade. "If it's okay with the sheriff."

Wade pointed toward me. "Take his sister back first. Andi Grace, I'll need to question Nate. Soon. If he didn't use the shovel to attack Corey, who did? Your brother could be a witness."

Now we were getting somewhere. A rush of relief washed over me. Wade thought Nate could be a witness instead of the murderer. "Don't forget Wendy was on the property as well as the driver of the dark SUV."

"We're checking out all leads. For now, Nate is at the top of my list to question."

The sheriff's words rang in my ears as I wound my way back to Nate's cubicle, following the nurse through the maze. Questions buzzed through my brain. Who would want to kill Corey? Did the killer try to frame Nate on purpose? Why?

If I could find the motive, maybe I could find the killer.

I'd promised not to help with the investigation, which I'd meant at the time. However, if he arrested my brother for Corey's death, I'd be right in the middle of another murder investigation whether Wade wanted my help or not.

Chapter Four

WRAPPED IN WHAT looked to be my red puffer coat and a check-ered red and black scarf, my sister Lacey Jane paced the front porch of my beach cottage when Nate, Juliet, and I arrived from the hospital. We parked then plodded up the driveway.

Nate's steps were wobbly and uneven. Juliet walked close to his side with a frown etched on her face. My brother didn't lack for attention. If you counted Sunny, there were four females looking out for him.

Sunny stood at the top of my stairs, eyeing us like a worried momma. Ears forward, eyes wide, mouth closed, standing on all four legs, and tail horizontal.

I trotted to her and knelt by her side. "It's okay, girl. We're all here." Nate had insisted on leaving the hospital against the doctor's advice to stay for observation.

Sunny barked and licked my face before heading to Nate.

I stood back and observed the two of them. Nate's stiff movements and Sunny's cautious response. She remained at his side as he climbed the steps to my front porch with the white wooden columns and protective railing. Years earlier, I'd bought this house and made a home to raise my siblings. As an added bonus, we were close enough to walk to the beach. Sunny and I strolled or ran on the beach almost daily. This was actually where my German shepherd and I first met. I'd been walking on the beach walk one day after my parents died. I don't know which of us adopted the other, but she'd become part of our family.

It'd be hard to let go of my beach cottage when my house was finished being renovated at the plantation. It made financial sense to move, but my heart remained at the cottage. My beautiful seafoam blue home with the cornflower blue hurricane shutters. Picking the color combination had taken weeks. To save money, the three of us painted it ourselves, which turned into a long labor of love.

"I'm so glad y'all are here. What took so long? Next time some-body's in the hospital, you better tell me right away. I don't appreciate being the last to know when something bad happens. Just because I'm the youngest doesn't mean I'm not part of this family." Lacey Jane held the door open for us, and once we were all inside, threw her arms around our brother. "Oh, Nate. I was so scared. Are you okay?"

He grabbed a chair with one hand and steadied himself before wrapping an arm around her. "I'm fine. It'll take more than a knock on the head to keep me down."

Sunny stood strong at Nate's side. She belonged to all of us.

Nate's eyebrows dipped down. He was probably trying to mask the pain from us. The middle-aged doctor had diagnosed him with a slight concussion and preached to us the importance of keeping an eye on Nate for at least twenty-four hours. Once we'd promised to keep him under our watchful observation, we signed the necessary paperwork and hightailed it out of there.

I touched my brother's arm. "Do you want to rest on the couch?" A fire crackled in the white brick fireplace on the far wall of my family room. White bookshelves filled with pottery, family pictures, and books occupied every available shelf. Nancy Drew, *Lassie, Call of the Wild,* and *Old Yeller* were some of my favorite childhood stories and were included in my collection. I loved the coziness of this room on a cold January day. Honestly, I loved this room every day, no matter what the season. Nate's response drew me from my thoughts.

"No, I'm fine. Hungry though." His voice lacked strength.

"Let's eat. Do you think you can sit at the kitchen table?"

"I've got a killer headache, but I'm not an invalid." He bent over to rub Sunny's side.

"Are you sure you shouldn't have stayed at the hospital?" Lacey Jane stared at Nate.

"According to the CAT scan, there's no bleeding in my brain. Doc said I needed to rest."

"Rest? That's all?"

Nate leaned against the chair. "You know it's only a mild concussion, right? Rest. Peace. Acetaminophen. Dark room. No TV or looking at my phone. He mostly focused on rest though."

"I'll feed you then we'll kick everybody out so you can have a quiet place to lay low." Lacey Jane moved to the kitchen and we followed. "I made chicken noodle soup and fresh chicken salad. Or I can make grilled cheese if you'd rather."

When I'd taken over raising my siblings after our parents died, Lacey Jane often fixed simple meals for us. "Chicken salad sandwiches sound good. I'm going to let Sunny out back and then help you pull it together."

Juliet said, "Count me in on lunch preparations."

Nate sank into a kitchen chair and gazed out the window to the backyard, where Sunny sniffed around the fence. His hair appeared redder, and the freckles popped out on his pallid complexion. He looked better than before but still not great.

While my sister prepared sandwiches, I pulled potato chips from the pantry, and Juliet sliced apples. She'd lived with us for a couple of years and was as comfortable in my home as the rest of us.

In no time we'd placed lunch on the table and said a quick blessing.

I stirred my soup, waiting for it to cool. "What do you remember, Nate?"

He chewed his bite of pimiento cheese sandwich slowly. "I was carrying large flowerpots from my truck to place around the front gate. They were filled with purple, yellow, and white pansies, which are hardy enough for the cool weather."

"Why were you carrying them?"

He tilted his head and squinted at me. "The wheelbarrow was full of mulch. I didn't want to spread it until the layout was perfect."

Now I felt stupid. "I didn't see any pots of pansies when we were looking for you."

"That's because I hadn't made it to the entry gate." He spoke like explaining something to a child.

Maybe I had the concussion instead of Nate the way I struggled to make sense of his morning. "Okay. Then what?"

"When I heard footsteps, I expected it to be you. The person got closer to me, and before I got a good look they whacked me in the back of my head. I dropped the ceramic pots and grabbed a tree to stay on my feet. You know when the cartoons show a character seeing stars?"

I nodded. "Yes."

"It's a real thing. I literally saw stars." He crumbled saltine crackers into his soup.

"Do you remember getting hit in the face? You've also got bruising there."

"It hurts, but I don't remember specific details." Nate reached for his Coke and drained the glass. "I planned to fight back but I don't think I got a swing at the thug before I was out."

My pulse picked up. "Are you certain it was a man who attacked you?"

He shook his head and winced. "I can't say for sure, but if it was a woman, I'll never live it down."

"Well, the good thing is, I can't rule out female suspects."

Nate glared at me. "You don't need to have a suspect list. The cops will handle it."

Lacey Jane said, "We all know you're going to make a list. Corey was a womanizer, and it wouldn't surprise me if his wife killed him. Make sure to include Erin."

"Oh, honey. I hope it wasn't his wife." I ran my hand along Lacey Jane's arm.

Erin Lane owned the coffee shop where my sister used to work. Daily Java served the best coffee around Heyward Beach, and nobody could come close to her delicious baked goods. "I wonder how Erin's taking the news of Corey's death? She's too young to be a widow."

Lacey Jane shrugged. "My guess is she's celebrating."

A shiver zipped up my spine. "Shh, you don't really mean that."

Red splotches tinged Lacey Jane's neck. "Fine. Maybe she's relieved. If she'd didn't do the deed, there's a long list of women Corey used and dumped. Being married didn't mean Corey stopped prowling."

"Don't talk ugly." How many times had our mother said the same words to us, and now I was repeating them? Although turning into my mother wouldn't be the worst thing in the world.

Lacey Jane frowned. "Again, I'm an adult and can say anything I want."

"True, but I wish you'd be kind. Please don't say anything the authorities can use to harm Nate. I understand why you feel the way you do, but we've got to protect Nate."

"You and Nate are the only two I told why I quit my job. I suppose Juliet knows."

Juliet reached for my sister's hand. "I accidently overheard you and Andi Grace discussing it. I didn't want to embarrass you, but I did confess to your sister. I'm sorry it happened, Lacey Jane. You can trust me. I never revealed your secret."

"I understand."

The public story was Lacey Jane left Daily Java to work for Marc while taking classes to become a paralegal. Working for Marc provided great experience for her, but the real reason she'd left the coffee shop had been Corey. He'd made a pass at her one afternoon when Erin left to run work-related errands. Erin's jealous streak was known by a few of us, and if her husband had been brazen enough to make a move on my sister, he'd probably made passes at other women. Lacey Jane kept the secret, fearing Corey would turn the situation around to make it look like she'd made a play for him. Instead of speaking up and rocking the boat, she'd quit her job.

I leaned my forearms on the table. "We've got to be careful your incident doesn't get out right now, for Nate's sake."

"I'd never hurt Nate. The three of us always stick together." She bit into her sandwich.

I rubbed her shoulder. "You bet we do."

We ate in silence for a while, but my brain wouldn't stop whirling. I couldn't help it. "Wade mentioned his deputy will handle the investigation. David Wayne."

"He's a good guy." Nate sipped his soup. "I don't know if you remember, but David graduated with me and played football at the college level."

Lacey Jane's frown disappeared. "Oh, I remember. He was a big deal. Not only did he play football, but he was a baseball player. Georgia recruited him to be a running back, and he eventually went pro."

It amazed me she knew so much about David when she'd never shown much interest in sports. "Why'd he return to Heyward Beach if he was a professional football player?"

Lacey Jane picked up her cell phone and tapped the screen. "This site says he played for the Falcons. The first time he took the field, he broke his back, which ended his career in football."

"I wonder if he's fit enough to be a deputy. Would Wade have hired him out of pity because of the broken back?"

Lacey Jane turned the screen so we could see. "He's on the sheriff's website and looks perfectly fit to me."

Juliet's eyes widened. "He questioned me today, and the picture doesn't lie. He's in good shape. I don't think he's quite that bulky, but the man is definitely fit."

"Fine, but what's underneath his good looks and muscles? Can he do the job?" The man was muscular with close-cropped jet-black hair. He was tanned, even in January. "Can he chase down a killer or defend himself in a fight? Why do you think Wade turned the case over to him?"

Juliet patted my hand. "During the investigation into Peter's death, Wade took the lead because he knew you. He told me he was doing it as a favor to you. Normally, he's busy with administrative things like budgets, personnel issues, and other paperwork. He trusts his detectives to investigate."

I suppressed a shiver. "Oh, man. I feel terrible. I thought I was his number one suspect and gave him a hard time. I should apologize."

"Circumstantial evidence pointed to you, but Wade didn't believe you could murder somebody. He wanted to make sure the real killer was caught."

A couple of things bothered me. Juliet and Wade had grown closer than I realized if she knew so much information. Also, how reliable was David? Would he keep digging until he caught the person responsible for Corey's death? Or would he take the easy way and arrest Nate?

I couldn't let that happen.

AFTER LUNCH, THE others left me home alone with Sunny. We'd decided to take turns watching my brother. Juliet took the first shift and drove my brother to his town house. Lacey Jane would relieve Juliet at suppertime. I'd asked to take the night duty so I could finish my schedule of dog walking appointments.

I knew where Erin lived, and I had a dog close to her that needed walking—oddly enough, Wade's dog. "Sunny, I'll be back."

My German shepherd opened her eyes and tilted her head.

"You enjoy your afternoon nap." I hurried out to my Suburban and managed to stay under the speed limit as I drove to the sheriff's house. His parents often helped take care of Duke, but they were spending a few weeks visiting their daughter in New York City. So Duke was on my afternoon walking list.

I pulled to a stop on the street in front of a charcoal gray house with white trim. Nice and neat. With house key, poop bags, and treats, I headed to the front door.

There weren't any obvious nosy neighbors. I rang the bell and knocked. When there was no answer, I used my key to open the door.

"Hello, anybody home?" It only took one time of interrupting an unsuspecting couple to learn to give plenty of notice. "Hello?"

The only reply was a bark from the kitchen.

I walked through the living and dining room combo. A new picture hung on one of the walls. Maybe a Christmas gift that he'd just hung. Closer inspection showed it was autographed. John Wayne. The Duke. All this time I'd imagined Wade had named his dog for Duke University, not the actor.

I continued to the kitchen and opened the crate, where the dog waited. "Hey, boy. Ready to go for a long walk?"

I filled his water bowl and placed it before him. His dog tags clinked on the ceramic bowl when he lapped up the last few drops. "Let's go."

A single bark was all the reply I needed before attaching his leash and walking into the chilly winter air.

Erin lived a few streets over. The sun blazed in the sky, and I lifted my face to absorb its warmth.

Duke kept a steady pace, except for a few periodic pauses.

"You're happy to be out and about, aren't you?"

A dark SUV drove past us and turned right onto Erin's street. It looked like the one I'd seen at Richard Rice Plantation, but there was a slight difference. This one didn't shine. It needed a wash and wax. My gut tightened. Coincidence or not, I'd keep it in mind.

I led Duke toward Erin's house. It was a cute yellow cottage with blue shutters. Somebody had even painted the concrete porch and steps a complementary shade of eggshell blue. Erin's white Prius sat alone in the driveway. Despite coming from money, Erin had a strong practical streak. Corey had been showy and enjoyed spending money. It was no wonder they had so many disagreements.

Erin's front door opened, and two ladies walked out with somber expressions. Behind them I spotted Pastor Mays speaking to Erin in the large entry hall. No matter how much I wanted the cops to arrest somebody for Corey's murder, intruding on the grieving widow and pastor would be in poor taste. My questions could wait.

"Come on, Duke." We retraced our steps to Wade's house, where we found his vehicle parked behind mine.

This time when I rang the doorbell, Wade answered. "Hey, thanks for walking Duke."

"Why are you home? Did I misunderstand?" I edged my way past him.

"No, you're good. A suspect vomited on me during interrogation, so I came home for a clean uniform."

My gag reflex kicked in. "Oh, yuck. Are you going to burn your dirty clothes?"

"No, but I'll let the cleaners handle it for me." He chuckled and followed me to the kitchen. "Andi Grace, I need to head out."

"No problem. I've got this. Have you started looking into the women Corey dated?" I poured kibble into Duke's food bowl and stepped out of his way.

His brow creased. "David is handling the investigation, and I can't discuss the case with you." He turned and left me standing in the kitchen with his dog.

I slumped. "Duke, I had so much to ask your master. Guess I'll have to deal with him another day."

Chapter Five

EARLY IN THE evening, Marc and I sat next to each other on my couch, drinking a blend of coffee from Peru with a sweet caramel flavor. I didn't worry it'd keep me awake because I doubted there'd be much sleeping between waking Nate every two hours and wondering who'd killed Corey. I figured if I got sleepy, Sunny and Nate's dog, Bo, would keep me from dozing.

A fire blazed in the fireplace, and soft light from two lamps added to the cozy atmosphere. I loved my home. A log popped.

In spite of the warmth from the fire and sitting next to Marc, I suppressed a shiver. "Do you think they'll arrest Nate?"

Marc sipped his coffee. "If the evidence points to him, yeah. Wade won't cut any corners before he presents the evidence to a judge for an arrest warrant."

"I forgot to tell you Deputy Wayne is in charge of the investigation. Have you met him?"

"Yeah. He's a decent guy. I've seen him kayaking around the Marsh Walk and on the Waccamaw River."

I laughed. "Do you like everybody interested in boating?"

"Not everybody. I've also seen David around the courthouse."

"I hope he finds the real killer and doesn't only look for evidence pointing to Nate." I took a deep breath. "I'm scared."

Marc leaned toward me until our shoulders touched. "Trust David to do his job right. I'm sure Wade will verify everything David presents to him before going to a judge."

"Wade wanted to arrest me last summer for Peter's murder. I fought him then, and if he arrests Nate, I'll fight him again." I remembered Juliet's words. She believed he'd taken the case to protect me. I wasn't convinced. Or maybe I didn't want to admit how I'd misjudged Wade. I dropped my head.

Marc reached for my mug and placed both of ours on the round vintage table I'd painted turquoise and converted into a coffee table. "Come here." He opened his arms to me.

I rested my head against his chest. I didn't like the shorter days of winter, but snuggling with Marc was a definite perk. The firm beat of his heart gave me a sense of calm. Steady, like the man himself. "Are you going to help me solve the murder?"

His chest rose as he took a breath. "I don't want you trying to find the killer on your own. I suppose you've started a list of suspects." He played with a long strand of my hair that'd escaped the ponytail band.

"You know me so well."

His chest rumbled with laughter. "We've traveled this road before. Together. You have no intention of waiting for David and Wade to arrest Nate. You'll start gathering clues right away."

"Will you help me?" My jaw tightened as I waited for his answer.

"I'll be your Watson."

I smiled. "Or you can be my Remington Steele. Or I'm Beckett and you're Castle."

"Just don't call me Agent Eighty-six."

"Who?" I still lay with my head against his chest.

Marc ran his hand up and down my arm. "He was on *Get Smart*. Agent Eighty-six was the clown who solved mysteries, and Agent Ninety-nine was the beautiful, smart sidekick."

"Nice. I may have seen a couple of episodes." Beautiful and smart. I could live with his compliment, although Marc hadn't said I was beautiful and smart. "You're definitely not a clown, and you're way more handsome than Maxwell Smart."

"Agent Ninety-nine can't hold a candle to you."

"Aw, you're so sweet. Thanks." I snuggled even closer.

"When do you need to be at Nate's?"

The last thing I wanted to do was end this special time, but being a realist, I knew it couldn't last. "I should head over soon. I'll ask him if he has any ideas on who'd want to kill Corey."

Marc shifted away. "We know Corey made some shady deals in the past related to the plantation. It could be a business thing."

"True." I hesitated, unsure how Marc would respond to what I needed to reveal. I twisted the teardrop turquoise ring around my finger and faced him. "I never told you this, but Corey made a pass at Lacey Jane while she still worked at the coffee shop."

His eyebrows rose. "He what?"

"Corey put the moves on Lacey Jane." I explained the situation.

"Why didn't she do something?"

"Fear." I lifted my hands, palms up. "I didn't push because she was old enough to decide for herself and young enough to be scared. I honored her wishes."

Marc ran a hand over his face and sighed. "If he did the same thing to another woman, we could have a motive besides money or business dealings."

"True, but it could also be additional cause for Nate to go after Corey."

"You're right." He stared at the fire. "How many people know about the incident between Corey and your sister?"

"Six. Lacey Jane, me, you, Juliet, Nate, and Corey. He's dead, so now there are only five."

Marc grimaced. "Five we know of. What if his wife discovered he put the moves on your sister? Then she'd have a reason to kill him."

I leapt to my feet and headed to my office. "Let's start an official list of suspects." I grabbed a new journal and pen and rejoined Marc on the couch.

"It's amazing how efficient you are when it comes to your business and murder."

I laughed. The man really did know me well. "I'm getting better at organizing. I even made my bed this morning."

"Nice." His grin made my heart cartwheel. "Who's first on your list?"

I opened to page one. "My top two suspects are Erin Lane and Wendy Conn." I wrote their names in big block letters.

"Wendy Conn?"

"Yes, she bought the salon from Juliet." I finished writing her name on my list. "I plan to pump Juliet for information on her. There are three main things I know about Wendy. She has a huge clientele of men, she's the biggest flirt I've ever seen, and men love her."

Marc stood and frowned. "Being a flirt is a far cry from murderer. Homewrecker maybe."

"A car exactly like hers left the plantation this morning as I arrived. A yellow Volkswagen with white daisies. The person behind the wheel drove fast and crazy, and we ran off the road. Of course, it's more of a narrow lane."

"I know how tight it is." Marc paced with hands in the front pockets of his jeans. He edged around the coffee table and toward the fireplace. "If the driver was Wendy, she was at the crime scene at the right time. You felt for a pulse, right?"

I nodded. "Yes. It was cool this morning, but the body was still kinda warm."

He took more steps, turned, and rubbed the nape of his neck. "The unofficial time of death is this morning."

I included the time to my notes. "I figured."

He said, "Did you see anybody else?"

"We watched a dark SUV drive by, and there was a fancy sports car in the back of the main parking lot. Juliet identified it as an Audi. On the way to the hospital we decided it might belong to Corey, because we've both seen it at Daily Java frequently."

"Daily Java is the best coffee shop around, so I don't think that's enough to go on, but I saw Corey driving a new R8 Spyder the other day. Was the car you saw blue?"

"Yes, shiny blue." I added this information to my notes. "If a Spyder is an Audi, let's assume it was Corey's car. It's possible Erin drove the Audi, but if so, then how did Corey get there?"

"Don't forget the SUV you mentioned." Marc rubbed his palms against each other, creating a sandpaper sound.

"Right. Marc, why do you think Corey was at the plantation so early?"

Marc sighed. "He was the CEO. Maybe he called an early meeting."

"For the board of directors or staff?"

"Either."

I reflected on his words. Early meeting? Something didn't fit. I needed caffeine. "How about more coffee?"

"No thanks. I won't be able to sleep, and I can't afford to hit the snooze button tomorrow morning. Water would be nice, though." He followed me to the kitchen.

Dirty dishes from lunch filled the sink. I'd skipped supper, but even if I'd eaten, I probably wouldn't have gotten around to washing dishes. They weren't at the top of my priority list. "Water. No problem." I pulled a clean glass from the cabinet and filled it with purified water.

"Thanks. Why did you decide to meet Nate at Richard Rice Plantation for mulch? Wouldn't it have been easier for him to bring it to you?"

I leaned against the kitchen counter. "Juliet has guests lined up for this weekend at the B&B, and we were in a hurry to freshen the landscaping before they arrived."

"You didn't want to pay Nate to do it for you?"

"We're on a tight budget." I lifted my hands palms up. Even though

I'd inherited a plantation, the financial picture was fuzzy.

Juliet was helping me convert the plantation house I'd inherited from Peter Roth into a bed and breakfast. I was also converting one of the barns into doggie day care and boarding, which is another reason it didn't make sense for me to live in my beach cottage. Selling my home would give us more cash flow, but the idea of living in the main house filled me with dread. Big and ostentatious wasn't my idea of a home. Where would I relax and just breathe?

"Gotcha."

It was my turn to pace now. "I still need to spread the mulch before Friday evening. I also have my day job, and I want to track down the murderer."

"You don't have to find the person who killed Corey. Most people would let the cops handle the crime."

"I'm not most people." I flashed him my list. "I'll get up early and stay focused, which should give me time to dig deeper into each of these people."

"Aren't you supposed to keep watch on your brother tonight?"

"Not a problem. I can do both. Researching on my laptop will help me stay awake."

"You need to be more careful this time." He ran a finger along my shoulder.

His touch sent a lovely flutter through me. "You remember I always suspected Corey was the person who broke into my house when the dogs escaped last summer."

"Yeah." His gaze met mine.

"If it was him, what was the purpose? We never figured out his motive, if it was actually Corey. I've still got my notes from Peter's murder."

"What kind of information are you talking about?"

"I took notes on the gambling ring and Richard Rice Plantation. I'll gather up my research files and take them with me."

Marc crossed his arms. "What do you think you'll find?"

"I don't know. After we caught Peter's killer, I never looked at the files again. What if there's a clue in my notes that'll lead us to the person who murdered Corey? And what if I could've prevented Corey's murder by studying the files sooner?"

"You need to be discreet. The fewer people know you're trying to catch the killer, the safer you'll be."

I swallowed hard. "Good point. I won't go blabbing all over town like I did before. Mum's the word."

"Good to know. Why don't you let me follow you to your brother's place?" He took my hands in his.

"Do you think I'm already in danger?" I squeezed his warm fingers.

"Corey was murdered today, and Nate was injured. Let's at least *try* to keep you safe."

I didn't argue. It'd be stupid not to take extra precautions. "Thanks, Marc. You're always so good to me, and I hope you know how much I appreciate you."

He smiled, sending warmth from our hands down to my toes. "Caring about you is the easy part. Keeping you alive and safe is where it gets dicey. Do you feel like it's safe to stay with your brother, or should y'all come stay with me?"

"Nate will be more comfortable in his own bed, and since the doctor said he needs to rest, that's where he should be. I'll be extra cautious." Marc made a good point about staying safe. If the person who attacked Nate earlier didn't realize my brother was unable to identify them, they might come back to finish off the job.

Chapter Six

EARLY WEDNESDAY morning, I stepped out of Nate's town house rental to walk our dogs. Sunny and Bo each wore non-pull harnesses attached to leashes. My breath was visible in the beams of streetlights. The sun hadn't risen yet, but I wanted to start tackling the items on my calendar. Dog walking, helping Juliet prepare the bed and breakfast for guests, and investigating Corey's murder.

Bo headed for a red winterberry holly shrub bordering Nate's sidewalk. After finishing his business, he tugged in the direction of the town house.

"No, boy. We're going for a run. You need to burn off some energy."

Nate had saved Bo from a shelter in Charleston months earlier. The dog must've known his hours were numbered because he'd proven his loyalty to Nate often. Throughout the night, the faithful black lab followed Nate from room to room and slept beside him when my brother rested. The sweet dog's bedside manner amazed me.

Sunny lurched forward, but Bo held back.

"Sunny, stop." I knelt down and ran my hand over Bo's back while my dog stopped and waited patiently. "Hey, boy. Nate's going to be okay."

Bo gave me a soulful look.

I smiled and rubbed his back. "Let's go."

We joined Sunny, who sat a few feet from us, and the three of us jogged down the empty damp street. The dogs were about the same size. Bo had a stocky body, but he didn't struggle one bit to keep up with my German shepherd. The cool, quiet morning made me want to crawl into a nice warm bed. I needed sleep, but my day was booked. I'd even agreed to give one dog a bath for an elderly couple. They'd caught me at a weak moment, but they were always so appreciative and tipped well. Little Snickerdoodle was their baby.

Lights cut through the predawn fog and darkness, and a vehicle appeared up the street. A dark SUV drove slowly toward us. I led the dogs to the sidewalk, getting us out of the path of possible danger. Tinted windows obscured the driver's identity, but I figured out the moment he spotted me. Tires squealed as the SUV picked up speed, blinding me with bright lights in the process.

I blinked a few times then followed the movement with squinted eyes. The color of the vehicle was black, navy, or maybe dark gray. It wasn't a Suburban, but I didn't know what the model was. It passed me, and I turned. Mud on the license plate made reading the tag impossible, and the vehicle zoomed out of sight before I identified the make. However, a small, square sticker flickered on the bottom corner of the back window as it passed a streetlight. Two squiggly white lines at the bottom of the decal and something white above it. The hair on my arms stood at attention. Was it the same vehicle I'd seen leave Richard Rice Plantation the previous morning? If so, why was it on Nate's street before the sun had risen?

I wanted to run after the SUV, but it'd already vanished. I studied the town houses and single-family homes nearby. Not an obvious surveillance system in sight and not even one of those plastic signs in a yard declaring the occupant had invested in a home security company for protection. I had no room to complain. I didn't have a system and had only beefed up the window and gate locks in the past year when somebody attempted to break into my home. The reason I'd been suspicious Corey was the culprit back then was I'd spotted a tall man running down my street in dark sweats on a hot summer night. Corey matched the man's build, and he'd run in high school and college. My theory was Corey wanted to remove evidence proving his involvement in criminal activities.

Sunny barked.

"Sorry, girl." I allowed the dogs to take the lead, and I followed, keeping a laser sharp focus on my surroundings. If the SUV reappeared, I'd get something useful to identify it. No more regrets for letting it get away.

JULIET ARRIVED AT Nate's place an hour later, carrying cups of coffee and a bag with the logo of the island's new donut shop. "Good morning."

"Morning. Let me take that so you can get out of your coat." I reached for the bag and coffee cups in a cardboard tray.

"Where's Nate?"

With one hand on the wooden rail, Nate lumbered down the stairs before I could answer. On a normal day he would've galloped—his head must still hurt. "Do I smell coffee?"

Juliet smiled. "Coffee, crullers, and I got you some morning specials. A maple cake donut with real pieces of bacon on top."

"Yum. Did you go to Donut Dreaming?"

"Yes, but I can't make it a daily habit or I'll pack on the pounds in no time." She patted her flat belly.

"Sweet." My brother remained standing at the bottom of the stairs. "I mean sweet about breakfast. Not you. I mean, I can't imagine you gaining weight. Uh . . ."

I cleared my throat. "Good luck getting your foot out of your mouth." I moved to the small kitchen, and the dogs followed me. When Nate and Juliet didn't appear, I called out, "Come on, you two. I've got questions."

Juliet and Nate walked into the kitchen. She had her arm linked through his. With a tender smile, she asked him, "Did you get any sleep?"

"Not really. It seemed like Andi Grace woke me up every time my eyes closed."

"It may be old school, but I didn't want you to slip into a coma." I signaled with my hands for them to sit at the vintage Formica and chrome square kitchen table. Four matching blue-green vinyl chairs waited to be occupied.

"Your old-school methods kept both of us from sleeping." Nate's grumble came out raspy.

"Sleeping wasn't on the to-do list. My job was to keep you alive. You've got an appointment with the doctor at eleven." I sat across from Nate and sipped my coffee. "Umm, this is good. Donut Dreaming is going to give Erin a run for her money."

Juliet said, "I don't think she's got anything to worry about. The line at Daily Java was out the door."

"People are probably hoping to get in on some good gossip. Although her coffee and baked goods are delicious." I reached for a cruller.

Juliet placed the bacon donut on a plate and slid it to my brother.

"Let's get down to business. Nate, were you expecting to see Corey yesterday morning?" I asked.

"Not exactly." He shook his head and winced. "You never knew when he'd show up. He always wanted to verify you were doing the job right, even if he didn't know what he was talking about. I didn't expect to see him yesterday, but I wasn't exactly surprised."

"You actually saw him?"

"Yep. We had a conversation, too."

I opened my journal and clicked my pen. "What'd you discuss?"

"First, he asked if it was too cold to plant the shrubs I'd brought over. I told him we were sprucing up for Valentine's Day festivities. Asher Cummings had worked with me on the design and presented the plan to the board. They approved it. I didn't need Corey showing up at the last minute, questioning me."

"Why Valentine's Day?"

"They're hosting a fundraiser dinner and dance."

"I hope you didn't share your feelings in the same tone of voice with the deputies." I noted this on a fresh page.

"Don't you think I'm too old to be scolded?"

"I'm simply pointing out how your words might sound to the sheriff's department." I smiled. "Yes, you're a grown man, and I'm proud of you. We've never been in a situation like this, and we must be careful what we say and do."

He grimaced. "You're right. This headache is killing me."

I moved to the cabinet and pulled out a bottle of acetaminophen, poured a glass of water, and placed the glass and two white tablets by him. "It's time for more."

He popped them in his mouth and swallowed them down. "Corey told me they'd be taking bids soon on the next landscaping project. I was to let him know beforehand if I was interested. He could make sure my bid was accepted—if I knew what he meant."

Juliet wiped her hands on a napkin, her brow furrowed. "What did Corey mean?"

Nate gripped his paper cup with both hands. "He wanted me to offer him a bribe, and in return, I'd win the bid."

My pulse leapt. "We've heard he liked to take bribes."

Nate set his coffee to the side and reached for the donut. "I didn't offer him a cent. Corey initiated the conversation and tried to get me to pay him. Crazy, huh? I want a job. Hence, I want to make money. Not offer him a kickback."

Juliet huffed. "It sounds like Griffin isn't being paranoid."

I turned my attention to her. "What do you mean?"

"My brother never could get a project no matter how low he cut his profit margin. He suspected something underhanded."

I looked from her to Nate. "It sounds like Corey was truly involved in bad business dealings."

Nate said, "Afraid so. Unless he was testing me. Which I doubt."

I added the information to my notes. "He shouldn't have gotten a monetary reward for giving you, or any bidder, a job. If we've heard these rumors without having any connection to Richard Rice Plantation, surely somebody on the plantation board knew what was happening."

"Knowing and proving are two different things." Nate picked up his coffee cup and slurped.

"Did you notice anything strange when you talked to Corey?"

A few seconds ticked by before my brother answered. "You know, I think his words were garbled. In fact, his movements were kinda slow. I briefly wondered if he was hungover, but I was too ticked to put much thought into his condition."

I jotted down the information. "Juliet, tell us more about Griffin's interactions with Corey."

"Griffin was ready to move back to Heyward Beach. He said it was time to face the bad memories and get on with his life. He's tired of running from the pain of our past. I really hoped this was the opportunity I'd been waiting for."

"I'm so sorry." I sighed.

Juliet and Griffin had a horrible upbringing. Drug and alcohol addictions afflicted both parents.

Juliet placed her finger in the dip over her top lip, a move I'd learned she made to avoid crying. "He had it worse than I did. Daddy took out his anger on him the most. He was the oldest and a boy."

Nate reached over and squeezed her hand. "Y'all did a good job of hiding the truth about your parents while we were in school. If my dad had been in the same condition, I'd have wanted him to take out his aggression on me instead of the girls. Griffin's a good guy."

Juliet met my brother's gaze. "Yep. He's one of the best, but so are you."

I held my breath and watched the sparks bounce between Nate and Juliet. If the attack on my brother convinced him to ask Juliet out, it might've been worth it.

Nate's face turned almost as red as his hair. "Thanks, Jules."

Time to interrupt the romantic tension. "Griffin approached Corey about a job?"

"Yes." Juliet wiped a stray tear away with her napkin. "I was so hopeful it'd work out, but Corey didn't waste any time hinting a kickback would increase his chances of winning the bid."

"If Corey was still alive, I might take a swing at him." Nate picked up a crumb and popped it into his mouth.

A vague creepiness settled on my shoulders. "The killer used a bat-like weapon and swung at Corey." I turned to a new page in my journal. "Nate, who around Heyward Beach played baseball in high school or college?"

"Too many to mention. It'd be easier to list who didn't play ball. For instance, Marc. Although he may have played wherever he grew up." Nate finished his donut and pulled another daily special out of the paper bag. "These are delicious. You're right Jules, it's got real bacon. Big chunks, too. How do they keep it fresh and not soggy?" He took another bite.

Juliet blushed. "I don't know, but I'm glad you like them."

"It's my new favorite donut." After a big bite, Nate spoke, despite his mouthful of food. "Your theory is flawed, Andi Grace. If you only consider athletic guys, you're leaving out all the women as suspects."

I snapped my fingers. "You're right. It could be a woman softball player."

Juliet said, "Or a woman scared for her life."

"True. Maybe Corey threatened a woman and she took a swing at him."

Juliet tore little strips off her paper napkin then wadded it up and set it to the side of her plate. Something was bothering her. "Juliet? What's wrong?"

She took a breath. "Before I came to live with y'all, did you know about my situation?"

I shook my head. "Not really. I suspected something was off, but I never dreamed how bad you had it." After high school Juliet had moved in with us to help with expenses when she could. We'd become a support system for each other.

Juliet reached for her coffee cup and avoided eye contact with us. "Plenty of people knew what was happening. More than once I had to defend myself against my dad and his friends. Thanks be to God we lived to adulthood."

"Jules, I had no idea." Nate handed her a fresh napkin.

"It's in the past, but I'd love it if Griffin could move back to Heyward Beach. It'd give us an opportunity to strengthen our relationship. Kinda like a fresh start without any guilt."

I squeezed her hand. "Hey, if you keep getting people to book rooms at the B&B and I get people to board their dogs with me, we'll hire Griffin at our plantation. We've got buildings to improve or demolish. The dog barn needs more attention if I want to expand my business. The more money we make, the more projects I can hire Griffin to handle."

"My brother is always up to a challenge, and so am I. If the plantation isn't a success, it won't be because I haven't tried. In February, I plan to attend bridal shows in Charleston, Georgetown, and Myrtle Beach in hopes of convincing people to have their weddings at Kennady Plantation. I might even venture up to North Carolina to spread the word."

"I'm impressed. If you need company, let me know." I smiled at my friend.

Nate pulled a jelly donut from the white bag and raised it to his mouth. Red jelly squirted out the side and dropped onto the table. "Oops."

I'd learned years ago not to get between my brother and food. "Anything else you two can think of for my notes?"

Nate held up a sticky finger. "The three of us know Corey wanted me to offer him a bribe. I refused. If David learns about this, do you think it'll make the cops more likely to arrest me?"

I shook my head. "I have no idea."

Juliet said, "We should be prepared for the worst. There's no way you're the only person Corey approached about kickbacks."

"You're right. Thanks." The tense set of Nate's shoulders seemed to relax. "Sis, one of my men will lay the mulch for you this afternoon. I can run over with Juliet after my doctor's appointment to make sure it's done right."

"No, I trust your employees. You only need to focus on getting better."

"Yeah, yeah, yeah. I can only take so much mothering in one meal." Nate shot me a grin.

"Sorry, it's a habit. Plus, I want you to get well soon."

"Yes, ma'am." He saluted.

I stood and tossed my trash into his wastebasket. "I'm heading out. Do you mind if Sunny stays here with Bo for a while?"

Nate reached for another donut. "Suits me."

I left Nate and Juliet sitting at the kitchen table with the dogs at their feet. The time had come for me to walk clients' animals and gather clues. I was determined to find the killer before the sheriff arrested Nate.

Chapter Seven

I'D WALKED ALL the dogs on my morning schedule and fed tropical fish for a family taking a Caribbean cruise. Before entering Daily Java, I inhaled a deep breath. Facing Erin wasn't going to be easy.

Mid-morning customers filled the dining area, and two men sat on the patio despite the cool January temperature. My goal was to order coffee and ask questions.

When I entered the coffee shop and approached the counter, a young woman I didn't recognize greeted me. Dark curls were pulled back in a ponytail, and her face was perfectly made up. "Good morning."

"Morning. I'd like a large coffee."

She gave me a toothy smile. "Would you like to try our Crème Brulee specialty blend? Or maybe a dark chocolate mint latte?"

"Hmm. Chocolate and coffee? Sounds delicious. I'll give it a try." I looked at the name stitched on her apron. "Uh, is your name Lacey Jane?" What were the odds she had the same name as my sister and now worked at the same coffee shop?

"No, ma'am. I'm Hunter Langdon." She rang up my drink. "Your total is four dollars and twenty-five cents."

I handed her a five. "Why don't you have your own apron?"

She shrugged. "They keep promising me one, but it's no biggie. Here's your change."

"You keep it." I held up my hand palm out. "Is Erin here this morning?"

"Oh, no, ma'am. I guess you didn't hear." She looked each way then back to me. "Yesterday, her husband died unexpectedly."

More like was murdered, but I didn't correct her. I considered my options while the girl who couldn't be twenty-one prepared my drink. Erin's absence could work to my advantage.

"Here you go." She slid a paper cup my way.

"Thanks. How's Erin doing?"

Nobody had entered the shop behind me, and Hunter leaned against the counter. "I was here when the cops came in. They followed her to the office, and I heard her scream. It was awful."

Erin was either shocked or a good actress.

"I'm so sorry. Is there anything I can do for her? I'm a dog walker. Does she have a pet?"

Hunter shook her head, and black curls bounced. "I don't know of any pets."

The bell on the door tinkled, and I shot a glance over my shoulder. A middle-aged woman looked toward the tables and hurried over to a group of women in deep discussion with Bibles open, sitting at a booth.

I turned back to Hunter. "Did you know Corey well? Did you like him?"

Her eyes widened, and she glanced around the coffee shop. "I'd never speak ill of the dead."

"But?"

She lowered her voice. "He was a big flirt."

I whispered, "Did he ever make a pass at you? Touch you?"

"Gosh, no. I have three brothers who taught me to scream bloody murder if anybody tries to lay a hand on me." Her eyes sparkled. "I earned my blue belt in karate and know where to kick a guy to inflict the most pain, if you know what I mean."

I smiled. "I have a brother, too. They can be protective." I sobered at the thought. Yeah, if word got out about Corey making a play for Lacey Jane, it could harm Nate. The cops might see it as motive for Nate to kill Corey.

Time was wasting, and I didn't think I could get any more out of Hunter. I slipped her my business card. "If you think of anything I can do for Erin, please call me. Or if you need to talk about the situation, I'd be happy to listen. I've got a younger sister, and I'm a good listener."

"Are you a therapist?"

I laughed. "No, just trying to be helpful."

"Oh, yeah. You're a dog walker." She smiled. "But you're easy to talk to."

"Thanks." I waved and walked out to my 2010 Suburban in the parking lot and studied its frame. The mysterious black SUV had more curves and soft lines, but what was it?

I glanced across the street toward the beauty salon Juliet used to own. No lights shone, but I strolled over to check it out. Sure enough, it didn't appear as if anybody was inside. To be certain, I knocked on the glass door and waited for a response. Nothing.

Weird. Why would Wendy be closed on a Wednesday?

I sipped my coffee and moseyed along the sidewalk until I reached Paula's Pickings, owned by Regina Houp, the original owner's niece. Regina probably wouldn't be thrilled to see me, but I decided to risk her displeasure. I entered the store and browsed while she rang up a customer.

When the store was empty, I took a deep breath and approached the woman. "Hi, Regina. How are you?"

Her eyes narrowed, but she displayed good Southern manners. "I'm recovering from Peter's death. Although not as well as you."

I counted to ten in French before uttering a response. Peter had broken his engagement to Regina weeks before his death. She must still be upset over the failure of their relationship, but it wasn't my fault he ended things with her. Instead of dignifying her comment with a response, I switched to what I really came to find out. "Lovely Locks isn't open. Do you know why?"

Regina let out a deep sigh and rolled her eyes. "Wendy didn't open yesterday or today. She called and told me she'd tried to contact her customers, but if any showed up here I should inform them she'd be closed until further notice. As if I have nothing better to do than be her secretary."

Wendy had a lot of gumption to tell Regina what to do. "The merchants around Heyward Beach often help each other out. Maybe she thought you wouldn't mind." Wait, why was I trying to defend Wendy's actions?

Regina's eyes narrowed, and she gave a slight shake of her head. "If you don't need anything else, I've got work to do."

"Sure. Thanks, Regina." I returned to the salon and sipped my coffee. Unsure what I hoped to find, I peered through the glass door again.

"Whatcha doing?"

My heart skyrocketed to my tonsils. I jumped and turned to see Marc. "Good thing I had a lid on my coffee or else one of us would have stains on our clothes."

He raised his own cup of coffee. "You didn't answer my question."

"I wanted to talk to Wendy, but the salon is closed. She didn't open yesterday either." I repeated what I learned from Regina. "What are you doing?"

"I was on my way back to work after meeting with a judge on the mainland and decided to stop for coffee. I saw your vehicle and came to find you. Glad you're alive and well." His gray eyes sparkled, and his navy suit highlighted their blue tones.

"You can't go wrong with coffee or Coke."

"Yeah, I'm figuring that out. You and your sister won me over to the dark side."

"Good to know. We'll try to get you eating dark chocolate next." The thought I'd had even a tiny impact on Marc weakened my knees. There was no doubt I was interested in the man, and he'd seemed to care about me until he set up his law practice on the island. We didn't see each other near as much as we had in the summer, leaving me confused about his true feelings.

"Never. Dark chocolate is evil."

I laughed. "Not hardly. You must not have tasted a good brand."

"It tastes bitter, and the devil is bitter. He can't get to heaven so dark chocolate is the devil."

I laughed. "You've got to be kidding."

"Yeah, I am, but I don't like the taste. Let's agree to disagree about dark chocolate." He flashed his amazing smile at me. "Do you have time to talk?"

"Sure. What's up?" I sipped my minty latte.

He pointed back to the coffee shop. "Is it too cold for you to sit outside?"

"I don't mind the brisk weather. Besides, the wind isn't blowing, and it feels good to be in the sunshine."

When we reached the street, Marc took my hand and didn't release it until we sat at a patio table at Daily Java. "What have you discovered with your investigation?"

Holding Marc's hand rocked my equilibrium, but he appeared calm and collected. I leaned back in the chair and tried to act like holding hands with Marc was no big deal. "Erin was here when the deputies came to inform her about Corey's death. And Corey indicated to Nate he could get him more business at Richard Rice Plantation if Nate would give him a bribe."

Marc whistled. "That's not good."

"I know it makes a stronger case against Nate, but he's innocent." I squeezed my coffee cup.

"What else have you got?"

My heart raced, and I avoided eye contact. If I told him more, how would it affect his career?

"Spill it. I won't be upset."

It unnerved me how well Marc read me. "When I took Sunny and

Bo for their early morning walk, a dark SUV drove down Nate's street. I couldn't see the driver or the car tags. The only identifying mark was a sticker on the back windshield. It's one you might have for a neighborhood, work, or country club."

"Anything else?" His relaxed posture reassured me.

"It was like the driver couldn't figure out his GPS and was looking for an address at o-dark-thirty. When the driver spotted me, he sped away."

"Do you think he was looking for Nate's place?"

"Yeah. What are the odds the day after Corey's murder, a vehicle is casing Nate's street for anybody else? It could be the killer wanting to finish off Nate in case he saw something yesterday morning."

Marc held up his hands. "Hold on, let's not jump to conclusions. In case you're right, though, it might be best to always have somebody with you for a few days."

"Me? Why?"

"You were at the plantation around the time Corey was murdered. You solved a murder last year, and the killer may be aware of your skills. Also, you're Nate's sister. He may have shared information to incriminate the killer. Neither of you should be alone for the next few days."

"Impossible. I've got dogs to walk, a business to run, and a plantation to take care of."

Kennady Plantation was mine. Peter had left it all to me and only a pittance to his family. I'd almost rejected the gift when I learned Peter's flawed reason for choosing me. Marc had convinced me I could do a lot of good with the property, and he'd been right. Juliet thrived taking charge of the B&B. I'd never seen her so happy. I'd also created a way to provide a place for Dylan King to live as well as work. With his dad in jail, Dylan was turning his life around, and I was proud of him. Converting the barn into a doggie day care allowed me the dream of dog training, boarding, and grooming. One stop for all your pet needs.

"What's going on at your plantation?" Marc raised the paper cup to his lips.

"We have our first guests coming tomorrow, and I need to work on the landscaping near the house. Nate mentioned he'd send a crew to spread mulch, but he's got more important things to deal with. Juliet's brother is going to come inspect my buildings this weekend and see about converting the old outside kitchen to a little house where I can live. Dylan's working on the stables, and I'm teaching him how to train dogs. I'm impressed with what a hard worker he is."

"He needed to direct his energy to something good." Marc smiled.

"You're right. Bad decisions usually catch up with you."

Marc hadn't drunk much of his coffee.

"Is your drink okay?"

"It's a little bitter."

"I've already heard your philosophy on dark chocolate. Don't ruin coffee for me. Did you add sugar and cream?"

He shrugged. "Don't real men drink their coffee black?"

"Stay right here." I laughed and moved inside the coffee shop with his drink. A warm shot of heat slapped me in the face, making me glad we were sitting outside in the fresh air. Not every January day was this pleasant. I added cream and organic sugar, stirred well, and hurried back to Marc. "Try this."

He sipped the doctored-up brew, and the frown left his handsome face. "Much better. I guess I'm not a coffee purist."

"There's no shame in enhancing your coffee. If you read the menu, there are many choices."

"Such as?"

"Look at the board next time you come here. There's Surfer Dude, Cowboy Up, Need for Speed and even Home Run. They don't sound like sissy drinks to me."

"Okay, but what's in them?" A slow smile formed.

"Marc, read the menu and pick one that appeals to you. Caramel, mocha, lavender, candy bar flavors and coconut are just some of the options. Do you like that?" I pointed to the coffee in his cup.

"Yeah. What'd you do to it?"

"I only added cream and sugar." I leaned back and sipped on my latte.

My phone vibrated on the table, and Juliet's picture popped up.

Marc pointed. "Go ahead and answer."

"I normally wouldn't be so rude, but she's with Nate." I swiped the button. "Juliet, is everything okay?"

"No. David took Nate in for questioning." Her voice wobbled.

My heart sank. If only I'd had more time or been smarter, maybe I could've prevented this from happening. I pushed the button for speakerphone. "Marc's with me and listening."

"What's going on?" He glanced from me to the phone.

I sighed. "The deputy took Nate away."

Marc leaned forward and lowered his voice, speaking into the phone. "Juliet, did David say Nate was under arrest?"

"No." Juliet sniffed.

"Good."

I pushed my chair back. "I'm heading to the detention center."

Juliet said, "Hurry. He needs you. I'll watch the dogs."

"Do you want to go with us?"

There was a long pause. "No, I'll stay here, but let me know what happens."

Our connection ended.

Marc stood. "I'll drive you."

"Are you sure? What about Chubb? What about work?" I'd convinced Marc to adopt his golden retriever the previous summer.

"I took him to doggie day care this morning. We go twice a week. It helps his socialization skills. Plus, he's a bit more mellow at the end of the day."

"I plan to have doggie day care at my place one day."

He tweaked my nose. "I'll be your first customer."

I stood and reached for his hand. "Thanks, Marc."

"For what? Driving you over or letting you take care of Chubb?" The twinkle in his eyes made me smile.

"Both. You really are the nicest person." Tears filled my eyes, but I blinked them back.

He slipped his arm around my shoulder and led us off the patio. "Shh, let's keep that our little secret."

Chapter Eight

MARC AND I SAT across an oak desk from Wade. David stood in the corner of the sheriff's office with arms crossed over his chest, frowning.

Experience had taught me to give the sheriff time to say his piece before I questioned him. I mashed my lips together to prevent myself from interrupting.

Wade's deep voice penetrated the room. "There wasn't a lot of blood on the shovel, but what we have matches Nate."

"Isn't that a good thing? He couldn't have hit himself in the back of his head."

Marc reached for my hand. Message received. Shut up.

"The sheriff narrowed his eyes. "The blood on the hedge shears belongs to Corey. Nate's fingerprints are all over both lawn tools, he was at the scene, and he had a motive for the murder."

My scalp tingled. "Wade, where was the blood exactly?"

"The blade of the shovel and the blades of the hedge shears."

Yuck. Bile rose to my throat as I remembered seeing Corey's body. "Do you mean the killer stabbed Corey with the sharp part of the shears?"

"Yes. We're arresting Nate today. I'll inform you when his arraignment is. You'll know more then."

"Got to keep your voters happy?" Oops. My face grew hot. Momma would've been ashamed of me. "Sorry."

With elbows on his desk, Wade steepled his fingers together. "But you thought it. At least we know where you stand on the issue."

My throat tightened. "You saw Nate yesterday. Are you looking into who clobbered him? It's obvious the same person who killed Corey is the one who attacked my brother." My voice grew shriller with each word.

"Andi Grace, you best settle down." He pointed a finger at me. "Marc, if you're Nate's attorney, you can talk to him in a bit."

Marc nodded. "Thanks. For the record, I am representing Nate."

Wade stood and motioned us toward the door. "I'll see y'all later."

"You can count on it." I clamped my mouth shut. It wouldn't help

Nate if I antagonized Wade and David.

David made no move to leave with us.

Marc cleared his throat and latched onto my elbow. He remained silent until we reached the waiting area. He leaned down enough for us to be face-to-face. "Couldn't help yourself, I guess."

I stood close enough to Marc our noses almost touched. "I'm sorry. He makes me so mad. I mean, he can't seriously think Nate killed Corey."

"I honestly don't know, but if he's going to keep his job as sheriff, he has to remain fair and impartial."

"Hmm. Fair and impartial? Corey didn't possess those characteristics. It might be part of the killer's motive."

Marc led the way to two scarred wooden chairs. "We shouldn't assume anything."

"Right, but knowing the motive will narrow my suspect list."

He checked his watch. "He was a ladies' man. If it's a romantic reason, there's a whole range of emotions. Jealousy. Anger. Betrayal."

"My romance theory didn't hold water on Peter's death." I looked around the depressing room. This was the second waiting room I'd sat in for my brother. Both times I'd been afraid. At the hospital I was scared for his physical health. Here, I feared he'd rot in prison. *Lord, please help us find the truth.*

Marc reached for my hand. "It's going to be okay."

"If you say so." The sentiment was sweet, but his words didn't reassure me.

"Wade indicated only I can see Nate right now. Why don't you do something useful while I wait?"

I hated leaving my brother, but Marc was right. "Okay. I guess it's a good thing we decided to each drive our own vehicles over."

"That's right. I'm learning you never know what might happen with legal issues."

"Will you call me after you talk to Nate?"

He nodded. "Yes. We can meet at my office."

I squeezed his hand before releasing it. "Thanks for helping. You're always so good to me."

"I wouldn't have it any other way." His smile helped thaw the icy cold fear flowing through my veins.

I left the building with determined steps. Once I reached the sanctuary of my Suburban, I called Juliet. "Hey, where are you?"

"I'm still at Nate's house with Sunny and Bo."

"Do you know where Wendy lives?"

"Sure."

I started the Suburban. "I'm coming to get you, and we're going to pay her a visit." At least, I hoped we'd find her at home.

Juliet didn't answer right away. "Shouldn't I be here when Nate gets home?"

"Marc is waiting to speak to Nate now, and it doesn't sound like Nate's coming back today."

"Oh, no." Juliet moaned.

Even with my own stomach in knots, I had to reassure my friend. "Let's focus our energy on finding evidence to prove Nate's innocent."

"You're right. I'll be waiting."

Thirty minutes later, Juliet and I pulled in front of a nondescript brick house on the west side of Highway 17. The place looked deserted, and there was no sign of the cute Bug Wendy drove. I parked in the driveway.

Juliet released her seat belt. "I should go by myself. She's used to me."

"No way. We stick together." Sticking together became my motto after facing a killer alone last summer.

"Fine." She hopped out and hoofed it to the front door, while I was still exiting the SUV.

I joined her on the front stoop as she pushed the doorbell for the second time. I watched for movement around the windows. "Can you hear anything?"

"No, nothing." She waited a few seconds before pushing the doorbell for the third time.

"Let's look around back."

She sighed. "If I didn't care so much for you and Nate, I wouldn't agree. I feel like a trespasser. Or a peeping Tom."

"She may be the only person who can prove Nate's innocence. What if Wendy witnessed Corey's murder?"

Juliet's gaze met mine. "What if she's the killer?"

I'd considered that. "Anything's possible." I led the way through the grass to the backyard. A rusted old chain link fence enclosed the space. The brownish green grass added to the unkempt look of the property. A big black wooden shed filled the back corner of the yard, and paint peeled off the planks. "Does the shed look large enough to hold her Volkswagen?"

"Maybe." She tried the latch on the gate, and it opened.

I grabbed my friend's arm and squealed. Juliet had become more assertive since taking charge of the B&B, but going into the backyard uninvited was a bold move for my friend. Very bold.

We entered the space and veered in different directions. I spied tracks through the tall grass. "Juliet, look."

She hurried to my side. "What?"

"These are tire tracks. Do you think they look wide enough for car tires?"

"It's possible. Do you have your phone? We can measure them with an app."

"Good idea." Juliet always impressed me with her brilliance. "Hey, look at the patch of dirt by the shed door. I bet we can bet a better measurement there."

Calculating the width of the tracks with a phone app wasn't as easy as it sounded. On my hands and knees, I held the phone in different angles and finally came up with my best guess. "It's about eight-and-a-half inches. At least I think."

I studied the tracks and pounded the side of the building with my fist. "Do you think Wendy killed Corey, drove home like a maniac, hid her car in here, and disappeared?"

"We know she was driving crazy when she ran us off the road."

I stepped to the shed door and pulled on the combination lock. It didn't budge. I spun the dial but didn't feel any stop points. "Do you remember Wendy's date of birth?"

"Not off the top of my head." She swiped the screen on her phone. A few seconds ticked by, and a bird sang its garbled song. "Here it is. October second, nineteen ninety-three."

I tried those numbers. "No luck."

"Try Christmas or New Year's Day. Maybe Valentine's Day."

I tried different combinations, but nothing worked. When a breeze blew over my skin, I realized I'd been perspiring. I shivered. "I don't think we're going to figure it out."

"Let me keep trying some of her favorite holidays. When we worked together, she went all out decorating for special occasions. Even obscure days like greeting card manufacturers invent."

I moved away and looked at the house. It was a simple one-story red brick ranch. No shutters in back. The concrete patio was cracked, and there was a metal table and rusty chairs. With a little work, the place had the potential to be attractive.

A flutter at the right window caught my attention. "Juliet, I think somebody's inside. Does she have a cat?"

"I never heard her mention a pet when we worked together. She mostly talked about good-looking men and who she was dating and wanted to date."

"Look." I pointed to the window. "I think the curtain moved. Maybe it was my imagination, but if Wendy has a cat, she'll come back for it. Right?"

"I suppose."

"Wait a second, if she parked the Volkswagen in the shed, how is she getting around? Does she have a second car?"

"Not that I know of. She loves her Bug."

We stood in the backyard and stared at the house. My breathing became shallow. Was somebody inside? Or had my imagination kicked into overdrive?

"Do you think Wendy's in there?" Juliet moved closer to me.

"Kinda, but if she is, why didn't she answer the door?" My stomach churned, and I needed an antacid.

Juliet faced me. "I'm going to knock on the sliding glass door. Maybe she'll answer if I go alone."

"Again, I'm not letting you out of my sight."

"I understand, but stay here."

"Only if you promise not to go inside without me." I gave her my most stern look.

"I promise." Juliet crossed the spacious yard and tapped on the glass door.

A siren wailed in the distance. I didn't know the difference between cop cars, ambulances, and fire trucks, but the wailing grew louder.

Goose bumps stole over my arms. "Juliet, run."

She swung around and must have trusted my instincts because she broke into a jog.

I met her at the gate. "I think a neighbor called the cops on us."

We raced to the Suburban, but a sheriff's car blocked the end of the driveway.

David Wayne exited his Dodge Charger, and a grin broke through his somber face. "Busted."

Chapter Nine

I LEANED AGAINST my SUV and bent my knee to prop the bottom of my foot against the door. I hoped I looked more casual and less guilty than I felt. "Hi, David."

"Andi Grace, I didn't expect to see you again so soon." He nodded to me and turned his attention to the other side of my Suburban. "Who's with you?"

"Juliet Reed. She's my friend."

With one hand on his holster, he called out. "Ms. Reed, please join us."

Juliet walked around the hood and stood beside me. I expected her to be shaking like a leaf, but she lifted her chin. Again, her boldness impressed me.

"Ladies, I got a report of breaking and entering."

I said, "We rang the doorbell. Never entered the house. We didn't even touch the door handle. You can test for fingerprints."

"Maybe I'll do that. The sheriff warned me you were feisty. Care to explain what you're doing here?"

I pushed off my Suburban and stood straight. "We told Sheriff Stone a car like Wendy's ran us off the entry road at Richard Rice Plantation yesterday morning. We came to ask Wendy a few questions. Is she on your suspect list?"

"I have no intention of sharing my suspect list with you, ma'am."

I rolled my eyes. "You can call me Andi Grace. I'm barely older than you. If Wendy didn't kill Corey, she might've seen who did."

"What were you doing in the backyard?" The deputy's hat shadowed his face, making it impossible to read his expression.

"Come on, I'll show you." I couldn't wait to hear his thoughts.

First, he spoke into the microphone clipped onto his shoulder. His words were mumbled, but I thought he said he didn't need backup.

Juliet stood closer to David than I did. "Please release Nate. He didn't kill Corey or anybody else."

The deputy's stiff posture relaxed a bit. "We've got a system and it works pretty well. I can't just release Nate because you ask me, but I won't quit looking into Corey Lane's death. Now, what did you want to show me?"

Juliet rewarded the man with a smile. "I think you'll find it exciting."

I doubted it, but I followed the two of them.

When we reached the tire tracks, Juliet took my phone and showed our measurements to David, and they walked around the yard. She even snapped pictures with my phone of the patterns in the grass and dirt. Again, I studied the house. If the call had come from Wendy, wouldn't she be watching out of a window to see what was happening? "Hey, David, who reported us to you?"

"Anonymous call."

His answer didn't surprise me. "Can you trace it? Did it come from Wendy's phone? Or maybe Lovely Locks Salon?"

"Not at liberty to say." He knelt beside a tire track and ran his fingers over the bent blades of grass.

I moved closer to the deputy. "Did you see my phone measured the width of the tires?"

"Ms. Reed suggested the tire tracks match Ms. Conn's Volkswagen." David frowned. "It's a standard-sized tire. The first three numbers on a tire size are the width of the tire in millimeters. If you convert your inches to millimeters, you'll find eight and a half inches is close to two hundred fifteen millimeters."

"Nice round number. Seems appropriate." I would've looked up the Bug's tire size on my phone except Juliet still held onto it. "Juliet and I think it looks like Wendy drove her car, or at least some vehicle, to the shed. If you open it, I bet you'll find her Volkswagen." I'd thrown Juliet's name in the mix because she didn't seem to irritate him as much as I did.

The sound of a guitar chord from my phone signaled an incoming text, but David held my iPhone. He glanced at the screen. "It's Marc Williams. Your brother's attorney, right?"

"Yes."

"Seems like a good time for you ladies to leave before I have to arrest you for trespassing."

"You're blocking us in the drive."

He handed the phone to me. "I'll move my car so you can go."

I glanced at the message. **Come to my office when you can.** I slipped the cell phone into my pocket. "David, aren't you going to at least find Wendy and question her?"

"Marc Williams is going to have another client if you don't get out of here." He stalked to the front driveway and slid into the Charger, moving it so we could leave. When we jumped into my SUV and pulled away, David returned to the driveway.

I watched him in my rearview mirror. "Thank goodness he's sticking around to investigate." I drove away, staying well under the speed limit. No need to risk David giving me a speeding ticket.

"Maybe he'll catch Wendy."

"Hey, do you have a thing for David?" Since we all graduated together, it seemed safe to call him by his first name unless he was with us.

"No." Her answer came out too quick, and when I darted a look at Juliet, her face had grown red.

"Hmm. I haven't asked about your love life for a while because I was hoping you and Nate might get together. I didn't want to sway your decision, though."

"Nate hasn't asked me out on a date. Simple as that."

I drove toward Marc's office. "If he asked, would you say yes?"

"The point is, he hasn't asked. We spent a lot of time together in the fall, and he had plenty of opportunities. It seems like the attraction is one-sided."

"Hmm. If David asked you out, what would you say?"

Juliet adjusted her shoulder strap and angled in my direction. "I could do a lot worse than dating David Wayne. He's good-looking and nice and smart." Chin in the air, she glanced at me. "You won't make me feel guilty, either."

I wasn't giving up. "You know Nate hasn't really dated anybody seriously."

"He's always got girls hanging around him."

"Maybe so, but he's not dating them. Despite having two sisters, he's awkward with women."

I turned into the parking lot of Marc's office. He'd found an old accounting firm office available for rent. Nothing fancy, but its set-up provided decent space needed for his law practice. I'd helped him decorate the space. Marc was a boat man, making it easy to come up with a sophisticated nautical theme.

Once inside, Rylee Prosser greeted us with a smile. She worked three days a week as Marc's office manager and was proficient at her job. "Good afternoon, ladies."

"Hi, Rylee. I think Marc's waiting for us."

The woman blew long auburn bangs out of her middle-age eyes and smiled. "Yes, he's expecting you. He and Lacey Jane are in his office. Can I get you anything to drink?"

"I'm fine, but thanks." I knew my way around. I should because I'd helped him furnish the place. Manly, sturdy furniture with sparse décorations. All pictures had a boat theme. I'd even given Marc a regatta sailboat canvas picture, and he'd placed it in his office, claiming it made him happy.

Juliet followed me down the short hall from the foyer and waiting room combo to Marc's private office. I tapped on the door before walking into the space with three large windows looking out to a pond with a fountain. "Hi."

Lacey Jane sat in a leather chair across the desk from Marc, going through a stack of files. "Hey, Sis. Juliet."

"Hi, sweet girl." I laid my hand on her head for a second. Her fair coloring and slender frame were so different from my body. She always seemed fragile to me, and I wasn't positive my opinion was due to her being the baby in the family.

Marc stood and motioned to two wingback office chairs I'd helped him find at an upscale consignment store. "Have a seat. You got here fast." He remained standing until Juliet and I each settled into the chairs in front of his desk. Lacey Jane left the files and retrieved a sturdy ladder back chair from the far wall and joined us.

I crossed my legs. "David ran us off, but at least he's considering Wendy as a person of interest."

Marc closed his eyes and squeezed the bridge of his nose. "You and David crossed paths?"

I nodded. "Afraid so."

"David may not be as patient with you as Wade was last summer. Please don't get sideways with him."

"I'll try to do better. How's Nate?"

Marc laid his hands flat on the desk. "He's shook up and still dealing with the headache from his concussion. He wanted me to tell you three he can rest in jail as well as he can rest at home. As long as y'all take care of Bo, he'll be good."

"Of course I'll take care of Bo." With a sinking heart, I gripped the arms of the chair and willed myself not to cry. "This can't be happening."

Lacey Jane slumped in her chair. "Oh, but it is."

I reached over and squeezed my sister's hand. No matter how confident I tried to appear, the stress of the last two days had drained me. "What about bail?" My voice caught.

"There's a bond hearing tomorrow. Nate doesn't have a criminal record and he lives in the area. He'll probably qualify for bail, but the judge often sets the amount so high it's hard to raise the money."

Doom and gloom.

Nate's arrest was bigger than I was. There were obstacles impossible for me to handle. A warm tear flowed down my face and splashed onto my thigh.

Juliet reached over and squeezed my free hand. "Trust in God. He'll get us through this."

Marc's gaze connected with each of ours before he walked out of the office through the double white doors calling over his shoulder, "Be right back."

I looked at Lacey Jane and Juliet. "You're right. God has protected us all of these years, and we can trust Him again."

Lacey Jane burst into tears. "How? Do you understand how serious this is?"

Even though my sister was the baby, she was taking paralegal classes and might have deeper insight than I did. "Nothing's too big for God."

Juliet stood and faced us. "The four of us will find a way to prove Nate is innocent. We're smart, and this isn't the first murder we've investigated."

"You're right. We'll figure this out." I swiped away a tear. "We're not going to let the fear of striking out keep us from playing the game."

"Hey, Babe Ruth said something similar." Marc returned with Rylee on his heels. "I should've asked, but I know Andi Grace loves coffee and took a chance y'all do, too. Rylee brewed a fresh pot."

Rylee placed a tray with four mugs of coffee on the credenza made from reclaimed driftwood. It looked masculine and outdoorsy. On the tray was a white carafe and a variety of sweeteners and cream. In no time, we'd each prepared cups of coffee and taken our places with mugs in hand and tears under control.

The next hour we focused on strategy for getting Nate released. With everything in me, I believed finding the killer was the best way to free my brother, which led to the topic of possible suspects.

The alarm on my phone beeped, alerting me of my next dog walking appointment. "I've gotta go. Juliet, do you want a ride?"

"If you don't mind taking me to Nate's, I'll pick up my car and the dogs then head to your place. The Plantation. Not your beach house."

I stood. "Lacey Jane, are you going to be okay?"

"Don't worry. I've got an online class tonight to distract me. I'll be fine." The smile she tried for morphed into a grimace. "Who knows, after this I may decide to go to college full-time and apply to law school."

Not being able to pay for Lacey Jane to attend college killed me. Student loans scared her, and I wanted to help. I only needed to get Nate out of jail and make a profit at the plantation, then maybe I could scrape up enough money to help pay her way. Even thought I'd inherited Peter's place, the money involved was a gray area. I couldn't offer to pay for my sister's education until I understood my finances. "I know you'll be fine, sweetie, but call me if you need to talk."

"Yes, ma'am." She lifted the file she'd laid to the side earlier.

Marc stepped around the desk. "I'll walk y'all out."

Juliet detoured to the restroom. "I'll meet you in a bit."

I suspected she wanted to give me a few minutes alone with Marc. "Okay."

Outside, he opened my door for me. "It's going to be all right. Do you want to do something tonight?"

"Related to Nate's case?"

He chuckled. "I know you well enough to realize you're not going to do anything except focus on the murder until the killer's caught. Not that it's a good idea, but trying to talk you out of it is a waste of breath and energy."

"You're exactly right. Thanks for understanding. The three people I most want to speak to are Wendy, Erin, and Asher Cummings."

"Asher? I'm sure you don't suspect him. Are you hoping he can help you find another suspect?"

"Yes. Plus, he worked with Nate on the landscaping. Not physically, but presenting the plan to other board members." I took a deep breath. "I'm more scared than when I wanted to catch Peter's killer. I need more suspects."

Marc opened his arms, and I melted into his comforting embrace. "One step at a time."

"I know you're right, but my little brother's life is at stake." It didn't matter Nate was six-foot-two-inches and twenty-seven years old. He'd always be my little brother, and I felt responsible for him.

One way or another, I'd take care of my siblings, get Nate's freedom, and find a way to help Lacey Jane with college expenses if she truly wanted to go to law school.

Chapter Ten

THERE WEREN'T MANY restaurants open for dinner in January in Heyward Beach. Marc arranged for us to meet Asher at a seafood restaurant in Murrells Inlet. After a dinner spent discussing college basketball and eating fresh-caught grouper, we ordered coffee.

Butterflies fluttered in my belly. How would I bring up the murder? It wouldn't be fair to let Marc start the conversation.

Asher stirred cream into his coffee. "I've enjoyed this meal with y'all, but the last time we got together it involved Peter Roth's murder. What's the occasion tonight? Possibly Corey Lane's death?"

"Yes, sir."

Marc grinned. "Andi Grace has always said you're one of the smartest men she knows. Can you shed any light on people who might like to see Corey dead?"

Asher looked in the distance and rubbed his jaw. "You know I was suspicious of how he managed money for Richard Rice Plantation. I remained on the board in order to keep an eye on the man." He shot a glance toward me. "For the record, I didn't kill him."

I sat straighter. Why was he so quick to declare his innocence? "I never thought you did, but do you have a suspect in mind?"

"Garland Davis is a possibility. Most people call him Ben. He owns a small construction company and accused Corey of taking bribes. Couldn't prove it, though. Corey's a slippery one. Uh, was a slippery one." Asher's tone implied he didn't think much of the dead man.

I took notes in my journal and started a fresh page with Ben Davis's name at the top.

Marc said, "Anybody else come to mind?"

Asher took a sip of coffee and drummed his fingers on the table. "I hesitate to say this in case it muddies the waters."

I looked up. "Go ahead. I'll list it as gossip."

He nodded and leaned forward, propping his forearms on the table. "They say Corey was a womanizer. He chased anything wearing a skirt. If it's true, you might want to look at his wife."

"I'd already considered Erin, but when I went to the coffee shop and her house, I missed her. I won't give up, though." Was Erin capable of murdering her husband then framing Nate? I knew for sure my brother was innocent, and I'd follow up on every possible clue. Had the killer meant to cast suspicion on Nate, or was it an accident?

Laughter sounded from the bar. Two women sat there with three men trying to attract their attention. I'd never gotten into the bar scene. Maybe because I'd taken charge of Nate and Lacey Jane after our parents died in a car crash. Whatever the reason, it seemed kinda sad to watch the five people trying so hard to hook up.

A woman sat at the end of the sleek wooden bar staring into a small glass filled with gold liquid. Dark hair pulled into a neat chignon. Low-cut dress and earrings sparkling so much they were evident across the room.

My pulse accelerated, and I grabbed Marc's forearm. "Erin's at the bar. Far stool."

Marc and Asher both twisted in their seats.

I stood. "Excuse me, I'll be right back."

Marc reached for my hand. "Andi Grace, wait. Don't do anything you'll regret."

"It's fine. I'm only going to pay my condolences." I slipped away from the men and made my way to Erin. I sat on the empty seat beside her. "Erin, I'm so sorry about Corey. Is there anything I can do for you?"

She spun toward me with eyes blazing. "I think your family has done enough. Thanks to Nate, I'm planning my husband's funeral."

My heart began to staccato. "Nate's innocent."

She stirred her little red straw in the drink, and ice cubes rattled in the glass. "He wouldn't be sitting in the detention center if he wasn't guilty."

"I know you must be in a lot of pain, but the killer is still on the loose. It wasn't my brother."

Erin stood, tall and confident. "I know Nate and Corey had an argument. Don't try to convince me he's innocent. He's in jail, which is exactly where he belongs."

My hands shook, but I wouldn't let her see how her words affected me. I rose to my feet and lifted my chin. "He didn't kill Corey, and you might want to be careful until the real killer is caught."

Her eyes grew wide. "Is that a threat?"

"No, of course not." I relaxed my body to look more approachable.

"Erin, I'm concerned about your safety. We don't know why Corey was murdered. What if the killer comes after you next?"

"I don't believe you." Erin's nostrils flared, then she reached for her drink and tossed the alcohol in my face. An ice cube hit my chin. "Face it, your brother is a killer."

Despite the cold drink, heat infused my body. I held my hands to my sides.

Everybody in the room stopped talking and stared at us. Some even pointed. Whispers started.

From the corner of my eye, I saw Marc approach.

"I'm so sorry, ma'am." The dark-haired bartender handed me a stack of napkins then turned his attention to Erin. "Lady, you need to leave."

Erin's gaze bored into mine. "I'll see you in court." She stormed out of the restaurant.

Marc appeared at my side. "I shouldn't have let you approach Erin. Are you okay?"

I wiped my face and blotted my blouse, but didn't answer his question. "Who knew those little glasses held so much liquid?"

The bartender passed me a white towel. "It's clean. Do you want me to call the cops?"

I shook my head. I didn't want to draw more attention to Nate's situation. "No. Forget about it."

Asher joined us with my purse in one hand and our jackets in the other. "I paid the bill. Let's get out of here."

Marc pulled out his wallet. "I can't let you pay. We invited you."

Asher helped me on with my coat. "You can treat me another time. Tonight, we need to skedaddle."

I laughed, never imagining a dignified man like Asher would say skedaddle. "Thanks."

In the parking lot, I faced the older gentleman. "I'll look into Garland Davis. If you think of anybody else—"

"I'll let you know." He walked away with a wave.

Marc and I hopped into his truck, and he turned on the heat. "What a shock. You sure you're okay?"

"Yeah, but I'd like to get into some dry clothes." I shivered, and he turned the heat to full force.

"It should warm up soon." He turned the radio on to a country station.

"Do you mind taking me home?"

"Sure." It didn't take long for him to reach Highway 17 and step on the gas.

"Do you think Erin was a little over-dramatic? Did her reaction seem sincere? Or was it an act?" I burrowed my hands into the pockets of my coat.

"It's possible she'd had too much to drink."

"If so, she's driving under the influence." I replayed the scene in my mind. "I'm not sure she was drunk. Her words weren't slurred, and her eyes were clear. Not even bloodshot, like a woman who'd spent the day crying."

"Okay, we'll say she was sober. What was her motive for causing a scene?"

"I don't know. If she's guilty, her insistence on Nate being the killer deflected the attention from her as a suspect."

"If that was her motive, I'm not sure she got the response she was hoping for."

I had an idea. "Marc, turn around."

"Why?" The truck slowed, and he switched on the blinker.

"I want to go back to the restaurant and see if she's a regular there."

"Again, why?" He pulled a one-eighty and drove north.

"It seems odd she'd sit alone at a bar instead of surrounding herself with friends and family after Corey's death. Is it something she does frequently?"

"Like when Corey didn't come home at night?" He lowered the volume on the radio.

"Exactly. If not, why did she go there tonight?"

He turned off the highway. "Definitely strange."

In a short time, we were back in the restaurant's bar.

The bartender came to us right away. "You're back. Did you decide you want to press charges against the other lady?" His accent told me he wasn't from around here.

I shook my head. "No, but I do have a few questions. What's your name?"

His shoulders drew back and his tone became defensive. "Why? Are you going to sue me? I only work here."

I crossed my hands over my heart. "Oh, no. I just wanted to talk to you. No lawsuits. I promise. I'm Andi Grace Scott, and this is Marc Williams."

"Blake Marshall. What'd you want to know?" His posture relaxed.

"Hey, bartender." A young man waved his hand in the air.

Blake shrugged. "Duty calls. I'll be right back."

I settled onto a barstool, and Marc took an empty one next to me.

A few minutes later, Blake returned. "Your question?"

"Does the woman who threw her drink on me come here often?"

He took a deep breath. "I've seen her before, but it's usually when she and her husband are waiting to get a table. Most of the time they order a fancy wine. Never beer and rarely hard liquor."

"She wasn't drinking wine tonight."

"No, ma'am. She ordered scotch on the rocks."

Marc said, "Did she have a lot to drink?"

"The scotch was her first, and I don't think she ever took a sip. Every time I checked on her, she was only twirling the glass in circles. I'm sorry she threw the drink on you. Most of my customers are more likely to throw a punch than their booze." He wiped the spotless bar top with a clean rag.

I was afraid if I took notes, Blake would stop talking. I committed his answers to memory. "Had she been here long? Was she meeting somebody?"

"I'd say she was here an hour. You may have noticed her ice cubes had begun to melt." His gaze stopped at my wet top. "Or maybe not. I asked if her drink was okay, and she assured me it was fine."

"What about somebody else?"

He shook his head. "Not tonight. I thought the older gentleman might join her, but she was all alone."

Marc leaned closer. "Older gentleman?"

"Yeah, I guess he's her husband."

"Like how old?"

Blake pointed to his chest. "I'm forty-one, and this dude looks at least twenty years older than me. If he isn't, he needs to work out or eat better or something."

On a hunch, I opened my phone and searched for a picture of Corey on social media. "Is this the man you usually saw her with?"

"No. Your guy is much younger." He gripped the white cloth. "Hey, I don't want to get anybody in trouble."

"You're not." Marc slid a fifty toward Blake. "Can you describe the guy she was usually with?"

Blake's forehead crinkled, and he drummed his fingers on the bar. "Yeah. Maybe he's not all that old, but the dude is totally bald. Got a brownish goatee. Might be around fifty. Smooth skin for a guy."

The description didn't match Corey in the least. Erin's husband was tall and lanky with thick wavy hair. "Did you hear his name?"

The bartender shook his head. "If I did, I don't remember."

Marc leaned closer to Blake. "Does he come here often by himself?"

"I only ever saw him with that woman." His eyes widened, and he smiled. "Actually, now that I think about it, he favors the guy in the *Die Hard* movies."

"Bruce Willis?" Who around Heyward Beach resembled the handsome actor?

"Hey, barkeep." One of the guys called out.

"Barkeep? Really?" Blake muttered then ran a hand over his face. "Sorry, but I've got to take care of them. Can't afford to lose my job."

I had more questions, but I didn't want to take up any more of his time. I slid him a business card. "Please call me if you think of anything else."

"Will do." He stuffed the card in his shirt pocket.

As we made our way to Marc's truck, I zipped up my jacket. The damp material of my top stuck to my skin and gave me a chill. "That was an expensive conversation for you. I'll pay you back."

"We gathered valuable information. It was worth fifty dollars, and it's my treat."

Somehow, I'd make it up to him. Most likely with free dog care because preparing fancy meals wasn't my thing. "I want to let David know what we learned. Maybe he can look at security tapes or something and find the bald man."

"Do you think Erin was having an affair with the dude?" Marc made his voice sound like Blake's.

I smiled. "It's possible she discovered Corey wasn't faithful and decided to step out on him. Tit for tat, or some such thing."

"Your theory would give Corey a reason to murder Erin or the bald man. Not the other way around, unless Corey confronted his wife."

"One thing I remember about Erin growing up was she didn't like to share. She always brought the best lunches to school but never allowed anybody else to eat part of her meal. Even if she had leftovers, she'd smash them back into her pink polka dot monogrammed insulated lunch box. If Erin wouldn't share her brownies with us, why would she share her husband with other women?"

Marc held the door for me then rounded the front of his truck and slid into the driver's seat. After starting the truck and cranking up the heat, he stared off into space.

I gave him a couple of minutes to collect his thoughts. Despite the warm air pumping out of the vents, I shivered. "What are you thinking?"

"There's a divorce attorney who works here in Murrells Inlet."

"And?"

He faced me in the shadows of the truck's cab. "The man I'm thinking of is bald, and I always felt like I'd met him before."

"Why? Does he look like Bruce Willis?"

"Kinda. Which could be why he seemed familiar to me. It's possibly the same guy the bartender referred to."

"What's his name?" I pulled my notebook from my purse.

"Norris Gilbert. If he was meeting with Erin, maybe she was planning to divorce Corey."

I scribbled down the name but something didn't make sense. "If she wanted a divorce, why kill him?"

"To protect her assets?"

"So maybe Erin has two motives for murder. An unfaithful husband and trying to protect her money from a messy divorce." I looked out the window toward the gaily lighted marsh walk. "Daily Java is a popular place, and Erin has tons of friends in the area. Add that to a rich and powerful family backing her, it won't be easy to prove she killed her husband."

"Keep an open mind." He rested his elbow on the console and leaned closer to me. "Maybe it's as simple as she wanted to divorce Corey. There's a lot of difference between divorce and murder. We need to consider other suspects."

"Like who?"

"Let's find out more about Ben Davis."

"Are you saying forget Erin? You saw how she can react when angry."

"That's true. Maybe she was angry at life and the loss of her husband, and you were a convenient target."

"You're not the one she doused. I'm not going to remove her from my suspect list anytime soon."

"I'm only suggesting we keep an open mind."

"Got it. Open mind. At this moment, my list of suspects includes Asher, Wendy, Ben, and Erin."

Marc looked over at me. "Wait a minute. You're back to suspecting Asher?"

"I like him, but he wasn't happy with Corey. There's more going on between the two of them than he's letting on."

He put the car in drive and pulled from the lot. "If so, you'll figure it out."

I hoped his faith in me was warranted because my brother's life was on the line.

Chapter Eleven

THE NEXT MORNING, I awoke under a pile of quilts. Sunny breathed in my face, and I smiled. Thank goodness for minty dog treats. "Good morning, girl."

She licked my cheek.

I rubbed her head and laughed. "Let's get this day started." My alarm hadn't buzzed, which told me it wasn't even six, but I'd wanted an early start. Five thirty, according to my watch.

In no time, I had coffee brewing. Sunny returned from her morning ritual in the backyard with a happy bark and headed to her food and water bowls. She munched on her kibble while I ate yogurt with fruit and granola, and searched the internet for more information on Wendy.

Where had she gotten enough money to buy the salon from Juliet at such a young age? She came from a blue-collar family in Upstate South Carolina. An older sister lived in Columbia. According to social media, the girls were close. They'd posted pictures doing everything from drinking coffee together to parasailing. If you believed the posts, they were close. I wasn't convinced, because I'd never met the sister, and Juliet had never mentioned her.

The coffee maker beeped at the same time my phone buzzed.

A text from Marc came through. I'll be in court this morning. Can you meet for lunch?

I called him instead of texting. "Good morning."

"Morning." He cleared his throat. "Why are you up so early?"

The sound of his voice warmed my soul. "I've got a lot to do. What about you?"

"I wanted to take Chubb for a run. I'm worried I don't spend enough time with him."

"Take him to work this morning. Chubb loves riding in the truck with you. I'll swing by later and pick him up. He and Sunny can enjoy the new dog play area at the plantation while I spread mulch." Nate had promised to get the grounds ready for me, but he was stuck in a jail cell. "Lacey Jane can keep an eye on Chubb until I finish my morning schedule."

"You don't think she'll mind?"

"No. She loves animals almost as much as I do."

"What about lunch?" His voice sounded hopeful.

"How about dinner instead?" My day would be packed, and as much as I wanted to have lunch with Marc, it didn't seem possible.

"Sounds like a plan. Let's touch base later."

Yes. Knowing I'd see Marc later added joy to my day. "Okay. Don't forget to take Chubb to work."

The dog barked in the background, and Sunny's ears perked up.

Marc chuckled. "I won't. Have a good day, Andi Grace."

His warm tenor sent chills up my spine. The man was a mystery, and he'd spent most of his life growing up without love and affection. Maybe he didn't know how to show he cared. Or the problem could be mine. Was I longing for passion, and he was treating me with respect?

We'd both experienced many changes the past year. More than likely, neither one of us was ready for a romantic relationship. I'd focus on the fact Marc wanted to help me find Corey's killer, and he wanted to have dinner with me. Baby steps were still steps. "You too. See you later."

I stirred mocha creamer and sugar into my coffee and looked up Erin's social media accounts. Midweek macchiato was the name of her blog and she posted every Wednesday. The posts were consistent and focused on coffee and bakery items. I read the cheerful post and wondered if she'd written a lot at one time and scheduled them to appear like clockwork on Wednesdays. Surely she wouldn't have been so upbeat the day after her husband was murdered.

I switched to other forms of social media. Most of the internet pictures were of her and Corey. Erin looked fabulous in every single shot. Nothing like the woman who'd thrown her drink in my face.

Hundreds of pictures appeared on Facebook. I toggled down through them, scanning for a bald man. No such person appeared. I changed to Instagram, where Erin featured food and special coffees she served at Daily Java. I viewed all of them and refilled my cup. Sunny snoozed at my feet, and I transitioned to searching for Corey.

His theme was sports and fun, and Erin was in most of his pictures. He'd even included a photo of them with Marc and me back in the summer.

Corey grew up poor, and making lots of money was a priority for him. Had shady business dealings caused his death or his unfaithfulness to his wife?

My heart stopped.

I tapped on a picture of Corey and Erin. They seemed to be at a party. Most of the people in the picture wore smiles and held drinks. I zoomed the picture. In the background stood a bald man. The picture was grainy but clear enough to see he was perfectly bald with a goatee. I saved the picture then emailed it to Marc with a short message asking if the man was Norris Gilbert.

I turned my printer on and made a copy of the bald man.

My phone rang. "Marc, did you get the picture? I think we should go back to the restaurant tonight and verify it's the man Blake mentioned."

"I doubt we need to bother Blake again. The man in the picture is Norris Gilbert, bigshot divorce attorney. Only the wealthy can afford his rates."

Oh, yeah. Now I was making progress. Too bad there wasn't anybody around to fist bump. "Erin inherited the coffee shop from her grandmother. She comes from a family who's not afraid to work, and they have the Midas touch."

"It sounds like paying Norris wouldn't be a problem for Erin."

I scribbled more notes on my pad. "Exactly."

"You did a good job finding the picture. It connects Erin and Norris."

"Thanks." My heart fluttered at his compliment. With a trembling hand, I tapped the circle on the screen to end the call. It was silly to be so taken with Marc, but I couldn't deny my feelings. I cared about the man.

I also cared about Nate, and I needed to get to work proving he was innocent. Theories were nice, but they wouldn't convince David Wayne. I needed concrete evidence to persuade him.

IT WAS ALMOST noon by the time I arrived at my plantation with Sunny and Chubb. I continued to find it hard to grasp the fact I owned a plantation. I would use the place for good. The first thing I'd done was give Juliet the job of being in charge Kennady Bed and Breakfast business in the main house when she asked. I'd agreed before she reconsidered.

At the side of the house was one of Nate's landscaping trucks. I'd figure out what was going on as soon as the dogs were settled. I attached leashes to their collars and led them to the dog area.

Dylan's background in construction helped the barn conversion move quicker than I'd expected, and for the last couple of months,

Griffin had spent his weekends helping.

The dogs and I stepped into the barn. "Dylan, you here?"

His voice came across the open space with a slight echo. "Yeah, in the office."

We joined him. "Can I leave Sunny and Chubb with you for a while? They can play in the doggie yard."

He jumped out of the antique 1940s black banker's chair. I'd inherited it along with everything else. "Yes, ma'am. Yes, ma'am. Nate's dog will enjoy the company." He stretched out his hand for the leashes.

"If the three of them give you any trouble, holler, but I'm sure they'll be fine."

Dylan nodded. "Don't worry about us none. I got it."

I returned to the main house. Not big enough to be a mansion, and as far as plantations went, it might be called modest. Still, it was more house and land than I needed. I found Juliet in the kitchen. "What's going on with the landscaping?"

"At Nate's request, Marc arranged for some of Nate's men to come over and take care of the mulch and landscaping. I'm sure they're overworked with Nate out of commission, but I couldn't stop them."

"My back thanks you." Between his concussion and arrest, I didn't know how my brother had time to think about me. He was so sweet—I had to get him out of jail. "What are you working on?"

"I'm washing the new bedding and towels so they'll be fresh and soft for our first guests. Try a muffin." She pointed to a plastic container. "And I've got coffee ready if you're interested."

"When am I not in the mood for coffee?" I laughed.

"Never. Homemade biscotti is in the jar and your favorite creamer's in the fridge." Juliet folded a fluffy white towel in fourths and smoothed it out. "I wanted colorful towels. A different shade for each room, but my research suggested whites were easier to keep clean."

I poured a mug of coffee and added creamer. "Makes sense to me. Somebody is bound to get mascara on them."

"For sure, and that's why I ordered little packets of makeup wipes to distribute in the bathrooms." She paused. "Do you think I should iron the pillowcases?"

"How wrinkled are they?" I opened the biscotti jar and snagged one with chocolate chips and pecan pieces. I picked up my mug and moved to the round kitchen table. Sunlight streamed through the bay windows and a large vase of daisies in the middle of the table added to the warm atmosphere.

Juliet held up a pillowcase. "Not terrible."

"Maybe this time iron them because they're our first guests and we want good reviews. Next time pull them out of the dryer sooner and see if they're less wrinkled."

"Should I iron the sheets?"

"No. The outer blankets will cover them so nobody will see the wrinkles." I dunked the biscotti into my coffee then took a bite. Coffee and chocolate were two of my favorite things. "Yum. This is so good. Did you buy this at one of the local bakeries or Daily Java?"

"I made it myself."

"Whoa. I'm impressed." I sipped my coffee while Juliet set up the ironing board and turned on the iron.

"What are you going to do now since you don't have to spread mulch?"

"Good question. I may go talk to Dylan about how the dog kennels are coming for our overnight guests. I can't wait until we're up and running."

"Griffin is coming tonight. His business partner offered to buy him out which will free him up to leave Charleston and move here. Of course, he'll stay in my quarters and wants to talk to you about where you want to live on the plantation. Are you still considering the old kitchen?"

"It seems spacious enough, but I'd like to hear Griffin's ideas. He's really willing to leave his business?" I licked a dab of melted chocolate off my thumb.

"Definitely. He and his partner have different business philosophies. Griffin doesn't believe in gray areas." She ran the iron over the board and tested the spot with her hand. "The man is also having an affair and wants Griffin to provide alibis to his wife."

"That's terrible." I rubbed my neck. Was faithfulness possible these days? How did people get the courage to marry when infidelity seemed rampant?

"I agree, but if it brings him back to Heyward Beach, I can't complain."

I massaged my temples. Marc seemed like one of the good guys. If our relationship grew, would it survive all the demands of life? Could I give him enough attention between my business and the plantation? "Am I taking on too much at once?"

"What do you mean?" She placed the first pillowcase on the ironing board and set to work.

"We're starting the B&B." I held up a finger for each of my concerns related to business. "I want to convert the barn to a climate-controlled building for my dog business. I probably need to live here to take better care of the dogs. Once Griffin has a place converted for me, I'll need to sell my house and move."

"And let's not forget Nate."

"I can't forget about his situation. It's terrifying, and I need to be smart because this is scarier than when I thought Wade suspected me of Peter's death."

Juliet stopped ironing and looked at me. "It's because you feel responsible for your brother. Don't forget, no matter how much you love Nate, God loves him more."

"You're right." Mug in hand, I headed to the back door. "Do you want to go question Wendy with me later today?"

"You betcha. I want Nate out of jail as much as you do."

"You're a great friend." I left Juliet alone in the kitchen. Once outside, I spotted all three dogs in the fenced-in play area. Sunny lay on the concrete pad observing Bo and Chubb. Despite Chubb's size, he was still a puppy with all the rambunctious ways of a young dog. Bo did his best to keep up with Chubb, and I laughed. The two ran under a plank supported by two barrels, then they raced around the circumference of the play area.

Most of the time Bo was a calm dog. Did he miss Nate? Was the black lab afraid he might be replaced by a younger, more energetic pet like Chubb? Or was he only having fun and reliving his glory days as a youngster? Whatever the situation, Nate would never give his dog away. Poor Bo. Even he was suffering at the hands of Corey's murderer.

What about Erin? We were only thirty, but had she worried Corey was going to leave her for a younger woman? Had she hired a divorce attorney in order to make the first move? I'd ask Wendy if Corey mentioned divorcing Erin.

Dylan appeared and filled three water bowls.

When the dogs moved toward him, I slipped into the building. Our office was short on frills. An old wooden file cabinet, the vintage chair and two wooden bank chairs from another era. A new laptop on the antique writing table was the piece not fitting the décor. Fancy new office furniture wasn't in the budget and probably wouldn't be until I was comfortable with my inheritance. These pieces I'd found in the main house and old barns scattered around the property.

I honestly had no idea what to do with all the buildings. Most leaned to one side or the other but somehow managed to remain standing. I'd love to have an expert tell me what was valuable and of historical importance. Maybe I could pick Asher's brain one day.

I opened the laptop and pulled up my dog walker email account. Two families had booked online for me to watch their Westies because they wanted to go skiing over the weekend. I clicked the arrow to reply. **I'll be happy to watch Heinz and Chloe for a long weekend next month. You can count on me. We'll firm up details the week before.**

I didn't get many overnight jobs in the winter and was thrilled with the prospect. I often watched the Westies when their families traveled. Best friends had adopted them as puppies from the same litter, which made it extra fun to take care of them.

I opened the big desk drawer on my right and searched for my file on expanding the plantation. With the original sketched plan in hand, I walked through the barn.

Dylan had built special stalls for the dogs who'd stay with us. Potty-trained animals got to stay in kennels with pet carpet. Each one had at least some kind of ground cover, depending on the animal's needs. A pet owner wouldn't find nicer kennels in the state of South Carolina.

We'd designed indoor play areas for rainy days. Low walls would allow me to see all of the different sections at one time from almost any spot.

Sunny barked and appeared at my side.

"Hey there, girl. Are you tired of those silly boys?"

She batted her eyes at me.

"Need to get away from all of the testosterone? I don't blame you. Boys are a mystery." I scratched behind her ears. "Like Corey's death is a mystery."

Sunny rubbed her head along my thigh.

"Good girl." My German shepherd's ability to gauge moods astounded me.

My thoughts returned to the murder. What about Erin and Wendy? Erin's outburst the night before convinced me she wasn't as nice as she pretended. Wendy loved men, but it didn't mean she was a killer or even having an affair with Corey.

I shook off the notions and finished comparing the drawing of the dog barn to the current reality. Lots of hard work had gone into this place. A safe shelter for animals, allowing them to have a haven until we found them a good home. It'd also be a place to train animals to become good pets.

Dylan appeared. "What do you think?"

"It's coming along nicely. Will you be here for a while?"

"Yes, ma'am. The fence man is coming this afternoon."

"Good. I'll leave the dogs with you and pick them up later."

I needed more answers from Wendy. If it took ironing pillowcases for Juliet so she could hurry up and leave with me, then I'd pick up the iron and work until every one of them was smooth.

Whatever it took to prove my brother's innocence was what I'd do. David might believe he was leading the investigation, but he didn't really know me. I'd track down every clue or trace of doubt. There was a killer roaming Heyward Beach, and I intended to find him or her.

If the killer had only wanted Corey out of the way, they might've stopped at hitting him with the shovel or whatever they'd used. Stabbing him in the chest led me to believe it was personal. Even if the motive was business-related, it was still personal. While I wasn't an authority, I'd read books and watched enough crime shows to believe strong emotions were behind the killer's motive.

If passion killed Corey, I'd match the passion and prove Nate's innocence. Nobody would stop me until my brother was free.

Chapter Twelve

THE SIGHT OF Wendy driving her Bug down Highway 17 in the opposite direction sent my heart into overdrive. "Where's she going?"

Juliet dug her phone out of her coastal-themed Vera Bradley hipster purse. "Let me give her a call."

I pulled a U-turn and followed Wendy southward, mashing the gas on my Suburban and whizzing past several vehicles in the slow lane. In the distance, I spotted her little yellow car. "There she is. We can catch her."

"Good, because she's not answering."

"Is she one of those people who doesn't talk while driving?"

"Not a chance. Many times, she phoned me on her way to work to say she was running late. She doesn't care about laws that might inconvenience her."

We gained ground until I was close enough to see details of the daisy decals on the car. Visible through the back window were suitcases and cardboard boxes. "It looks like she's packed for a trip. Or a move."

"I'll say. If you pull alongside her, I'll roll down my window and get her attention." She pushed the button, lowering the passenger window.

"She may be ignoring us on purpose."

"At least let me try." Juliet's hair whipped in the wind.

I hit the gas to pull up by the Bug and then slowed to match Wendy's speed. "It's a good thing there's not a lot of traffic right now."

Juliet lowered her window and waved her arm. "Wendy, it's us."

The Bug sped up, and I did too.

"Wendy, it's me. Juliet. Pull over." She motioned with her arm. "Get off the road."

Wendy darted a look our way and swerved toward us.

I yanked the steering wheel left and slowed, not wanting to end up in the median. My SUV bumped along on the warning divots. "She must be crazy to think she can run a Suburban off the road with her little car."

"I doubt it's the craziest stunt she's ever pulled."

The Bug returned to its lane, and I eased off the shoulder and back onto the road. Soon we were side by side.

Juliet pointed to a consignment store parking lot. "Pull over there. We need to talk."

The little car slowed.

I pulled behind Wendy and signaled my intention to turn onto the access road. I followed her to the consignment store's parking lot, and we both stopped at the farthest corner from the door.

She jumped out without turning off the car or shutting the door. "Are you trying to get us all killed?"

My heart leapt. "Hey, you're the one who came into my lane."

Juliet got out of my SUV and faced Wendy. "We've got some questions for you. If you're really innocent of Corey's murder, you'll be glad we're trying to catch the real killer. Did you murder Corey?"

"No." She looked at the ground and kicked a rock with her braided wedge sandal.

"We saw you at the plantation." Juliet's voice was strong and firm.

Wendy still avoided eye contact. "I knew Corey had an early morning meeting with one of the board members. He was stressed out about it, and I decided to surprise him with coffee. From the new donut shop. Not Daily Java. It'd be weird to buy coffee from his wife to give him when he's planning to divorce her for me."

"He was going to divorce her or vice versa?" Juliet's voice remained calm.

"He wanted the divorce because Erin was a terrible wife. Always nagging him about money, and she grew up rich. Corey had mentally checked out of the marriage and was only waiting until a judge said they were officially divorced."

"He filed for divorce?" I doubted it.

"Yes."

Juliet raised her hand to stop me from asking more. "Wendy, were you planning to get married?"

"I don't know." Wendy shrugged. "I've never been one to settle down."

"What happened when you showed up at the plantation? Did you give Corey the coffee?"

I enjoyed watching Juliet question her former employee.

Wendy's eyes grew wide. "I walked around and found Corey near the entry gate where you pay to tour the mansion. He looked dead, and I took off."

My pulse quickened. "Did you even check for a pulse?"

"No. I didn't want to be accused of anything."

Juliet glanced over Wendy's shoulder toward the Bug crammed full of stuff. "Looks like you're packed for a long trip. Where are you going?"

"None of your business!" Wendy yelled so loud customers in the shop probably heard her. "Leave me alone, Juliet."

I joined the two of them. "Shh. You may want to hold it down before somebody calls the cops."

Wendy eyed me. "How do I know you won't try to blame me for Corey's murder so your brother will be off the hook?"

I counted to ten in French. "We're looking for the truth. If you're innocent, you've got nothing to fear from us. Are you leaving town?"

Wendy's shoulders slumped, and her face turned from red to ashen. "I'm scared, and it seems like a good option."

"What are you scared of?" I softened my voice.

"What if the killer thinks I saw her?"

"Why do you think the woman was a killer?"

"Corey liked the ladies, which is why, deep in my soul, I didn't really expect him to settle down with me. At first, I thought maybe we could make it work. Then I discovered there were other women besides me. It's possible he couldn't be loyal to one woman, which is why I figured a woman killed him."

Wendy might know more than she realized, and I needed to earn her trust. "You never considered a man killed Corey?"

"Not really. I assumed it was Erin."

I took a deep breath. "Did Corey ever say if Erin had filed for divorce?"

"No." Wendy stepped closer to us and looked around before speaking. "Corey claimed he wanted to divorce Erin in order to be with me. I played along, but what a liar. He probably spent time with a different woman every day. It's not surprising he got killed. He had a mean streak, but very few people saw it."

"He and Erin seemed so in love last summer. Did something happen?"

Wendy shrugged. "Who knows? Besides being mean, he was sneaky, but I loved him. I hate myself for caring so much, but he oozed charm when he tried."

It didn't sound like true love. More like a sick, twisted relationship. "Sneaky about things besides his love life?"

"He was a gambler. Not a good one, either. It's possible he owed somebody money."

Juliet crossed her arms. "Usually loan sharks want their money back and don't try to kill you. Let's rule out gambling as the motive, and we'll assume you're not the killer and neither is Erin. What about somebody you were dating? Maybe a man you broke up with in order to be with Corey? Or what about a man interested in you who wanted to eliminate the competition for your affection?"

Wendy's shoulders drooped, and she leaned against my SUV, crossing her arms around her middle.

I had to give Juliet credit for considering another man in Wendy's life as a suspect. The VW was still running, so I slid into the driver's seat and shut off the engine. Curling irons, scissors, hair products, and rods for perms filled a plastic bin on the passenger seat. A baseball bat handle was near the gear shift. Shoes on the passenger seat and floorboard looked like the work of a panicked woman. Bags and totes filled the back.

Juliet said, "Wendy, were you seeing more than one man?"

One tear trickled down Wendy's cheek. She didn't even swipe it away. Instead, she looked at the sand and gravel parking lot. "I need to get away from Heyward Beach. This town isn't good for me. Not if I want to stay alive."

I nudged Juliet to get closer to Wendy.

Juliet slipped a thin arm around the woman's shoulders. "You can trust us. We want to help."

Wendy's eyes remained downward. "What if I tell you something, and it puts you in danger?"

My stomach somersaulted. "Have you talked to the police about this?"

A truck zoomed by on the highway with the bass blaring.

She flinched and turned pale. "No."

Was Wendy about to give us some good evidence, or was she playing us? "Let us help you. Please."

Wendy looked right and left. She clenched the top of her shirt and breathed in through her nostrils. "I have an apartment in Myrtle Beach." Her words were so soft, I leaned closer.

Juliet frowned. "But you have a house. Why do you need two places?"

A black SUV pulled into the parking lot.

Wendy turned her back to the vehicle as if she didn't want to be recognized.

I might have laughed if the situation wasn't so serious. The yellow Volkswagen was a dead giveaway to her identity. I studied the occupants of the SUV.

Two middle-aged ladies climbed out of the vehicle and headed into the store. I didn't recognize either, and when I looked at the back, it had New York tags. Probably not the SUV from the morning Corey was murdered, but they were both dark.

Wendy moved to her car. "I've got to go."

I latched onto her arm. "What about the apartment? Are you going there?"

"It's not safe there either."

"Why?"

"The other man rented it for me. It was our place to get together. You're going to think I'm a horrible person, but he's married. The apartment helped us keep the affair secret."

What was wrong with Wendy? Why was she dating two married men? "Was the other man in your life jealous of Corey?"

Wendy shrugged. "I don't know. I didn't think he knew about my relationship with Corey. Until—"

"What? Did he do something?"

"He started acting jealous a couple of weeks ago."

Juliet frowned. "Jealous? What'd he do?"

"He asked where I was and who I was hanging out with. He asked me to meet him at the apartment, then he texted and said something came up. I began to wonder if it was his way to stop me from seeing Corey."

What a creep. "Who's renting the apartment? Where is it? Exactly."

Wendy dug her purse out of the car and pulled out a key chain. She removed two keys. One was silver and the other gold, and she thrust them toward Juliet. "House key and apartment key. I don't have time to keep talking. I need to hide. If it's my other boyfriend, he may come after me next. Maybe you can find a way to stop him from killing me."

Juliet gripped the keys. "No. You need to tell Deputy Wayne what you told us."

She shook her head vehemently. "Not a chance. I'm too scared."

"Scared of who?" I blew out a breath. "Never mind. The authorities can protect you. Give me a chance to call the sheriff."

"They didn't protect Corey."

Juliet said, "That's not fair. I doubt he asked the cops to guard him."

Wendy thrust her chin out. "I'm leaving, and you can't convince me to change my mind."

Juliet jangled the keys. "Where are you going? And where is the apartment?"

"It's safer for me if nobody knows, but if you figure it out be careful." She got into her little car. "Don't follow me."

I gripped the top of her car door. "Be careful, Wendy. We're here for you if you change your mind."

"I won't." She wrenched the door from my grasp and slammed it shut.

After she sped away, I sighed. "Either Wendy truly is scared the killer is coming for her next, or she just gave the performance of a lifetime. What do you think?"

"I've seen her lie to customers as often as she told the truth. If I was a member of the jury, I doubt I'd convict her, though. I believe she's afraid."

"If she is, we need to focus on other suspects. Starting with the man who rented the apartment for her in Myrtle Beach. Let's go to Wendy's house and see if we can find a clue."

Chapter Thirteen

WE STOOD IN the living room of Wendy Conn's home, gazing at the disarray. An overturned laundry basket on the couch with articles of clothing strewn about. Coffee table, love seat, and recliner were littered with unmentionables, socks, and T-shirts. There was even a pair of shorts on the kitchen counter. It looked like a tornado had ripped through Wendy's house. "What a disaster. I guess she was in a hurry."

We moved from room to room.

Juliet said, "Hurricane Wendy hit the bedrooms and the bathroom, too." Unmade bed, drawers opened, and more unmentionables scattered on the floor. Cosmetics on the counter and toothpaste stains in the sink.

"What a slob." Even I wasn't as messy as Wendy.

"Funny thing is, she's neat at work. Let's keep looking."

On the other side of the kitchen, we ended up in a sunroom. Sunshine battled its way through simple woven bamboo blinds. The tidiness of the room contrasted with the chaos in the rest of the house.

"Well, what do you know?" Juliet stood by a treadmill in the corner. An orange towel was draped over the handle of the expensive machine. "She always cared about her figure. I can't count the number of diets she tried, and she worked out at some gym in Myrtle Beach."

"Wonder why she had fitness equipment here if she belonged to a gym?"

"She's OCD about her appearance." Juliet shrugged. "Until today though, I thought she only worked out where she could flirt with men."

I giggled. "Oh, you're bad."

"I prefer to call it realistic." Her smile widened.

I touched a bright blue resistance band on a hanging organizer next to other bands of multiple bright colors and different shaped handles. A white board hung next to it with a workout schedule. Open shelving held a yoga mat, fitness magazines, some kind of rubber block, hand weights, a mirror, and towels. "Despite the lack of big equipment, this place is amazing."

Juliet sat in a swivel chair at a small white desk tucked into the corner of the room. "Let's see what we can find here."

Two plastic file boxes sat under the desk. "Slide one of those over, and I'll look through it."

"Here you go." Juliet pushed the box to me and opened the top drawer.

I sat on the wood floor and crossed my legs in yoga fashion. "I wish Wendy had been a little more specific when she gave us permission to search her house. It would've been so much easier to name the other man."

Juliet snorted. "One of the other men. Who knows how many men she's juggling?"

I lifted the lid off the file box and fingered through the papers. "I've never understood why a person is unfaithful to their spouse. Don't wedding vows mean anything?"

"It's not too hard to get a divorce these days."

"True." I paused at a file of recipes tucked between hair styles and product ratings. Nothing seemed suspicious. "Why couldn't she date single men?"

"Maybe the secrecy adds to the thrill. At least we know why she never posted pictures of them on social media." She stood. "I'm going back through the house to look for pictures."

"Good idea. There doesn't appear to be anything important in this box. It's all fluff. I'll look for an apartment contract or some kind of receipt with the mystery man's name." I exited the office-slash-exercise room. In the kitchen, I gathered clothes and placed them in a chair. With all of the mess, I'd need to be methodical in my search. Not my strong suit. The eating table became my station for miscellaneous junk.

I opened drawers and, on the third try, found the catchall. I removed keys, pens, tape, and magnets. A bulky envelope of coupons caught my attention. Sorting through it, I found a stash of pictures. "Bingo."

There were photos of small children, older adults, and the salon. My hands stilled at a picture of Wendy and a man at a resort. The guy wore a Clemson Tigers ball cap and sunglasses, making it hard to identify him. Scratch that. Impossible. No way to tell if he was old, young, handsome, ugly, hairy, or bald. I placed the photo to the side and sorted through the rest of the pictures. The only other one I thought merited keeping was of a resort in Hilton Head. With my phone, I took a picture of the photo and the stranger.

After I finished searching the kitchen, I headed to the master bedroom. If Wendy's romance was supposed to be secret, it wouldn't make sense to display her Romeo's picture to the public.

I made her bed and placed piles of clothes on it as I systematically went through the room. A drawer full of jewelry slowed my search. I opened each little box. Some pieces appeared to be junk, and some looked like better quality. No green tarnish. I'd always heard the more karats in gold, the less likely it was to turn colors.

I lifted a black velvet box the perfect size to hold a ring or earrings. No jewelry filled the space, but there was a folded-up note. In small neat script, I read, "This ring is a symbol of my love. Soon we can tell the world about our relationship. Give me a little more time, and I promise it'll be worth the wait. Love you!"

No name. I gripped the box. "Who are you?"

Juliet entered the room. "Are you on the phone?"

"Arg. No. Look at this." I thrust the note to her. "It was in this box."

Juliet scanned the short message. "You've got more than I found."

"Do you want to help me in here? I wish I had more time, but there are a couple of dogs I need to walk."

"I'll look in the closet. You know, we have the house key. We can always come back later."

"Unless the killer shows up to look for evidence while we're gone." I opened a white cardboard box then a red fuzzy container. Pearls. I wouldn't know a real one from a fake, but if they were fake, they were beautiful.

Juliet walked out of the closet. "I don't guess Wendy sent us here so she'd have time to escape."

I paused. "Maybe. Which takes me back to wondering if she killed Corey."

"What if the note is from Corey and not the mystery man?"

I had no idea what Corey's handwriting looked like. "Whether Corey's in love with Wendy or playing her, it works. She continues to see him. Then maybe she gets tired of waiting and takes up with Romeo."

"His name is Romeo?" The pitch of her voice rose. "He's either a newcomer or not a local, because I would've remembered that name."

I laughed. "No, I'm just calling him Romeo for now. He falls for Wendy hard enough to pay rent for an apartment where they can get together in private."

The doorbell rang.

"Do you think it's the killer?" I dropped to the ground and tugged

Juliet down with me.

She clutched my hand. "Would a killer ring the doorbell?"

I pulled my phone from my jeans and texted Marc and Lacey Jane. Somebody should know where to look for our bodies if it was the killer. "Don't make any sounds. Maybe they'll leave."

The bell rang again, and then the person pounded on the front door. "I know you're in there. This is Deputy Wayne. Open up."

I hurried to the entryway and Juliet followed a few steps behind. When I opened the door, his hand was raised as if he was going to knock again. "Yes?"

He placed both hands on his belt. "I got a report of intruders. Should've guessed it was you."

I held up the keys Wendy had given Juliet. "We have permission to be here."

His gaze darted from me to the keys I dangled in the air. "Likely story."

My phone vibrated in my pocket. I ignored the caller and remained focused on the deputy. "It's true. Feel free to call Wendy yourself."

"Andi Grace, you can't go through people's houses."

Juliet scooted between us. "We aren't intruding. Wendy gave us consent to go through her house."

David rocked on his feet on the front porch. A cool breeze blew past him and into the house. I shivered. The three of us seemed to be at some kind of standoff.

I waved my hand toward the living room. "Would you like to come inside?"

"Yes, I would." He spoke into the microphone on his shoulder, reporting his whereabouts to the unseen operator. When he stepped into the house, his head turned from one direction to the other. "Did Ms. Conn tell you to trash her house?"

I laughed. "You should've seen it before. We've straightened it."

"Where is Ms. Conn?" He pulled a small notepad from his pocket.

Juliet moved closer to the deputy. "She left town but refused to tell us her destination. I asked, practically begged her, to call you. Let's sit down, and I'll explain."

The good Southern manners my mother taught me made me want to offer the man something to drink, but this wasn't my home. I sat in one of the faded blue velvet chairs, and Juliet dropped onto the mustard-color couch. David sat on the edge of the other blue chair.

Juliet launched into the story of our encounter with Wendy.

I listened to every word to make sure she didn't miss any pertinent details.

Outside, tires screeched.

I looked through the window. Marc's red pickup truck whipped into the driveway. I rose. "David, do you mind if I run outside for a minute? My friend is here."

One dark eyebrow lurched up. "Why? You planning to throw a party or something?"

"No. I'm sure he was worried about me. It's Marc. I thought you might be the killer and texted him when you pounded on the door."

Marc knocked and entered the house before I opened the door. "Andi Grace, are you okay? Why didn't you answer my call? Why is there a patrol car here?"

My nose tingled, and tears filled my eyes. I managed a shrug but knew if I spoke, I'd cry like a baby. I usually took care of others, and here Marc was concerned about me.

He took me in his arms.

I held on tight. "Thanks for coming."

"Anytime. I wish you would've called me before you came over here."

David cleared his throat. "I wish she'd called me as well. Ladies, I know you've come here twice. Somebody called the law on you both times. In the future, maybe you should give me a heads-up."

I slipped out of Marc's arms. "Wendy gave us a key."

"Which is why I'm not arresting you for trespassing, but I will verify your story. Are you through here?"

I glanced at my watch. "I've got to get back to work, but I also need to finish my search in Wendy's room."

The deputy's nostrils flared. "What exactly are you looking for?"

"Wendy's mystery man."

"What? Who? Why?" His voice grew more thunderous with each word.

I held out the blurry picture I'd found in the kitchen. "I think this may be him, but I'd like to find a better photograph."

"Again, why?"

"Because I'd like to put him on my list of suspects."

"I thought the sheriff told you I'm in charge of the investigation." David held up his hand when I opened my mouth to speak. "Your assistance isn't needed. I understand you're concerned about your brother, but don't make me lock you up for interfering."

So many comebacks popped into my brain, but there was no need to antagonize David further. "I'm sorry, David."

"But?"

"I honestly thought it'd be all right to come here since Wendy told us it was okay. Your reaction makes me think she's a suspect. Are you close to releasing Nate?"

The deputy frowned, and his eye twitched.

"Time to go." Marc took my hand and led me outside. "You gave me a real scare when you didn't answer my call."

I hugged him. "Next time, I'll answer."

His arms tightened around me, reassuring me he cared. "I'd prefer there not be a next time, but I'll settle for a warning before you do something dangerous."

"I can do that."

"Break it up, you two." Juliet tapped our shoulders. "We should leave before David comes out."

Marc kissed my forehead. "Be careful."

"Don't worry. The rest of my afternoon involves hanging out with friendly dogs." Juliet and I left in my Suburban.

She slipped on her sunglasses. "Girl, he's crazy about you."

A momentary sense of joy filled me. "Good, because I'm falling for Marc."

It wasn't long before I'd dropped Juliet at her car and tackled my appointments. Walking the dogs added normalcy to my day, giving me a reprieve from the mounting stress. After the last appointment with a golden doodle, I headed to the plantation.

Once there I entered the barn-turned-dog-training center, Sunny and the others ran to greet me. "Hey, there. Have y'all had a good afternoon?" I rubbed on each one before standing straight. "Dylan, you here?"

No response.

I went to the dog yard and found him measuring the outdoor play area. He looked up. "Hi, boss."

"What're you doing?" I pointed to the stakes with twine connecting them into a rectangle.

"I looked online earlier and found some above-ground doggie pools. What if we converted the far corner into a water park for dogs? Of course, I'm planning for the summer."

It sounded messy but fun, and dogs liked to have fun. "Draw me up a plan and estimate on the cost and we'll discuss it."

"Yes, ma'am. Yes, ma'am. Now we'll still have room for a grassy area where we can train them." He bit his lip. "Maybe it's a crazy idea."

"No, it sounds good. Should we get some kind of fake grass?" How would real grass hold up to training a pack of dogs?

"Your brother won't like artificial turf." Dylan removed his ball cap and ran a hand through his hair before putting the cap back on.

"True." Nate believed there was nothing as good as the real thing. I glanced toward the main house and considered the work Dylan's dad had done to it. "Your dad didn't seem to think a lot of Corey."

He blew out a breath. "Tell me about it."

"Do you know why?"

"Corey made it hard to get hired for jobs."

I nodded. "Next time you see your dad, would you ask him if he broke into my yard last summer and led the dogs away with steaks?"

Dylan straightened his shoulders. "Ain't no way he'd do that. He may not be the best guy around, but he'd never hurt an animal."

"Even if he thought releasing the dogs made it easier to break into my house?"

He shook his head with force. "I can't imagine he'd do something so despicable. Your dogs could've gotten hit by a car and died." His smooth forehead crinkled. "Why do you care now if it happened last summer?"

"I'm trying create a list of suspects for Corey's murder. It wasn't Nate."

"It wasn't my dad either." Anger laced his words.

I held up my hands. "I know, Dylan, that's not why I asked. What what if Corey broke into my house last summer? I kinda forgot about the incident when Peter's death was solved."

He relaxed. "What are you trying to figure out?"

"I wonder if there's anything in the files pointing to Corey's killer."

Dylan cocked his head to the side. "I know you put yourself in danger when you tried to find Peter's killer, but don't get yourself hurt trying to solve another murder."

I met his gaze. His dad was in prison, and his mother had served time for kidnapping Dylan when he was a child. To my knowledge, he didn't have siblings. So maybe he didn't understand the need deep in my soul. "I've got to help my brother, and the best way to get him out of jail is to find Corey's killer."

His scratched his jaw. "Even if it puts you in harm's way?"

I swallowed. "Even if."

Chapter Fourteen

AFTER TAKING Sunny and Bo to my cottage, I showered and changed clothes. On the outside, I was presentable. Inside, I was a nervous wreck.

Marc picked me up and soon parked his truck a few houses down the street from Erin's. "You sure you want to do this instead of going out to dinner?"

People flowed in and out of Erin's place like the tide. Cars filled her driveway and were scattered along the street. She was a hometown girl who deserved support from the locals. Despite our altercation at the restaurant, I wanted to pay my respects. I was sorry for her loss. Nobody should suffer the death of a spouse at such a young age.

I nodded. "It's the right thing to do. Erin is my friend. Was my friend. Who knows what we are now, but I need to see her."

"Not a problem. If this many people are stopping by her house, can you imagine how packed the funeral will be?"

"It'll be standing room only. Even if people didn't like Corey, they love Erin and her family." I placed a hand over my fluttery stomach. "When my parents died, people overwhelmed us with food. Some of my mother's friends came and cleaned the house for me. Dad's friends made sure my car was in good shape. Heyward Beach people show up and pitch in during a crisis."

"Good to know." We hopped out of his red Chevy Silverado and met on the cracked sidewalk. Roots from a birch tree had broken the concrete squares leading up to Erin's house.

As we walked, Marc pulled on his suit jacket. A navy tie and light blue shirt complemented his taupe suit. Whether Marc wore a suit or dressed in casual clothes, there was no denying how handsome he was. Ooh, la, la.

I wore a conservative navy suit I'd found deeply discounted the year before. A white blouse and black pumps completed my outfit. Classic and simple. Not my usual attire. I'd even curled my hair instead of pulling it back into a ponytail. "There are quite a few people here. Maybe I can step into the bathroom and look for clues."

"What kind of clues?" His fingers circled my arm, and I stopped.

"Didn't I mention the handkerchief at the plantation? It was somewhat close to Corey's body with lipstick smeared on it. I'd like to see what shades Erin has in her bathroom." How could I have left out such a little detail?

"I would've remembered. Why is it important?"

"It was white cotton and had a slash of red on it. Maybe scarlet. Anyway, it was like a woman had kissed a man and he wiped it off his face."

Marc's eyebrows rose. "And?"

"What if it belonged to Corey? What if the smear really was lipstick? Don't you think it's a good clue? Do you carry a hanky?"

An older couple walked past us, and Marc scooted closer to me. "In the summer, I usually keep a bandana in my pocket for perspiration. Most of the time, I don't carry one. What about your brother? Could it be his?"

I shook my head. "He's not dating anybody right now, and I've never seen him with even a bandana, although he carries hand towels in his truck. I've seen him wet one with water and run it over his face and neck."

"Sounds like the hanky isn't his."

My breathing hitched in my chest, and I pointed to a dark gray SUV. "Marc, do you know who owns this vehicle?"

"Can't say that I do. Lots of SUVs around here."

I snatched my phone out of my purse, turned to camera mode, and snapped pictures of it.

Marc nudged me. "People are coming."

I stopped taking pictures. "Thanks."

"Let's go see Erin and get your snooping over with." He reached for my hand. "You look nice."

My neck grew warm. "Thanks. You look pretty spiffy yourself."

Two women carrying foil-covered casserole dishes crossed the street and reached Erin's driveway at the same time as we did. We paused to allow them to enter the modest yellow house first. The visitors claimed Erin's attention, and I broke out into a sweat waiting to speak to her. It was rare for my nerves to get the best of me, but they were winning the battle.

"Are you okay?" Marc touched my shoulder. "You look pale."

I leaned against the nearest wall and kept my voice low. "I think I'm going to be sick."

He moved me away from the others. "Let's find you a bathroom."

I leaned against him. The worst thing I could do was pass out in Erin's home and cause a disturbance.

Phyllis Mays approached us from behind. "Everybody's heading to the living room for a prayer. Oh dear, Andi Grace. What's wrong with you? Do you need to sit down?"

"She doesn't feel so good. Can you direct us to the nearest bathroom?"

My stomach gurgled so loud Phyllis stepped back. "I think there's someone in there. Let's go back to the master bath. You might like a little privacy. Marc, you go ahead and join the others." She shooed him away with her fingers.

Marc's gaze connected with mine as if questioning what he should do.

"It's okay."

Marc nodded and walked away.

I trailed after Phyllis through the master bedroom to the en suite. "Thanks, Phyllis. I was fine earlier."

"You've had to deal with a lot of death in your life. This could be grief raising its ugly head. I'll come back to check on you in a bit."

I locked myself in the bathroom and gripped the marble vanity. If I could only cool down, it might help. Shrugging out of my jacket and letting it hit the tufted bath rug, I studied the cool tile floor. No, I couldn't lay on Erin's floor. I turned on the sink and ran cold water over my inner wrists. It helped a little, so I leaned over and splashed my face with water. Yes. That helped. I continued until I felt my damp blouse stick to my skin.

I turned off the water and checked my reflection in the mirror. Horrors. Black mascara ran down my face. I plucked tissues from a box on the counter and worked to remedy the damage. I finished and focused on my damp hair. If only I had a couple of bobby pins, I could fix the mess well enough to disguise the wetness.

I froze. The only way to work on my hair was to look into Erin's bathroom drawers for what I needed. What I longed for was an icy Coke and to be sitting at home. Debating wasn't helping my stress. I stared at the top drawer. My hand hovered near the handle. Yes, I'd wanted to look for clues, but not this way. Overhearing a conversation or seeing a framed photograph of Corey with a suspect had been my goals.

My stomach chugged, and I glimpsed at my reflection again. Limp damp hair. There weren't many options. The damage had to be repaired.

I opened the drawer.

Toothpaste, inhalers, nose spray, prescription vials, and bobby pins. I snatched up four and finger combed my hair into place, securing it with Erin's hairpins. Yes. I reached down to close the drawer. One of the pill bottles snagged my attention with its drowsy warning. Diazepam. I leaned closer to read the label. It had Corey's name along with directions to take it for anxiety. I almost laughed. Maybe I needed a prescription for myself if the thought of facing Erin could throw me in such a spin.

Somebody knocked on the bathroom door. "Who's in there?"

Time to face the music. I retrieved my jacket and opened the door. "Hi, Erin."

Her mouth dropped open. "What are you doing?"

"I came to tell you how sorry I am about Corey's passing."

"In my bathroom?"

"Yeah, about that. When I got here, I felt kinda sick."

"So you came into my personal bathroom?"

"The other one was occupied. I didn't want to cause a scene." I held onto the doorframe to steady myself. "I'm really sorry for your loss, Erin."

"I know you never liked Corey."

This was getting worse by the second. "That's not true. We double-dated with y'all. Remember?"

She squinted. "It doesn't mean you liked him."

"You and I've always been friends, and we're both local businesswomen. We need to stick together."

"I feel like you're up to no good."

I lowered my voice. "How well did you like your husband?"

"I loved Corey." She clenched her fists.

I relaxed my shoulders. "I understand, but did you like him?"

She backed up a step, and her eyes narrowed. "I suppose you heard the rumors he was taking money from Daily Java, but it's not true."

That nugget of information would go on my list. I hadn't heard it before. "Have you met with Norris Gilbert in order to divorce Corey?"

She paused. "You'll do anything to get your brother out of jail, won't you?"

"Nate's innocent."

"The cops wouldn't have arrested Nate if he was innocent."

"Innocent people get arrested all the time." My head pounded. How many criminals on death row proclaimed innocence until their dying breath? In South Carolina, lethal injection or electrocution were the ways inmates were punished. I shivered. To know Nate's life could end in such a way was unbearable. "Nate isn't guilty, and it seems like you'd want me to find the person who murdered your husband. What if the killer comes after you next for some reason?"

Erin's harsh laugh unnerved me. "Excuse me for trusting the police more than you. Now, get out of my house." She dug her fingers into my arm, and I headed toward the front door willingly.

Norris stood in the living room with his arm around a beautiful woman. Ivey Gilbert had been on the news often for her volunteer work in the community. The frailness of her body and the severe shortness of her hair didn't diminish her attractiveness. She smiled at him, and I realized she must be his wife.

Bile rose up to my throat. How could any man be unfaithful? What a two-faced, selfish, obnoxious nincompoop.

I hurried out and didn't stop until I reached the mystery SUV. I took more pictures of it, including the license plate. The vehicle was a Toyota Land Cruiser. Not a scratch on it, and the paint shone. Even the tires were polished. No sticker on the back window though. Drat.

I texted Marc. **I'm waiting for you at the truck.** Now that the confrontation with Erin had passed, I didn't feel as sick. Shaky, yes, but I wasn't ready to collapse or throw up.

"How do you feel?" Marc pushed a button on his key fob and the doors unlocked.

"Much better. I'm so embarrassed."

Marc opened the door and stood beside me. "I'm sorry you didn't get to talk to Erin."

"She tracked me down." I explained what happened, including her bringing up the rumors about Corey stealing from her business. "On my way out, I spotted Norris Gilbert. I can't shake the feeling he was meeting with Erin so she could divorce Corey."

"I'm sure Norris warned her Corey could take a big chunk of her money if they divorced. Instead of turning her wealth over, she could've decided it'd be easier to kill him."

"Most people don't resort to murder to protect their money." He slipped off his jacket, tossed it into the truck, then rolled up his sleeves.

I twisted my mouth. "Think about the situation. Erin has two motives. Scorned wife and financial woes."

"Even so, it doesn't mean she killed her husband."

I pictured tall, slender, gorgeous Erin. "It's hard to imagine she'd do such a thing, but she revealed her temper the other night when she threw her drink on me. Also today she was ticked to find me in her bathroom."

"I know Phyllis took you there, but you really can't blame Erin for being upset when she discovered you in her personal bathroom. Please, keep an open mind about her. Corey crossed lots of people. Erin's anger toward you doesn't make her a killer."

"You're right." I hopped up into the passenger seat. "I found prescription vials with Corey's name on them."

"You what?"

I pointed to my hair. "When my hair got wet, I needed to fix it. I didn't fake that little episode to snoop. I opened the top drawer by her sink and found bobby pins to fix my hair. A prescription bottle was rolling around with Corey's name on it. It was for Diazepam."

"It's for anxiety or nerves." Marc shut the door and jogged around the front of the truck then slid in behind the steering wheel.

"There were also inhalers and a nasal spray."

Marc signaled and pulled away from the curb onto the pothole-filled street without commenting on my discovery.

"Who all was in the house? I didn't speak to anybody but Phyllis and Erin. I assume Pastor Mays was there since his wife was. What about any of the deputies? Wade?"

"One question at a time. I didn't see anybody from the sheriff's department. Erin's parents were there, and Pastor Mays seemed to be consoling Erin's mom."

I rubbed my forehead. "How'd they get back so fast? They were taking a river boat cruise along the Seine River in France. One day I want to see the Eiffel Tower and all the historic buildings. It must be so beautiful."

"Are you sure about the timing?"

"That's the story going around town. The river boat stops in a different town each night. Granny Farris got some of her yummy recipes on her trips to France. They say she made friends with a baker in Normandy and they tried out new recipes together. Anyway, Clem and Gina Farris try to visit France once a year."

"If they make the trip frequently, it might've been easier for them to make arrangements to return home quickly. For now, we'll assume they were in France when the murder occurred." Marc stopped at the corner. "Where to? Should we schedule dinner for another night?"

"If you don't mind, I think so. I need to get home. Dylan took over my late afternoon dog walking appointments, but I need to check on Sunny, Chubb, and Bo." I relaxed into the leather seat. "You know

Dylan has really turned himself around."

"You deserve a lot of credit for the change in him. You've encouraged him and given him a job. Responsibility. A lot of times all a person needs is to have somebody believe in them."

"Sounds like the voice of experience." I smiled.

Marc's parents had died when he was young, and he'd bounced around the foster care system. One set of foster parents had helped turn Marc's life around.

Marc nodded. "Yeah. I'd hate to think how different my life would've turned out without Bobby Joe Wilkes. He didn't back down from my anger. Instead, he treated me with love and never gave up on me." Marc hummed a country song softly. His deep tenor calmed my nerves.

I closed my eyes. I'd been so blessed to have known my parents for eighteen years. They'd raised me to adulthood, and I'd never regret sacrificing college to keep my siblings with me.

The truck stopped, and I opened my eyes. We were sitting in front of my beach cottage. My home. Pressure built in my chest. "I don't want to sell my house."

"Then don't." Marc tilted his head to the side.

"It makes more sense to live on the plantation than to keep this place."

"Are you going to be happy there?"

I sighed. "If I hire Griffin to turn the old kitchen or garage into living quarters, it'll get him back living in Heyward Beach. Juliet will be so happy. I'm kinda stuck."

"You don't always have to do what's best for others. It's okay to say you want to remain here." Marc tapped the steering wheel. "Or you could rent the cottage out while giving life at the plantation a shot. If you don't like living there, you can always move back here."

My spirits soared. "Marc, you're brilliant. What a terrific idea."

"Su-weet. I'll take brilliant." He met my gaze and broke out into a wide smile. "Thanks."

"Do you want to come inside?"

"I'll collect Chubb, but I should go back to the office."

"This late?" My joy dimmed. "Are you glad you returned to practicing law?"

"I enjoy helping others, and I'm kinda good at it."

"Even with the long hours?"

"It's a special case, and I want to give it my best effort. This is so much different than working for my old firm. I feel like I'm making a positive impact in our little corner of the world. The hours don't bother me and being the boss allows me some flexibility. My only regret is not being able to spend more time with Chubb."

"Do you miss the boat business?"

He rubbed his chin. "To be honest, it's more of a hobby. I needed the time to figure out what to do with my life."

"I'm glad you're happy."

Marc walked me to the front door. Winter's short days dampened my spirits. Spring couldn't arrive soon enough, but I wouldn't wish my life away. "Do you have a long day tomorrow?"

He followed me to the kitchen and leashed Chubb while I let the others out in the backyard. "Afraid so. How about we meet for a late dinner? You can catch me up on whatever you've discovered."

"I've got a better idea. Meet me early for coffee at Daily Java and bring Chubb. He can hang out with me for the day."

"Again? Are you sure?" He walked to the front door with Chubb at his side.

"Absolutely. He's a lot of fun."

The tense set of his broad shoulders relaxed. "Su-weet. What time should we meet?"

"Seven thirty?"

"Great. See you then." He jogged back to his truck with his dog.

I locked the door and leaned against it. I missed spending as much time with Marc as I had the previous summer when I'd worked to find Peter's killer. Marc's life had revolved around building boats then, and the way he'd kept his guard up, it'd been a challenge to become friends.

Still, when I dreamed of a relationship, Marc's face was the one I imagined. *Que sera, sera.* Time would tell if we'd have a real relationship or not.

In the interim, I needed to feed the dogs and look into my other suspects, starting with Garland Davis.

Chapter Fifteen

THIS MORNING'S sunrise had been glorious, but white clouds now filled the sky. With Chubb in tow, I walked around the neighborhood where Garland Davis, also known as Ben, lived. According to my research, he lived on the mainland along the marsh in a middle-class neighborhood. Make that upper middle-class. The location of the modest houses made them pricey.

A white pickup headed our way. The driver wore a ball cap and held a phone in his left hand while his elbow was propped on the open windowsill. I'd researched Ben's company, and saw their red logo advertising Davis Construction on the door.

Great, I'd caught him leaving the neighborhood. I waved at him and moved into the street. "Mr. Davis?"

He stopped and put his phone to the side. "How can I help you?"

Either he was a gentleman or a good businessman. I kept a firm hold on Chubb's leash. "Are you Garland Davis?"

"Friends call me Ben." He eyed Chubb. "Nice dog."

"Thanks. I'm walking him for a friend. I need to talk to you about Corey Lane. I'm Andi Grace Scott."

He snorted. "If you're a friend of Lane's, you can call me Mr. Davis. Better yet, don't talk to me at all." He reached down and the window started rolling up.

"I wasn't his friend. You know he's dead, right?" I watched his mouth drop open then glanced at Marc's dog. Chubb remained at my side. Ears up and alert.

"Hold on." He pulled his truck to the curb and parked. "I been outta town a few days. You say Corey Lane is dead?"

I walked closer to his vehicle. "Yes. Murdered. Do you know who might've wanted to murder him?"

"Probably a long list, and I'd be on it." He rubbed his hand over his scruffy jaw and threw open the door, stepping onto the pavement. The man wore a flannel shirt buttoned over a gray T-shirt. Holey jeans that looked worn from work, instead of newly bought for a hefty price.

"Why?"

"You a cop? Aren't you supposed to identify yourself when you question somebody?"

"I'm a dog walker. Nothing else." I pointed to the golden retriever. "Meet Chubb."

"Then why are you so curious about Corey?"

I shrugged. "I knew his wife growing up."

"Gotta be more to it." He stretched out his hand for Chubb to sniff. Before long, the dog's tail wagged in approval.

"You might know my brother, Nate Scott. He's a landscaper."

"Yeah, I know him. Good kid." He crossed his arms over his tight-fitting flannel. The man was a little taller than I was, and he was super muscular.

"The authorities arrested Nate for killing Corey. He's innocent. I want to make sure the cops catch the real killer and release my brother."

I moved closer to Mr. Davis as a sleek silver car passed us.

He whistled. "There goes a nice ride. Fast, too."

My blood pressure rose. Why wasn't he focused on me instead of a silly car? "Mr. Davis, can we get back to Corey?"

"May as well call me Ben. Did I have a motive to kill Lane? Possibly. He was a racketeer. Ask anybody. He was always trying to get a little something under the table in order to give you a contract. I never stooped to his underhanded shenanigans, and I haven't gone out of business yet."

"If you had killed him, what would your motive have been?" I was curious, and it might lead me to somebody else with the same purpose.

"It hurt my business to keep losing bids—those kinda jobs are usually good work for my crew. Man's gotta stand for something, though, and I'm an honest man."

My respect for Ben grew. "It's good to know you're an honest businessman."

Chubb tugged on the leash, but I held firm.

"Thanks. I best get to work. Hope you can get your brother out of the pokey, but you're wasting your time thinking I killed Lane."

I wasn't ready to let the man go. "Do you mind if I ask where you were Tuesday morning?"

"In Wilmington at the Hampton Inn. I was there to bid on a job."

"So who do you think killed Corey?"

He shrugged. "Could be a dozen people. Maybe Wendy Conn. She did his hair and other things, if you get my meaning."

Another person suggesting Wendy. "Do you know much about her?"

"Has a sister in the upstate, I believe. No, it might be Columbia. Not sure, but I gotta get to work now." He jumped into the driver's seat.

I followed. "What about Asher Cummings? Would he have a motive to kill Corey?"

Ben laughed. "He's a straight arrow. You're barking up the wrong tree if you suspect him."

"Okay. Thanks, Ben."

He touched the bill of his ball cap advertising his business. "Have a good day now."

"You too." I crossed the street and returned to the sidewalk with Chubb at my side. If Ben was the killer, he'd completely snowed me. He seemed like a good old boy. Not a cold-blooded killer.

"Time for some serious exercise, Chubb. We can't let you get fat and lazy. Let's go. We've got dogs to walk." I picked up my pace and jogged.

Chubb joined me at the next three houses to walk a variety of dogs. The dogs played, walked, and lapped up water during our visits. It was good for their socialization skills, and Chubb enjoyed all of the attention from me and the other animals. At my last morning stop, I went to pick up Heinz, the Westie. After I attached a leash to his harness, we walked through an older section of homes near the creek.

Heinz's ears perked up, and he trotted beside Chubb. We veered to a sandy beach path. His owners knew how much Heinz enjoyed walking on the beach and encouraged me to take him. The sand wasn't too hot to burn the dogs' paws this time of year, and there was little chance they'd get dehydrated on our short January walk.

The wind blew my ponytail around, causing it to smack my cheeks. I zipped my sweatshirt jacket but enjoyed the cool breeze and the sound of waves lapping along the shore while my mind whirled. Could I live full-time at the plantation? I'd still be able to visit the beach, but would it be enough? Would I be miserable so far inland? Yes, but was it selfish to want to stay in my cottage?

A tall man ran toward us in shorts and a sweaty T-shirt.

I squinted at the familiar figure with a sense of dread. Yep, it was David. I waved and forced my lips up into what I hoped was a smile and not a grimace.

He reached us and jogged in place. "Andi Grace."

"Good morning, David. How are you?"

"Fine. Have you been staying out of trouble?"

"Yes." I gulped. "I ran into Ben Davis this morning. He didn't know about Corey, but if he had to guess, Wendy Conn is who he'd suspect to be the killer."

"Just happened to run into him?" He frowned.

I straightened my spine. "Did you know Wendy was having an affair with Corey?"

David's nostrils flared. "I'm handling the case. Not you."

Heinz barked at a seagull and tugged on the leash. Chubb barked at Heinz, as if to warn him not to interrupt.

"I even considered Asher Cummings, but he's so nice. Ben said there's no way Asher's guilty. What do you think?" I studied his expression, hoping for a clue.

His jaw jutted out, and he pointed to me. "I think you need to butt out before I arrest you for interfering in an ongoing investigation. Are we clear?"

Maybe I should've listened to Heinz and chased after the seabirds before I pushed David's last button. "Crystal. Have a good day, *Deputy Wayne.*"

He jogged toward the pier, and I led the dogs in the opposite direction. Marc had asked me to keep an open mind. So maybe Erin was innocent and Wendy was guilty. I didn't want to make the deputy mad, but how could I stand by and do nothing? Nate's future was on the line.

Chapter Sixteen

I TOOK HEINZ home then swung by Wendy's house. There was no sign of life at Wendy's place, so I drove to her shop. Closed. I hopped out of my Suburban and peered in the front windows. We'd assumed she left town, but with at least two boyfriends, who knew? Could she be hiding at another man's place?

"What are you doing?" Regina Houp's voice cut through me like nails on a chalkboard.

I slapped my hand to my chest. "Looking for Wendy."

"Her car's in back, but I don't think she's open." Regina watered planters of ferns near a bench in front of her shop.

My heartbeat sped up. "Thanks, Regina." Not knowing what to expect, I left Chubb in my vehicle with the windows down and wandered to the back of the building. No need to endanger both of us if I ran into trouble. Confronting Ben hadn't scared me, but Wendy made me nervous.

No signs of life in the loading area, but sure enough, her Bug sat there. I walked to her car and looked in the windows. The junk from our previous encounter had been removed. I touched the hood. Still warm.

I didn't want to spook her, so I sat on a step at Regina's loading dock and waited. And waited. And waited. What was Wendy doing in the salon? For a woman on the run, she didn't seem to be in any kind of hurry.

If I knocked on the back door, would she escape out the front? No doubt she could catch a ride with one of her many men. I remained seated, watching and waiting.

I reviewed my calendar on my phone. There was a cat to check on whose owners were out of town for the week. Later, I needed to walk a couple of dogs whose owners had gone hiking.

Squeak. The back door of the salon opened. A hunched-over figure, wearing a hoody and carrying assorted bags, emerged.

I hustled toward her. "Wendy."

She jerked. "Andi Grace, why can't you leave me alone? I told you everything."

"Not everything. I've got a few more questions." I took a calming breath. "Who signed the lease on the Myrtle Beach apartment?"

"You had a chance to find out when I gave you the key to my house." She pushed me aside and dumped the bags into the little yellow car.

"Deputy Wayne arrived and kicked us out. You've sure got nosy neighbors."

"What can I say? We watch out for each other." She elbowed me out of the way. "If you'll excuse me, I've got to go. I only returned to gather enough supplies to make a living."

"Who are you running from? The cops? Or the killer?"

"Both. I might not be the smartest person in these parts, but I know when to get out of town." She rubbed her upper arms. "Be careful, Andi Grace." She slid into the driver's seat and drove away.

I walked around the building and got into the Suburban. Marc's dog lay on a soft towel chewing on a bone. "Hey, Chubb. How're you doing? Let's go see a cat." I verified the address was on the other side of Highway 17. "Hmm, it wouldn't be impossible to swing by Wendy's neighborhood after we fed Whiskers. What do you think?"

Chubb barked and gave me a goofy grin.

An hour later, after taking care of Whiskers, I pulled into Wendy's driveway. I still had the house key, but my plan was to question the neighbors. "Let's go, boy. Time to turn on the charm and see what we can learn."

A man in overalls pulled weeds in the yard across the street. We walked his way with only one stop for Chubb to sniff around and relieve himself.

"Hello," I called out.

The man stood, pressing on his knees as he slowly rose. "Howdy."

"I'm Andi Grace Scott." I stuck my hand out.

He shook mine. "Frank Hoffman. You look familiar."

"I live on the island, and I run a dog walking business. I used to work for Doc Hewitt, but it was years ago."

He removed his Vietnam Veteran ball cap and ran a hand over his balding head. "I remember you. Used to bring my Berner into Doc, and you could always calm him down."

"A Bernese Mountain Dog. I remember Max."

"He was the best dog. He passed shortly after my wife did."

Chubb edged up to the man. Frank touched Chubb's head and gently moved his fingers in the direction his fur lay.

"I'm so sorry. Do you have a pet now?"

He shook his head. "Haven't had the heart to go through the loss again."

"I get it. I lost both of my parents at the same time in a car wreck. It's tough."

Frank pulled a faded red bandana from his pocket and blew his nose. "I don't recognize your dog. Is he new to the neighborhood?"

"No, he came with me. Wendy Conn is a friend of mine and the man she was dating was murdered this week. Wendy claims she's innocent, and I'm trying to find the real killer."

"Wendy hasn't been around for a day or two, but I've seen you."

"Yes, sir. She gave me a key to her house with permission to enter. It turns out Wendy was seeing another man."

"Who's the other guy?" He tugged the cap on and ran his fingers along the bill.

"Wendy was too scared to tell me, but I'm worried he might be the killer. What if he decides to kill Wendy too?"

Frank rubbed at the scruff on his chin. "There was a tall man with dark hair that came over late at night, and there was a bald guy. I haven't seen him in a while, though."

"Bald guy? Any chance he's a Clemson fan?"

"Yeah. He drove a Lexus with a Clemson tag on the front and a sticker in the back window." He chuckled. "I'm a Carolina fan myself, but I can't deny the Tigers have a talented team."

Bald Clemson fan matched Norris Gilbert, but there were lots of bald Clemson fans. "You haven't seen him lately?"

"Correct."

Was he the guy paying for the apartment in Myrtle Beach? I pulled a business card out of my jeans' pocket. "If you think of anything else, would you give me a call? Or if you'd like to visit my dogs, give me a shout." I described my vision for doggie day care and training facilities.

"I don't see as good as I did in my younger days." He looked at my card and tromboned it back and forth. "Andi Grace, I might surprise you and show up to help with your dogs." He rubbed Chubb's head.

"I'll be happy to see you. Thanks, Frank." I led Chubb next door to a white brick house with a faded red door and rang the doorbell. I checked my cell for messages and found nothing urgent.

Sally Mae Zorn, the church organist, opened the door and lifted her hand to her mouth. "I'll be right back." Her words were garbled, but in less than a minute the door reopened. "Sorry about that. You interrupted my morning nap, and I didn't have my teeth in."

"I'm so sorry." I didn't know if I was more surprised to see Sally Mae or the fact she'd been napping before lunch.

"Don't be. I have trouble sleeping at night and end up napping twice a day. Andi Grace. What brings you my way?"

"Mrs. Sally Mae, are you friends with Wendy Conn?" I couldn't imagine what they'd have in common, but who knew?

"Yes, she's a real sweetie pie. When I broke my wrist a couple of years ago, she came over and took care of my hair. Every day. Even washed and set it twice a week without accepting a penny in return. Since then, I've taken her muffins or whatever I bake. I also keep an eye on her." She narrowed an eye. "Why do you keep coming over? First time, I called the cops on you. Course I didn't realize it was you until they showed up. What were you doing?" Her dangling gold spiral earrings spun as she shook a finger at me.

Chubb growled.

"Easy, boy. It's okay." I rubbed his head before turning my gaze to Mrs. Sally Mae. "Wendy's in trouble. Corey Lane was murdered, and Wendy's worried the killer may come after her. She gave me a key to her house to look for clues. I'm trying to help Wendy by catching the killer."

"I know you helped catch the man who killed Peter Roth, but you're not a deputy, Andi Grace."

"Yes, ma'am. You're right."

"Would your interest in helping Wendy have anything to do with your brother being in jail?"

Busted. "Nate's innocent."

"I'd invite you inside, dear, but I'm allergic to dogs." Her penciled eyebrows rose. Despite her age and lack of teeth, the woman worked on her appearance and was very pretty. "Why are you here?"

"Did you see any of the men Wendy dated?"

"Well, I don't like to gossip." She looked right and left.

I pushed more. "I know about Corey, and I know there's a bald-headed man."

"Norris Gilbert." She blurted out his name and never blinked.

Goose bumps popped out all over my body, and I shivered. Norris Gilbert was Erin's friend and probably her divorce attorney. Was it possible he was Wendy's other boyfriend? "Right, Norris."

"He showed up at odd hours, but I haven't seen him in months."

I nodded and didn't contradict the elderly woman. "Is there anybody else?"

"Corey's the only one I've seen lately. Wendy's a lovely girl. It's too bad she only dates married men. I wonder if it's because her mother had a string of lovers who always left her? Maybe Wendy figures if she dates a married man, she won't get her heart broken."

That logic didn't make sense to me. "I don't get it."

She sighed. "Right from the start, Wendy must know the relationship is doomed. It's a way to protect her heart. Do you understand what I'm saying?"

There was some twisted logic in her words. "I guess that makes sense. Is there anything else you can think of to help me?"

"No, dear. Now, if you don't mind, I'm going to finish my nap. I need my beauty rest."

"Yes, ma'am. Thanks so much." I led Chubb back to the Suburban and gave him a another treat from the back where I kept pet supplies.

"Norris Gilbert." The man's name flitted through my mind to the tune of Handel's "Hallelujah Chorus." He was the bald man. I couldn't wait to tell Marc, but first I had two more dogs to walk.

A car turned onto the street. It was the first one I'd seen since arriving. The vehicle was a metallic beige Lexus sedan. A tasteful license plate on the front matched the color of the car, but it had a bright orange tiger paw. Clemson's logo was an orange paw print.

I froze in place.

By the SUV, Chubb munched on his dog bone in the grass.

The Lexus stopped on the other side of the street, and the driver's door opened. A bald man got out with a spring to his step and approached me.

The sight of the man made it difficult for me to swallow.

"Andi Grace Scott?"

My gaze darted around. Mrs. Sally Mae had said she needed to nap, but where was Mr. Hoffman in my hour of need?

Chapter Seventeen

MY LEGS SHOOK. "Yes."

The lean man's green gaze lasered in on me. "I believe you know Erin Lane."

Chubb dropped his bone with a little thump and stood alert. I didn't tell him to relax, like with Mrs. Sally Mae, because I had no idea what was about to happen. I wanted Chubb to look like a Brutus or an Axel. Fierce and loyal. Not sweet and loving.

"She's a friend." My stomach fluttered.

"Not according to Erin. She wants you to stay away from her. I argued for a restraining order, but she's not ready to take that step. Yet." He moved so close I could see the wrinkles around his green eyes and the flecks of gray in his goatee. His breath smelled garlicky. "Stay away from Erin. Don't come to her house or Corey's funeral."

Chubb growled and bared his teeth.

"Hey." Mr. Hoffman's voice boomed as he crossed his front yard with a slight limp. "What's going on? Andi Grace, is this man bothering you?"

"I'm definitely not comfortable with him standing so close." Relief poured through me, and I felt a little stronger with the veteran watching out for me. Safety in numbers and all that. I lifted my chin.

"No need to get riled." Norris raised a tanned manicured hand. "I stopped by to deliver a message."

"More like a threat. How did you know I was here?" Was he keeping tabs on me, or Wendy? A shiver crept up my spine.

"I have my ways." His sinister tone sent a chill over my body.

Mr. Hoffman pulled a cell phone out of his bib pocket. "I suggest you get out of here before I call the cops. Got 'em on speed dial."

"I'm leaving, but Ms. Scott, you better stay away from Erin. Or else I'll take action." He stepped away from me.

Like he'd taken action with Corey? "Legal or otherwise?"

He turned on the heel of his shiny brown crocodile loafers. "Legal, of course. Don't cross me."

Surrounded by Mr. Hoffman and Chubb, I decided to show some chutzpah. "What's your relationship with Wendy?"

Norris slammed the car door and drove away. Why wasn't he driving a dark SUV? Then I'd believe he was Corey's killer. The Lexus threw me off, and I wondered if there was a way to find out if he also owned a vehicle like the one I'd seen at Richard Rice Plantation the morning Corey was killed.

We stood together until the taillights of Norris's Lexus disappeared.

I faced Wendy's neighbor. "Frank, if I disappear, tell Sheriff Stone to look into Norris Gilbert."

"You got it, but you be careful around him. He's a mean one. A friend of mine got divorced, and Gilbert was his wife's attorney." He waved both hands down.

"Thanks so much for coming over. I hate to think what he'd have done if you hadn't shown up."

"I may look like an old man, but in my heart, I'm still a warrior." He saluted and headed back to his house.

"You were definitely a warrior today. Thanks, Frank." Once Chubb and I were inside my Suburban, I texted my two clients working second shift and asked permission to take their dogs to my plantation with me. I thought they might enjoy extra time to run around the fenced-in dog area, and I didn't want to chance another round with Norris. Both owners agreed when I mentioned it'd be no extra charge.

I also dialed David, but it rolled to voice mail. "Hi, this is Andi Grace. Please, don't be mad. I ran into Norris Gilbert, and he threatened me. Turns out he was also having an affair with Wendy. Maybe he killed Corey in a jealous rage. I can't rest until you release Nate."

Within an hour, I pulled into Kennady Plantation with Chubb, Harry, and Belle. I leashed all three dogs and headed for the barn.

Dylan met me at entrance. "Who ya got here?"

"The goldendoodle is Harry, and Belle is the beagle. Their owners won't be home until after midnight, and I thought they might enjoy some extra playtime."

"Cool." Dylan stepped back, allowing us to enter.

Sunny and Bo raced to us, barking with joy.

"Hey, there. Did you miss me?" I loved on Sunny before leading all the dogs to the play area.

A whimper sounded from a crate to my left. "Did somebody else drop off a dog?"

Dylan frowned. "We found her in a ratty cardboard box at the kitchen door of the main house. No note. Nothing."

I glanced at the other five dogs who sniffed each other. Harry and Belle began to explore while Sunny climbed to the top of the sliding board and scrutinized the others like a momma watching her babies. "Show me the newbie."

He led me to the crate. "I gave her a bath and cut some sand burrs out of her hair."

"Looks like people know how to find me, if they dropped her here. Thank goodness they didn't throw this sweet thing in the river." I studied the black, tan, and white puppy with a pink bow around her neck. "I take it Juliet's seen her."

"I didn't give her a pink anything. Should I run her to Doc Hewitt's for an exam?"

"Great idea." I pulled a twenty out of my pocket. "Why don't you grab yourself a pizza or burger before coming back?"

"Cool." His eyes sparkled. "I appreciate it."

"And I appreciate all you're doing around here. Are you still doing okay with your room?" We'd converted the tack room into a studio apartment with a kitchenette, bath, and main room.

"It's great. I found a couch at a consignment store and a TV on sale in Georgetown."

"Sounds like a home then."

"Yes, ma'am." He glanced at the dog. "Juliet started calling this little girl 'Pinky.' That okay with you?"

"Absolutely. I'm going to check our website for messages. If you see Juliet, tell her I'm in here."

"Sure thing." He took off with Pinky in a travel crate.

I settled down in my office, leaving the door open so I could hear the dogs. No new reservations, so I created a file with notes on Corey's murder. My head spun with the number of possible suspects. Erin, Wendy, Norris, Ben, and Asher. I shivered.

"Knock, knock." Juliet stood in the doorway.

"Hey, I heard you're adopting a dog." Thinking about the cutie patootie lowered my blood pressure.

"I don't have time to train a puppy and open the bed and break-fast."

"I can help train Pinky. What do you think about Kennady's Doggie Day Care? You'll run Kennady's B&B for people, and I'll handle animals."

"Great idea but long name. Have you noticed how many people

travel with their pets? They could board their animals with you and visit them while staying at the main house."

"You're right. I think we may be on to something." I jotted the idea on a sticky note.

"What are you working on?" Juliet leaned against the doorframe.

"Murder notes."

She shook her head. "I figured. Anything new?"

"Wendy's other man is Norris Gilbert. Erin's divorce attorney."

Juliet pushed off the door frame. "You're kidding?"

"Nope, and he threatened me to stay away from Erin. Restraining order and all that jazz." I replayed the scene for her.

Beep. Beep. Outside a car horn honked, and all the dogs barked.

I stood. "I wonder who's here."

Juliet shrugged. "The weekend guests called and said they're stuck behind a wreck in Savannah. They won't arrive until late tonight."

"They'll be starving by the time they get here."

"I'll have some light refreshments ready, but they plan to eat in Savannah and hope to hit the road when the wreck is cleared."

Beep. Beep.

"Somebody's not being very patient." I hurried to the door, and Juliet wasn't far behind.

Marc's red truck was parked next to my Suburban. He came my way, and my heart fluttered as we made eye contact.

Juliet squealed and rushed past me straight to the passenger emerging from the Silverado.

Chapter Eighteen

MARC'S SMILE STRETCHED across his handsome face, and I turned to see his mystery passenger.

Nate.

I hurried toward my brother. "Oh, my goodness. How'd you get out of jail?"

Juliet threw herself into Nate's arms. "I'm so glad you're here."

He hugged her long and hard.

We all stood in front of the truck, and I reached for Marc's hand. "How?"

"I convinced David he didn't have enough to keep holding Nate. Your brother's not free and clear, but he's out for now."

"David knows Nate didn't kill Corey."

My brother stepped away from Juliet. "Hey, Sis."

I wrapped him in my arms and found myself unable to speak. Tears spilled down my cheeks. Freedom. For now. Joy flowed through my veins, and if I could have done a front handspring, I'd have flipped all over the yard. This made me even more determined to track down the killer to assure Nate remained free.

He chuckled. "I can't breathe."

"Sorry." I stepped back and wiped my eyes. "It's so wonderful to see you. Have you seen Lacey Jane yet?"

"She came with Marc to pick me up. I told her not to skip her night class and convinced her I'd still be a free man when she got out."

"I'm surprised you convinced her."

Nate lifted one shoulder. "I told her she needed to get her degree so she could get other innocent people out of jail when she was an attorney or law clerk or whatever she decides to do."

"Well done, little brother." I couldn't stop smiling.

Juliet reached for Nate's arm. "Come to the house. I'll make you a good home-cooked meal."

Nate glanced at me as if unsure of my reaction.

I was willing to share him with Juliet. "Go. We'll join you after a while."

Juliet's eyes glowed. "I'll ring the dinner bell when supper's ready. Dylan found it in one of the old barns and hung it up for me to let guests know when a meal is ready."

"Okay, we'll keep our ears open." My jaw hurt from so much smiling. If the two of them finally got together as a couple, life would be even better.

They walked to the house holding hands.

"If he doesn't ask her out on a real date, I'm going to smack him."

"They seem to really care about each other."

"Yeah. He's had a soft spot for Juliet for years, but he worries if they date and it doesn't work out, they won't be friends anymore."

"I understand. It's a risk." Marc stuffed his hands into the pockets of his trousers.

"Want to see your dog? He's in the barn playing with the others."

He motioned for me to lead the way. "Thanks for taking care of him. If you need a reference, feel free to have potential clients call me."

"Thanks, I will. The dogs seem to enjoy Dylan's improvements." I stopped at the fenced-in play yard.

Chubb raced to us, and the others followed.

Marc laughed. "Hey, Chubb. How ya doing?"

Chubb barked, licked Marc's hand, then raced away, showing off for his master. He climbed the toy slide, slid down, jumped through a plastic hoop, and ran the dog-friendly obstacle course before returning to us.

Marc clapped. "Good job, Chubb."

I slipped Marc a treat to reward his golden retriever.

Marc lavished affection on Chubb, then the dog headed for the water bowls.

I asked, "How was your day?"

"Busy, but good. Seeing your face when you realized Nate was out was the best part."

"Thank you so much for bringing him home." I kissed Marc's cheek, and he wrapped his arms around me and touched my lips with his.

"Su-weet." He kissed me again. "This just became the best part of my day."

"Mine too." I held on another moment. "Do you have time to discuss Corey's murder?"

He laughed. "I should've known."

"Come on back." I led him to my office. "It's been an informative day. I met Ben Davis and ruled him out."

"I'm glad you're expanding your search for suspects."

"I tracked down Wendy, who was gathering supplies from her salon. She says she saw the body and ran. She truly seems afraid the killer will come after her. I believe her fear, which makes me want to rule her out. Although she still wouldn't tell me about the other man she was seeing."

"What else?" He crossed one ankle over the other knee and revealed bright blue socks with sailboats.

"How do you know there's anything else?"

Marc loosened his tie. "I can read you, Andi Grace. You've got more."

"Well, you're right. I wondered about Wendy's nosy neighbors and went to her neighborhood to see if anyone would talk to me. Chubb was with me the entire time and behaved very well."

"Good to know." He pointed at me to get back to my story.

"Frank Hoffman lives in the house across from Wendy and had seen a Lexus at her house often, but a few months ago, it stopped. This led me to wonder if he's our mystery man who rented the apartment in Myrtle Beach for their rendezvouses."

"Did Mr. Hoffman know the driver?"

"No, but he described the car perfectly." I rested my arms on the desk.

"How do you know it was a good description?"

"Patience. Our church organist lives next door to Mr. Hoffman, and she knew the owner of the Lexus. Guess who it is."

He sat straighter in his seat. "Asher? A board member? The mayor?"

"Norris Gilbert."

Marc's eyes widened, and he leaned forward. "You've got to be kidding me."

"No."

"Is that how you know Mr. Hoffman's description of the Lexus was accurate?"

"Are you ready for this?" At his nod, I took a deep breath. "After we finished talking to Mrs. Sally Mae, Chubb and I walked to Wendy's driveway, where I'd left the Suburban. That's when Norris drove up. He parked on the edge of the road and walked over to me."

"What?" Marc's hands gripped the arms of the chair.

"He warned me to leave Erin alone or he'd file a restraining order. His tone frightened me. Frank crossed the street and told Norris to leave me alone. Frank and Chubb protected me."

Marc stood and paced in my cramped office. "This is serious, Andi Grace. Norris is a powerful man. I haven't practiced here very long, but I know he's a force. Like a category three hurricane. You don't want to cross him."

"I think as long as I don't bother Erin, I'll be okay."

He ran a hand through his sandy blond hair. "Norris is married. Please tell me you didn't accuse him of having an affair with Wendy."

I replayed the conversation in my mind. "Kinda, and I asked how he'd found me. He said he has his ways. It made me think of a mafia gangster in the movies, except he didn't flex his muscles, pop his knuckles, or flash a gun. What do you think he meant? Does he have video surveillance on Wendy's house?"

"I doubt it."

"Then how did he know I was there?" Norris was an attorney. Not a cop or detective. "What about a tracker?"

"I find it highly unlikely, but we can check your SUV, if it'll give you peace of mind. Anything else?" Marc's pacing slowed.

"I'm mulling an idea over. Wendy's seeing two men. Norris is a bigshot divorce attorney. He can't let the public know he and Wendy are in a relationship. So he rents an apartment where they'll have more privacy. Then Erin hires Norris to be her divorce attorney. They discover Wendy and Corey are having a fling. Not only does Erin feel betrayed, Norris is also betrayed. He doesn't confess his affair to Erin, but he needs to eliminate Corey." I paused.

Marc nodded. "Right. Norris isn't faithful to his wife, but he wouldn't like having the tables turned on him. Keep going."

"Wendy's relationship with Corey gives Norris a motive. Say he's furious and tells her to end the affair with Corey. She must've refused because she was taking coffee to Corey the morning he was murdered. She saw the dead body and ran in case the killer spotted her. I think she's afraid Norris is guilty, and that's why she can't hide at the secret apartment."

"Makes sense. What else?"

I leaned back in my chair. "I think that's it."

He stopped pacing. "Then I suggest we look for a tracker on your car. I really don't believe we'll find one, but the smart move is to check."

Marc's intelligence was one of the traits I found attractive. I walked with him to the Suburban, reflecting on his good qualities, including how handsome he was. "You're still in your nice clothes. Tell me what to look for, and I'll do it."

Marc removed his tie and rolled up the sleeves of his button-up. "I've got this." He started at the front, stretching his arm out under the fender and, with a methodical approach, moved inch by inch around the car. I followed him to the point where he reached the back-hubcap area. "I don't believe it."

"What?" My heart beat faster.

"I found something."

I knelt beside him in the worn-down grass by my SUV.

On his knees and with his shoulder hugging the wheel well, Marc extended one hand farther under the vehicle. When he moved back toward me, he held a small gray box with what looked like spools on it.

"What is it?"

In unison, we stood.

Marc pointed to the circles. "These are magnets, which hold the box to your vehicle. Let's see what's inside."

I leaned close. "I don't know why I'm so nervous."

"That makes two of us." With shaky fingers, he opened the sturdy box. "Here's the tracker."

"How does it work?"

"Whoever put the device on your Suburban can monitor your location twenty-four hours a day. Seven days a week. It's probably connected to their phone or tablet. David needs to see this."

The dinner bell clanged.

My heart nearly leapt out of my chest, and I shrieked. "Oh, that startled me."

Marc shook his head. "It gave me a little jolt, too. Do you want to report this?"

I nodded. "You bet I do." I made a quick call while Marc brushed the dirt off his slacks. Then we trotted to the house to join Nate and Juliet in the dining room.

I'd barely started eating when the doorbell rang. I hurried to answer it. "Hi, David. Thanks for coming."

"What seems to be the problem?" His normal assertive posture was missing. He looked tired, in fact.

"We found a tracker on my Suburban, and I think Norris Gilbert put it there."

David held out his hands. "Whoa, you don't want to mess with him."

"Wait until you hear what happened. Norris showed up today out of the clear blue sky while I was at Wendy's. He told me Erin hired him to be her divorce attorney. Did you get my message about him having a relationship with Wendy?"

David sighed. "Yes."

"Come on, David. Didn't you become a deputy to catch the bad guys?"

"Norris Gilbert is an attorney. Having an affair isn't a crime."

I ran my hands through my hair. "You got me there, but I think more's going on. Will you at least look at the tracker?"

He shook his head. "Lead the way."

"Can Marc come with us? He's actually the one who found it."

"Sure." David waited on the front porch while I hurried inside.

"Marc, David's here and willing to see what you found."

Marc pushed back from a plate of meatloaf, mashed potatoes, and green beans and shook his head. "I hate to leave this delicious meal, Juliet. Thanks."

Nate stood. "Should I go with you?"

I shook my head. "No. You and Juliet enjoy supper. We'll be back." After a few steps, I turned back. "Hey, Juliet. Can you fix a to-go plate for David? He looks like he could stand a decent meal and some kindness."

"Even though he's the one who arrested Nate?"

I nodded. "I have faith he'll get to the truth."

"Whatever you say."

Marc walked beside me through the house. "Mighty nice of you to show compassion to David."

"He's working hard on this case." My hands shook.

"It's going to be okay. Take a deep breath." Marc took my hand as we walked to the SUV in silence.

David said, "What have you got?"

Marc opened the car door and pulled the tracker out of the console while telling the deputy exactly what happened. He passed the contraption to the officer. "My fingerprints will be all over it, but can you check for other prints or maybe see who is getting the tracking reports?"

"I'll look into it." He pulled a small evidence bag from his khakis and held it out.

Marc placed the tracker inside.

I raised my hand. "Would it do any good to leave it on my Suburban and see who shows up to get it when the batteries wear out?"

Marc darted his gaze at me. "No way. We're not putting you in any more danger."

David slipped the device into an evidence bag. "I agree, but I'll talk to Sheriff Stone. Maybe we can come up with a plan to catch the person by using this as bait."

"Awesome. Will you let me know when you catch the guy?"

"We'll see, but Andi Grace, I thought you would drop this once your brother was released. Spend time with him, and let me find the killer."

How unfair. "I ran into Norris before Nate was released."

His brows hiked, he studied me with a frown. "Whoever put the tracker on your vehicle isn't necessarily the same person who killed Corey."

I nodded. "Right. There are so many motives to consider. Gambling debts, taking bribes from contractors, and having affairs. When we find the motive, it'll be easier to determine who murdered Corey."

David scowled at me.

Marc reached for my elbow. "That's not how you let the sheriff's department solve the crime. Let's go finish our dinners."

"Sorry, David, you're right. I've got dogs to take care of, and you've got a murder to solve. You don't need my help. Message received. Thanks for coming out here tonight. I hope you have a good weekend."

"It'll be easier if I'm not worried about you getting yourself killed." He turned.

"Wait. I asked Juliet to fix you a plate. To go. I figured you don't have time for a social dinner."

His mouth dropped open. "Uh, thanks."

"You can go in the front door. Now that we're a B&B, people come and go frequently. Juliet's expecting you."

David walked toward the house.

We watched him go, then Marc placed his hands on my shoulders. "Our conversation with David went better than expected."

I tugged at the neck of my T-shirt. "I'm not going to relax until they catch the guilty person."

"Then let's hope they hurry up and find him."

"Or her. I followed your suggestion and considered other potential suspects, but I haven't completely ruled out Erin."

"If you've not ruled her out, I'm hearing you're not dropping your investigation."

"I can't let it go until I know Nate is in the clear."

An owl hooted in the woods.

Marc ran his hands down my arms. "Honestly, I'd be surprised if you backed down at this point."

His words touched my heart. He got me. Even better, he seemed to accept me. For now, it was enough. "Thanks for not talking me out of my investigation."

"I've learned. Please keep me informed, though."

"Informed of my whereabouts? Why?"

"Somebody needs to watch your back." He reached for my hand, and we walked to the house.

I could get used to having Marc look out for me. Not that I needed his protection, but it was nice to know he cared.

Jackie Layton

Chapter Nineteen

SATURDAY MORNING Sunny strutted into the dog barn at my side. Head lifted high and unleashed, she entered first. We'd picked up Chloe and Heinz so they could spend the day with us while their families snow skied at Sugar Mountain.

"Who's ready for some fun?" I opened the gate to the play area and unleashed the Westies.

Heinz barked and raced around the perimeter of the fence. Chloe sniffed and took her time investigating, while Sunny climbed to the top of the slide and watched over the other two.

"Sunny, you can play, too."

Her ears stood at attention, but she didn't leave her perch.

My phone buzzed in the pocket of my jeans. Asher's name flashed on the screen, and I headed to my office as I answered. "Hi, Asher. How are you this morning?"

"I'm cold and nursing my second cup of coffee. How about yourself?" His melodic tenor floated over the line.

"I've been walking dogs, which usually keeps me warm." I knew Asher hadn't called me to chat about the weather. He'd never asked me to care for a pet, but maybe this was the first time. I sat at my desk hoping to land a new dog-walking client. "How can I help you?"

"My daughter is about to announce her intention to run for state representative, and I thought it might be nice to do it at your place. If the weather cooperates, the front porch would be a beautiful setting. Stately. Your plantation is a tribute to our roots. At the same time, it also shows how two women can successfully run a business."

No wonder he was a successful businessman. Clear and succinct words stated his desire, and I wanted to be professional in my response. "What if we have bad weather?"

"The living room is spectacular. Would you be willing to set it up for a large gathering? Maybe serve a few refreshments? I'm confident it'll work."

His comments startled me until I recalled Asher's friendship with

Peter had made him familiar with the house we'd converted into the Kennady B&B. "I'd love to be able to provide the setting for her. We need to check with Juliet and make sure she doesn't have anything else planned. I guess you'll want as much press coverage as possible and photographers. What about political bloggers? Other politicians who support your daughter?"

Asher laughed. "We've got it figured out. We feel like a Wednesday is good for all of us. The sooner the better. What do you think?"

I hadn't heard Juliet mention any Wednesday guests. "Sounds good, but I want to run it by Juliet. Why don't you come by later? We can nail down everything you need. Refreshments. Lighting and furniture placement, if we have to move inside. I can rope off a parking area for the press and public. If we do it here, I want it to be perfect for you and your daughter."

"How does this afternoon sound? Hannah's spending the weekend with us. We could run out then. Of course, I'll text you first."

"Sounds great. I look forward to seeing y'all." We confirmed a time, and I hurried to the main house to alert my friend. She'd dreamed of ways to make the plantation profitable, and she'd be excited about a political announcement. "Juliet." I entered the kitchen and found her frosting a chocolate cake.

"Hey, there. Our first guests are delightful. They kept complementing the food. I helped them book a tour at the Mansfield Plantation in Georgetown, then I sent them off with sack lunches and smiles."

"Good." I found a clean spoon and swiped a little of the icing. "Yum."

"Stop it. This is for the guests which means you can't lick the bowl." She shook her head and laughed. "Do you need something?"

"Sorry. I never thought of that." I rinsed the spoon and placed it in the dishwasher. "How would you feel about hosting a political candidate?"

"What?" Her eyes widened.

I explained Asher's proposal.

"I love it." Juliet dropped the spatula into the bowl. "Griffin spent last night here, and he and Dylan are at the old kitchen going over plans to convert it into living quarters."

"Oh, uh, great." My spirits sank.

Juliet circled the island and placed a hand on my shoulder. "You know, I can run the B&B without you living on the premises."

"I know." I swallowed hard. "If we board pets, though, I probably should be here full time."

She shook her head. "Andi Grace, you're a beach girl. Specifically, Heyward Beach. Just because Peter left this place to you, it doesn't mean you have to live here."

"But—"

"No buts. Live here if you want. Otherwise, you can pay employees to live on the plantation and care for the animals at night."

"Yeah, but Griffin and Dylan are excited about converting the kitchen into living quarters."

"We can make it a honeymoon cottage or something."

I sighed. Was it time to start taking advice from Juliet and Marc? "I really do love my house."

Juliet laughed. "I know you do. It's a great home."

I glanced at my watch and noted it was mid-morning. "Maybe I'll take a short walk."

"Pray about your decision."

"Yes, ma'am." Juliet's faith was deeper than mine. I was often afraid of letting others down. My friend usually pushed me to seek God when I had to make a decision. The beach was the place I'd always felt closest to God, but it didn't mean I couldn't pray while walking the path along the Waccamaw River.

The wind blew my hair, and I secured it with a band from around my wrist before I saw a familiar figure jogging my way with his dog.

I waved and ran a hand over my messy ponytail. "Hi, Marc. It's nice to see you're actually taking a day off work."

He turned on his toe and walked beside me. "I promised myself not to get buried in work like when I lived in the city. Weekends are my time off."

"Good for you." I rubbed Chubb's back. "I missed you this morning, but I know you love your master."

Marc chuckled. "He swam in the river."

"What?"

"I took him to the dock, and before I knew it, he belly flopped into the water." Marc turned his ball cap around backward, giving me a clear view of his face.

Early morning stubble didn't take away from his handsomeness. In fact, it was downright attractive. Heat rose in my face. "It must've been freezing."

"Yep. He shook like a leaf on a shady fall day. I even heated some towels in the dryer to help him get warm."

I smiled. "Marc Williams, you're such a softy."

His eyebrows rose. "I know, but why wouldn't you expect me to be nice?"

I considered his question. "Maybe because I still feel like I coerced you to take Chubb."

He reached out and took my hand in his warm one. "I rarely do something I don't want. I think we're good for each other."

Butterflies took off in my belly. "I think we're good for each other, too."

His mouth dropped open. "Uh—"

My face grew hot. "Oh, you mean you and Chubb. Of course that's what you meant."

"I thought we were talking about the dog." His mouth turned up.

"Yeah, yeah. We are." I needed to get away from Marc and get my emotions under control.

"Andi Grace, knowing you makes my life richer."

Now he was just being polite. I met his warm gaze. Maybe his words were sincere. "What do you have planned for today?"

"I thought about calling the local amateur detective to see if she needed any help solving the latest mystery. How's the case going?"

I laughed. "Asher's bringing his daughter here this afternoon to discuss booking the main house for a political announcement. I thought I might see if he's got any ideas on Corey's murder."

"Is Asher running for office?"

"No, but his daughter is. Oops, I was supposed to keep that to myself. Good thing you're a lawyer and used to keeping secrets." How many times could I embarrass myself in front of Marc? I knew he was dependable, because he'd kept plenty of matters confidential for me in the time I'd known him.

Crinkles broke out around Marc's eyes and his dimple appeared. "Your secret's safe with me. I'm proud of you for considering other suspects besides Erin."

I shrugged. "You were right. She's the most obvious suspect, but there are others."

"I need to finish my run, but how can I help you later?"

"Can you find out where Wendy's mysterious condo is? If we can find it, I've got the key."

"Even if we find it, we can't barge inside."

My face grew warm. "I'll knock and if nobody answers, I'll try the key. Dog walkers are used to entering empty houses."

"Why go inside? You already figured out Norris was the other married man in Wendy's life. What do you hope to accomplish?'"

Good question. "I don't know. Maybe we'll find a clue. Norris and Wendy are both suspects."

"Okay. I'll call you later." He and Chubb jogged away in the direction of his house on the river.

I continued along the trail and wandered through old rice fields. Previous owners had tried different crops, but I had no intention of farming. Kennady's B&B, as well as the doggie day care, fit me better. I counted my blessings. If not for Juliet, I never would've been able to turn the place around. Partly because it wasn't my dream to run a B&B. Working with animals was another matter.

Back at the dog barn, I ran into Griffin and Dylan.

Dylan said, "Doc Hewitt said Pinky is ready to come home. Do you want me to go get her?"

"Yeah. Thanks, Dylan. Ask Doc to put it on my bill. I always pay him at the end of the month."

"Yes, ma'am. Yes, ma'am. See ya later." He left me standing with Griffin.

I faced Juliet's brother. "How's it going?"

"We're doing fine. The old kitchen has good bones. You can turn it into a small home, if you'd like."

"Any other options?"

He scratched his head. Thick dark brown hair covered Griffin's head and face. Full moustache and beard. He wasn't as tall as Marc, more like six foot. "It could be used for offices, but you already have an office in the barn. Maybe guest quarters for long-term guests. Say a couple wanting to spend the winter in the Low Country. The lighting is good, so an artist or author might enjoy an extended visit. There's also the possibility it could be a home for Juliet, but whatever you do with the building, it needs to make sense financially."

My gut tightened. "I know."

"It'd make a nice home for you."

"Let me think about it. Are you in the middle of any other jobs?"

"No, it's a slow time right now. I'd placed some bids at Richard Rice Plantation but missed out on all of their projects."

"Did Corey try to get you to offer him a bribe?"

Griffin's eyebrows shot up. "Yeah. How'd you know?"

I moved toward the barn door and waved for Griffin to join me. "I've learned a few things about Corey since he died."

Griffin matched his stride to mine. "A few months ago, I started hearing rumors about his shady deals. I've wanted to move back to Heyward Beach for some time, but I need work. Legitimate work. Nothing that'd lead me to prison."

"I guess you heard Nate was arrested for Corey's murder."

"I heard." He pushed open the door and held it for me.

"He's innocent." I took him back to my office.

"I know."

I glanced at the dogs snoozing on soft dog beds and didn't say another word until we entered my workspace.

Once we were seated at my desk, Griffin said, "There's no way Nate would hurt the dude, much less murder him."

I laughed. "I always liked you, Griffin."

His expression grew serious, no visible smile. "Even when I left Juliet all those years ago to fend for herself?"

I met his gaze and didn't blink. "You were a kid trying to survive. Nobody can blame you. Recently, Juliet told me your dad took his anger out on you more than anybody. There's no shame in leaving."

"I appreciate that." The straight line of his shoulders relaxed.

"Griffin, what do you think about Dylan?"

"He's had a rough go of it, but he seems like a good guy."

"He helped me convert the dog barn, but he doesn't have your experience. Juliet really wants this place to succeed. Can you help us?"

He leaned forward in his chair. "Be more specific."

"I need more kennels to board dogs. Let's convert the old kitchen into a small home."

"You're going to move in?"

I shook my head. "It still doesn't feel right, but I like your idea of renting it out. That'll help us make a profit sooner. How long to renovate it?"

Griffin took a deep breath. "Four to six weeks. I'll give it my full attention and shoot for four."

"You're not returning to Charleston?"

"Nope."

Okay, so he didn't want to discuss the situation with me. I respected him enough not to push. "Do you want to live in the main house with Juliet while you work here?"

"Your friend, Marc, offered to let me crash with him. Can I store my belongings in one of your other barns until I get a place of my own?"

"Sure. How much do you think the renovation will cost?" Would I have enough to cover the cost without selling my beach cottage?

"I know it's not easy to start a new business. Why don't you pay for supplies, and we'll create a payment plan for my salary?"

I flattened my hands on the desk. "No, Griffin. That's too generous."

"You didn't ask. I offered." He crossed his arms. "Besides, you're allowing me to work here and store my belongings on your property."

I grinned. "Juliet would love seeing you every day, but I'm going to pay you as much as I'd pay anybody else."

"It's all good. My sister will probably feed me. You'll need to deduct food from my earnings. I'm not paying rent for a while, and the commute couldn't be any easier."

"True. You can walk from Marc's place in about five minutes. Ten if you want to take in the beauty of the river." The arrangement seemed too good to be true. "Are you sure I'm not taking advantage of our friendship?"

"Positive. I'm going to spend more time in the old kitchen and draw up my plan. I'll present it to you tomorrow."

"Do you want to wait until Monday?"

He stood. "Naw, I want to get started. I haven't been this excited about a new project in a long time."

"Thanks, Griffin."

"No problem." He exited my office.

I called out, "Hey, do you have a dog?"

Footsteps thudded back. "No dog. No time. See ya."

I laughed. Somebody had probably warned him about me fixing up dogs with people. If I had to guess, Marc was the guilty party.

My phone vibrated, and Asher's name popped up with a text. Heading your way. My daughter got here sooner than expected.

Yes. I texted Marc and hurried to alert Juliet about Asher. I hoped the encounter with Asher would go well. The money would help us survive.

Chapter Twenty

THE SOUND OF gravel crackling alerted us to Asher's arrival. I stepped onto the front porch to greet Asher and his daughter. A black SUV parked in the shade of a stand of pine trees. I'd seen Asher's vehicle at night, but I hadn't seen it in the daylight. Could it possibly be the same vehicle I saw the morning of Corey's murder?

I'd invited Marc to join us, thinking this was a big deal—I wanted to share the experience with him.

Marc walked with Juliet and me to welcome Asher and his daughter. I elbowed Marc and tried to point without being obvious to the back of the SUV.

His eyebrows crinkled up, and he gave a slight shake of his head.

Asher and his daughter met us at the edge of the semi-circle driveway. If his big smile was any indication, the man was proud of his child. "Hannah, I'd like you to meet Andi Grace Scott, Juliet Reed, and Marc Williams."

We all shook hands with the slim dark-haired woman.

"It's nice to meet you." Her eyes sparkled, and she exuded warmth.

I said, "We're honored you'd consider making your announcement at the Kennady Plantation."

She nodded. "I wanted a place representing stability and South Carolina history. Like me. I've lived here my entire life, and I'm stable. I've got good plans, and I've heard you're giving the plantation new life while retaining its integrity."

"Yes. There won't be any farming, but I'll have a bed and breakfast and doggie day care." I felt at ease with Asher's daughter. "Let's go up to the front porch. You can see the river from there, and it's a beautiful setting. We'll also show you the living room, in case of inclement weather. Or you may even prefer to make your announcement inside."

Asher touched his daughter's shoulder. "Let's go, hon."

"Juliet's in charge of the house, so I'll let her lead the way."

"Follow me." Juliet waggled her fingers and led them to the house, talking the entire time.

I hung back to get a glimpse of the back of Asher's SUV. I did a double take, not wanting to believe my eyes.

A white square sticker. Waves. A dolphin.

"Marc." I grabbed his arm.

"Ouch. What's wrong?" He pushed up his aviator sunglasses.

"The sticker. On Asher's window. He's driving a dark SUV."

"Black Cadillac Escalade. Why?"

"It could be the one I saw at the plantation Tuesday morning. I know it's the same decal I saw the morning I walked Bo and Sunny at Nate's place."

"You think Asher had something to do with Corey's murder?"

I nodded.

His voice dropped. "I still can't believe it."

I paused. What would drive Asher to commit murder? "I know everybody says he's so upstanding, and he's always been decent to me . . ."

"But?" Marc crossed his arms.

"Why was he at the plantation early the same morning Corey was killed?"

"I'm sure there's a logical explanation."

"I'd like to hear it." I pulled out my phone and snapped a picture of the sticker, the SUV, and the license plate.

"Didn't Nate share his doubts about Corey with Asher?"

"Yeah."

"If you hadn't seen a vehicle like his Tuesday morning, you wouldn't be so suspicious of him. His explanation could be as simple as he wanted to support your brother."

I paused. I didn't want to think Asher would do this. "It's possible, but I still need to talk to him."

"After Juliet finishes with him and Hannah." He held up his hand to stop my reply. "We can ask, but it's going to be a respectful conversation. Calm and courteous."

I straightened my shoulders. "I won't come right out and accuse him of killing Corey, but I think he was there and knows more than he's letting on. I'll ask him about it in a *calm* manner."

Marc stared at the plantation house. "Although."

My heart skipped a beat. "Yes?"

"He might be able to explain why he was at the plantation, but why was he driving by Nate's house?"

"Very good question. Let's find out." I crossed the lawn with quick steps and climbed the front steps, where the others discussed the event.

My heart pounded hard while waiting to question Asher. We stood on the front porch, listening as Hannah discussed her vision for making the announcement. I tried to focus on the conversation and curb my impulse to butt in.

Juliet's eyes shone, and the smile never left her face. We needed the business, and this opportunity would provide a great way to advertise the B&B. The Kennady Plantation Bed and Breakfast was Juliet's dream, and success was her goal. I wanted the doggie day care to thrive. Both businesses needed to do well if we were going to survive.

Juliet led Asher and his daughter into the house. "You can see the main living room is large enough for a small audience and the press." Her voice faded, and the door closed.

I hung back, and Marc remained with me. The sound of barking could be heard in the distance. Happy noises. "It sounds like Dylan's letting the dogs play outside. I'm glad you brought Chubb over."

"It's nice he can come to stay and play with your dogs. By the way, I heard you've got a new one."

His words *stay and play* rang through my mind like a pleasant guitar chord. Would that be a better name for my doggie day care? Kennady's Stay and Play for your pets. I liked it and tucked it in the back of my mind. "Pinky. I plan for Juliet to adopt her."

Marc chuckled. "Juliet doesn't stand a chance if you're matching them. Like I didn't have a prayer of saying no to Chubb."

I winked at him. "I'm usually right about these things."

"Instead of a matchmaker for couples, you could call yourself a matchmaker for animals and humans." He made a funny face. "It doesn't sound as good out loud as it did in my mind."

I laughed. "Doggie Matchmaker. It's something to consider."

The front door opened, and Asher stepped out. "I don't want to be an overbearing dad. Hannah can handle herself with Juliet."

I said, "And vice versa. Juliet will do her best to make Hannah's vision a reality."

Asher tucked his large hands into his trouser pockets. "If I didn't trust y'all, we wouldn't have come here today."

"Thank you." I stepped back and swept my hand toward the rocking chairs like a gameshow hostess. "Why don't we have a seat?"

Marc adjusted the rockers so we sat in a small circle.

Asher sat in the nearest one but didn't look comfortable. He crossed and uncrossed his long legs. Swung his sunglasses around in his hand and leaned forward. "Is this some kind of intervention?"

"No, but I need to ask you a question."

"A question I can handle." He set an ankle over his opposite knee, showing off well-worn brown cowboy boots. "Shoot."

"Were you at Richard Rice Plantation on Tuesday morning? The morning Corey was killed?"

His face went flat. "Why?"

"I saw an SUV like yours leaving right before I found the body."

He rocked back and forth. The chair squeaked in a soothing fashion. A cool breeze wafted over my face as I gave the man time to answer.

At last he spoke, "Why are you asking me now?"

I explained about walking the dogs and seeing a vehicle like his with the same sticker. "I believe it was the same SUV both mornings. Then today I see you've got a sticker like the mystery SUV. It made me wonder."

Marc rested his elbows on the paddle arms of the rocker. "We're not accusing you of killing Corey, but we're curious."

I said, "I can't remove you from my list of suspects unless you share with me what's going on."

He nodded. "Yes, I was at the plantation Tuesday morning."

My heart leapt. "Why?"

"I wanted to talk to Corey about the financials. It seemed to me as if he was monkeying with the plantation funds. My company invested thousands of dollars in Richard Rice Plantation, and Corey couldn't explain to me where the money had gone. I've had my suspicions about him plenty of times."

Marc leaned forward. "How long?"

Asher shook his head. "Around a year. He began gambling, and he's not very good. I was suspicious he borrowed money from Richard Rice Plantation to pay off his debts. By borrow, I mean he took it. I was giving him the benefit of the doubt that he'd pay it back. Even if he returned the money, it's illegal. I'm on the plantation board, and we don't want to be involved in anything illicit. Plus, I convinced my business partners to donate to the plantation. There were many reasons we needed to right the wrong."

I rocked my chair. "Okay. I understand you wanted to confront Corey. Did y'all have the conversation?"

"No. I never saw him. I did see Wendy Conn run into the parking lot and take off like a bat . . . well, you know the expression."

"What'd you do then?"

He hiked his shoulders. "I walked back to my Escalade and left."

"Why?"

"I figured nothing good was going on, and with Hannah about to run for state representative, I didn't want to be involved in a scandal."

Made sense to me. "What about seeing you on Nate's street?"

"When I heard about Corey's death and the gossip surrounding Nate, I decided to see for myself. I didn't know if your brother was a gambler in cahoots with Corey. Did he have money belonging to Richard Rice Plantation? I didn't know."

I leapt from my chair. "Nate didn't kill Corey, and he's not a gambler."

Marc reached for my hand. "Easy, now. Asher doesn't know your brother and was looking for answers. Just like you." His tone left no room for argument.

The words stung, but I would've done the same thing in Asher's situation.

Asher said, "I didn't mean any offense. I wanted to see what I could learn."

I sat back down but didn't release Marc's hand. "About the murder or about gambling?"

"They could be connected. Bottom line? I need to find the missing money. It's not fair to my company that made the donation, and it's not fair to the plantation."

My thoughts raced as I peered out at the Waccamaw River. Trees lined the riverbank on the other side and the reflection of clouds rippled in the water. "Last summer, I took home some files from Peter's place. Uh, this place. Somebody broke into my beach house, and I always wondered if it was Corey."

Asher cocked his head to one side and studied me. "Why'd you think it was him?"

"I spotted a man running away dressed in black sweats, and he was about Corey's size. I never could figure out if he'd taken any papers or files because I hadn't thoroughly reviewed them before the break-in."

"Gotcha. I wouldn't put anything past Corey. Peter and I had many discussions about him. I know Peter kept a file on his suspicions. Have you come across it?"

"No." Peter was an emotional topic for me to discuss, but I hadn't found a folder with any information on Corey.

"Too bad." Asher dropped his foot to the wood slats of my front porch and perched his forearms on his thighs. "It wouldn't surprise me if Corey was the person who broke into your house—probably to get rid of incriminating evidence."

"Where do you suppose the file is now?"

"If Corey was smart he would've destroyed it. What about Peter's computers? Flash drives?" Asher's eyebrows lifted.

I hated to squash his hopes. "To be honest, once we caught Peter's killer, I didn't think much more about who broke into my house. I've had a lot to deal with."

Asher nodded. "I'm sure that's right. Inheriting an estate this big can be a gift or a burden. It seems to me you're making the best of it."

"I'm trying." I rubbed the back of my hand. "I don't want to be like a lottery winner who spends all of their winnings in the blink of an eye. I need to be smart with the gift Peter left me."

"I'm sure you will be responsible. After this little conversation, do you believe I'm innocent?" He made a circular motion with his finger.

The tension in my shoulders relaxed. "Yeah. I never really suspected you, but I thought you knew more than you were letting on."

"I'd prefer to keep this on the down-low. At least until Hannah makes her political announcement. Forever would be better. I don't want to be the reason she doesn't get elected, because I think she'll make a fine representative." He lifted his chin.

"I won't lie to the police, but I won't offer it up either. Besides Wendy, did you see anybody else at the plantation when Corey was murdered?"

He ran a hand over his face. "No. I parked on the caretaker's lane and planned to catch Corey by surprise. There was a shiny mountain bike propped against a large pine tree. It looked new, and I thought it odd somebody would leave it there."

"Did you notice the color?"

"Red. Shiny and bright even in the shadows of the pine trees."

Marc squeezed my hand then let go and stood. He started pacing back and forth. "Maybe the killer rode the bike to the plantation and killed Corey. They could've been trying to surprise him."

"True. Asher, did you see a handkerchief that morning? Specifically, a white one with a lipstick smear?"

He shook his head. "Afraid not."

I rocked in my chair. Thoughts raced through my brain. Marc continued to pace. Asher looked toward the river gently lapping the sandy shore. Each of us most likely contemplated Corey's murder.

At last I focused on the well-respected man. "Asher, I'm sorry to have sprung this on you. Especially today, of all days."

"It's good to clear the air. I'd rather confront an issue head-on."

The front door opened, and Juliet and Hannah joined us. Asher rose and stood by his tall daughter. "Well?"

"It's a go. I'm going to make my announcement from here. Juliet will provide refreshments and help with crowd control. I think it's going to be amazing." Hannah's shoulder-length hair was pulled into a sleek bun, giving her an air of sophistication. She exuded confidence, and I predicted voters would love her.

Asher's pride in his daughter was evident, but I found it amazing he believed nobody else would discover his secret. If his secret leaked, it wouldn't be my fault. Unless the cops asked. Then I'd have no choice but to be honest, but I'd already warned Asher I wouldn't lie for him. The man knew where I stood, so why did I feel guilty? I plastered a smile on my face. Maybe I wouldn't be the one who had to shatter his secret.

Chapter Twenty-One

WITH MY NOTES IN a drawstring bag on my back and Sunny at my side, I walked along one of the dirt paths on my plantation. Sunny had been with me over twelve years, and despite her age, my German shepherd still had a good amount of energy and enjoyed our jaunts.

I picked up a branch on the path and broke it into thirds. "Sunny, go fetch." I threw a stick as far as I could into the brown field. She barked and raced after it as a cold gust had me pulling up my sweatshirt's hood.

Sunny returned, dropped the stick at my feet, and sat. I threw it again, and off she went. After two more rounds of the same activity, Sunny was content to walk at my side.

Gray clouds drifted across the sky, and I shivered. My plan had been to sit on a log, watch the Waccamaw River, and review my notes on Corey's murder. But the temperature plunged faster than the local weather forecaster had predicted, giving me a chill.

I was running out of suspects. The cold seeped into my bones. Instead of sitting, I continued along the river trail.

Marc had urged me to consider more possibilities than Erin. I'd taken his advice, but it seemed like a waste of time.

I'd met and ruled out Ben Davis. Asher rolled off my list after his convincing argument for why it wasn't him. Wendy had insisted she was scared and it wasn't her. I scratched my head over her. The woman's love life was a disaster. Juggling two married men took talent. She could've had an argument with Corey about Norris. Or they might have argued about Erin. Either way, passions might have flared, and she hit Corey with Nate's work shovel. Or maybe in self-defense. I pictured the fight in my mind. Corey fell to the ground. Wendy panicked. When he didn't move, she covered him with mulch and fled the scene. It didn't explain the stabbing with the hedge shearers. If Juliet and I hadn't seen her, no one would ever know she'd been there. If Wendy was the killer, crime of passion fit for a motive. Bonk Corey in the head then stab him.

But what if the murder was related to money? Gambling or a business deal gone bad. Multiple professionals had told me Corey wanted kickbacks before he'd award a project. Nate and Griffin were two who'd confided in me, and I believed them. According to Asher, Corey had snowed most of the board members of Richard Rice Plantation. Asher wanted the truth revealed and the money returned to the foundation.

Sunny's ears perked up, and her tail wagged.

The sound of guitar playing interrupted my thoughts. Real music. Not a radio. I picked up my stride and followed the sound toward Marc's property. His land had belonged to Kennady Plantation but had been sold off decades earlier. Marc had bought his parcel because of its location on the river. He had a dock and boathouse, making it easy to get on the water whenever he wanted, and the main house was close to River Road.

The shed's garage door was open. Inside, where Marc usually spent time building boats, he sat strumming a beat-up guitar. Chubb lay on a mat with his eyes closed, his tail swishing along the floor in time to the music. Marc wore a faded long-sleeve T-shirt. *My Boat My Rules.*

His sense of humor made me smile. A stranger might think Marc was an inflexible brute. I knew different. He was kind and willing to adjust to situations.

Marc balanced the guitar on his right leg and strummed a country ballad. More old-school than popular. I tapped my foot to the rhythm. When he finished playing, I clapped.

His head jerked up. "Didn't realize I had an audience. I'll have to charge admission next time."

I smiled and wound my way around the saw horses holding a wooden kayak to stand by him. "I'll gladly pay."

"Save your money for fancy coffee. I won't be holding any concerts." He laid the instrument on a worktable and ambled back toward me with his special athletic grace that always made my mouth go dry. "Whatcha doing here, Andi Grace?"

My face grew warm. I pointed to Sunny. "We were walking and thinking about Corey's murder when we heard the music. I couldn't help myself. I had to find the source."

"You always have to satisfy your curiosity." He laughed. "I should've known you'd be working on the murder. Have you solved it yet?"

Chubb circled around us and nudged Sunny. The two scampered outside and chased each other around the trees.

"There are plenty of ideas and theories bouncing around in my head, but I don't have any real proof."

"Have you got time for coffee? We can discuss what you know for sure. To catch the killer, we need to separate truth from notions."

"Notions?" I couldn't help but smile. Sometimes Marc sounded like an older man, which made sense because his favorite foster home had older parents. Bobby Joe Wilkes had passed years before I met Marc, but from the stories I'd heard about his foster parents, they were wonderful.

His gray eyes darkened. "If you don't want to discuss the murder with me, you can just say so. No need to get insulting."

I reached for his hand. "I didn't mean that. The truth is, I love it when you talk like an old man."

He shook his head but his mouth twitched. "You're digging your hole deeper."

I didn't know how to turn the conversation around without revealing how much I cared for this man. But I didn't think he was ready to hear my heart, and I sure wasn't ready to lower my defenses. "Maybe we should change the subject. Coffee sounds great."

"No change of topic is needed if you're worried you offended me. I can usually hold my own." Still holding my hand, Marc turned toward the path leading to his house and chuckled. "Chubb. Come."

"Sunny, let's go."

The dogs appeared and walked beside us. Sunny held her head high and strutted with dignity as if I didn't know she'd just behaved like a playful puppy scampering all over the place. "To catch the killer, I'll need to see beyond their public persona." I explained my revelation to Marc. "Is Wendy playing me? She acts scared and innocent, but is she?"

"If a woman is having an affair with a married man, how innocent can she really be?"

I held up two fingers. "Corey, and don't forget Norris."

"Right. Two married men."

"Norris is old enough to be her dad. When you consider he rented a place for them to meet, you've got a sugar daddy affair."

"Not all sugar daddies are married. There are some legitimate relationships between older men and younger women." Marc released my hand, ran up his front steps, and opened the door. "After you."

The dogs followed me inside and headed to Chubb's water bowl. Sunny was familiar with Marc's place and made herself at home. "I might rename her the Grand Dame."

"It suits her regal demeanor." Marc moved to the coffee maker. "Caffeine?"

"Why not?" I sat on a barstool at the kitchen counter and pulled my notebook from the bag. "Norris was Wendy's sugar daddy, and Corey was her regular boyfriend, even though he was married." I drew a tree with their names.

Marc glanced at me. "Wendy was treading dangerous waters when she decided to take up with married men."

"And now she's running scared. Erin, Norris, and his wife all have reason to be angry with her if they're aware of her affairs."

"Ivey Gilbert's a cancer survivor. Her hair's growing out, and she made a speech recently at a luncheon I attended."

I pounded my notebook. "What a jerk. She's fighting cancer, and he's having an affair? Ivey's the one who needs to get a good divorce attorney."

Marc pulled two blue ceramic mugs from the cabinet. "I don't think she has a clue. She seemed happy and at peace. She told us how terrified she was when the doctor informed her she had breast cancer. After praying, she decided not to give in to the fear and to fight with grace."

"Arg. How could Norris have deserted her when she was fighting for her life? What a creep."

"Settle down, now. We don't know if Norris was supportive or not. Maybe he gave up possible cases to spend time with Ivey. Except for the affair, he might be a decent husband."

I leapt to my feet. "Are you defending him?" My voice came out in a screech.

Marc held his hands up in surrender. "Heck, no. I'm only saying I admire his wife. You'd like her, too. The point I was trying to make is I don't believe Ivey would kill Wendy. She's more of a pray-for-your-enemies kind of woman."

I drew a line through Ivey's name and counted to ten in French to collect myself. "Not Ivey."

"Thanks for trusting me." He placed a sugar bowl in front of me and poured coffee into our mugs before pulling milk from his refrigerator. "Go back to Corey. Let's consider all of the reasons to kill him."

I turned my notes to Corey. "Despite his charming personality, there's not a lot to like. He's smart, and he knows how to manipulate people."

"Was smart."

"What?" Whoa, Nellie. I tightened my grip on the mug. How could I forget? I'd been consumed for days trying to figure out who killed him. "You're right. Corey's dead."

Marc stood behind me and rubbed my shoulders. "Andi Grace, you don't have to solve his murder. The sheriff's department can handle it. They're trained and know how to do their job."

I leaned into the shoulder rub. "I know, but it's my brother they've questioned."

"Still, there's no shame in trusting the system." The massage ended, and he sat next to me. "Most of the time it works."

"Even you've got to admit *the system* is flawed at times." I wondered if he was thinking about growing up as a ward of the state. "For example, despite the imperfections in the foster care system, there are good people working for the best interests of children. Look at how you turned out."

"A confused loner with trust issues." He lifted the mug to his lips.

Tears welled in my eyes. "How can you not see what an amazing man you are? You use your degree to help the underdogs in this world. You left a corporate firm and focused on the everyday person. You helped me find Peter's killer, and now you're assisting in my quest to find Corey's killer. You're a productive part of society and one of the good guys. A small-town hero."

Tension crackled between us. Our gazes locked. My pulse pounded in my neck. Could he hear my galloping heartbeat?

The dogs approached. Sunny came to me, and Chubb went to Marc's side and whined.

Marc reached down and rubbed the lab between his ears. "It's okay, boy." The tightness of his jaw disappeared, and his face relaxed.

"Maybe I should go." I didn't want to fight with Marc. He needed to be loved and cared for. My fingers ached to weave their way into his wavy hair. My arms wanted to cradle him. My lips wanted to kiss him and lessen his sadness.

"No. Let's work on your case. I don't know how we got off track." He reached for my notebook. "What else do you know about Corey?"

"Hold on." I needed some space to pull myself together. I moved away from him and let the dogs out to play in the backyard. With slow steps, I returned to my seat. "Corey was smart about business but not necessarily moral. According to Peter and Asher, he gambled. Badly. He managed to get on the board of Richard Rice Plantation. Remember how passionate he was with Erin last summer?"

Marc nodded. "He couldn't keep his hands or eyes off her."

"The night we got together with them, they seemed all lovey dovey, but I saw them arguing when they thought nobody was watching."

"It makes you wonder if true love exists." He rubbed his palms together.

I stopped writing. "I need to believe it exists."

"Then why aren't you married?"

"Between raising my siblings and trying to survive, there wasn't time to date. Why aren't you married?"

"I've never been one to date just to be dating."

My neck grew hot. "Right. So, back to Corey."

"Did you find time to go through your files from Peter?"

"Not yet. I think the file Asher mentioned is missing. Juliet turned Peter's office into a guest room. I imagine his other files are probably in one of the old barns."

He drummed his fingers on the counter. "You got time to look for them? If Asher and Peter were building a case to get rid of Corey from the plantation board, we might find something important."

"Looking through the files means the motive is related to business."

"Or not." He drained the last of his coffee.

I sipped the rest of mine and considered his challenge. I'd been leaning toward love or jealousy for the motive. Would the files provide a clue, or would it turn into a waste of time? If nothing else, maybe we could rule out business as the motive. "I'm willing to give it a shot."

Chapter Twenty-Two

WE ENDED UP AT my house with takeout pizza and boxes of files we'd found in a ramshackle barn on Kennady Plantation. We spread the boxes out on the coffee table, kitchen counter, and kitchen table. Sunny snoozed on her big pillow, and Chubb lay at her side.

Marc finished off the last slice of supreme. "Delicious." He patted his flat belly.

"Yes, but now we need to face the music." I waved my hands toward the file boxes. "You're more organized than I am. What's the plan?"

He laughed. "How do you eat an elephant?"

"Say what?"

"One bite at a time. Same way we tackle this. One box at a time. We're looking for anything with Corey's name, gambling, or Richard Rice Plantation."

I giggled and lifted the lid on the closest box on the kitchen counter. "You're so corny sometimes."

"Are you just now figuring that out?" Marc took the box next to mine and smiled. "Can we listen to some music or something to drown out the sound of dogs snoring?"

"I think there's a basketball game on TV." I checked my app. "Georgia plays Kentucky in a few minutes."

"Sounds good."

I found the game on the TV in the family room and raised the volume so we could listen from the kitchen. "Kentucky's up eighteen to six."

He nodded. "That's a decent lead."

"Would you rather sit on the couch and go through these?"

"It'll be easier to focus without the game in front of me." He tugged on my ponytail. "Working next to you is enough of a distraction."

I fanned myself with the file in my hand. Ooh, la, la. "If you keep talking like that, I won't be able to concentrate."

He winked at me. "I'll behave."

Disappointment hit me harder than I expected. I glanced at the box Marc examined. "Have you found anything?"

"Besides evidence mice have eaten some of the papers?"

"Ugh." I shivered.

"You need to find a storage unit for anything important."

The statement put a crushing weight on my chest. "More money I don't have. Let's hope there's not much important in here."

Marc pulled a chair over. "If a file looks important but not related to the case, put it in this chair. Otherwise, it's going to the shredder. I get monthly shredding at the office. We'll add your papers to mine."

"Great. Thanks."

We worked in a comfortable atmosphere. If the game crowd cheered, Marc wandered into the family room to catch the replay.

By the time the game ended, most of the files had been designated to the shred pile and placed in the back of Marc's truck. Only a few were left when Marc whistled. "You're going to want to see this."

I sat down and read the pages he'd handed me. "This is bad."

"Well, we've found the evidence we needed to prove Corey was embezzling from Daily Java."

"Real proof. That stinks. Thinking it was possible versus knowing he really did it are two different things. If he'd steal money from his wife's business, it'd be easy to imagine him stealing from the plantation." I sank into my chair. "Poor Erin. No wonder she needed Norris."

"Makes sense to me. She inherited Daily Java from her grandmother. Right?"

I smiled. "Yes. She was closer to her grandmother than her parents. They were kindred spirits. The coffee shop was more than a business. It was a gift of love from Granny Farris. Erin dropped out of college to take over Daily Java despite her parents' objections. Adding more coffee options helped modernize the place, and so did updating the name from Kathy's Patisserie to Daily Java. Also, Clem and Gina Farris didn't want Erin to marry Corey."

"Giving Erin financial motive as well as personal stakes." He squeezed the bridge of his nose and shut his eyes.

"Wait a minute. You're the one who told me to consider other suspects." My hands fisted and slammed onto my hips as if they had a mind of their own. I recalled my mother doing the same thing often when we found ourselves in trouble.

"That was before we knew Corey stole from her business. More than a business. A gift of love. You're right. Corey was a jerk."

"I feel bad trying to prove Erin is the killer."

"But?" Marc quirked one eyebrow up.

"I can't let Nate go to prison for a crime he didn't commit." My hands dropped down.

"Of course you can't. We need a plan." He looked toward the dogs. Seconds ticked by, then Marc snapped his fingers. "It's Saturday night. Want to go bar hopping?"

If he'd said skinny dipping, I would've been less shocked. "What? Is this boring you? I don't usually hang out at bars." I straightened. "Do you?" How well did I know this man?

"Relax, Andi Grace. I don't make a habit of cruising bars. Let's see if we can learn more about Erin and Corey."

"Oh, now I get you. I need to wear something nice if we're going out."

Marc still wore his faded T-shirt and jeans. "I've got a change of clothes at the office. I'll run over there and be back in twenty minutes."

"Make it thirty and lock the door on your way out." I hurried to my bedroom to shower and change.

BY NINE WE WERE dancing at the closest bar and restaurant. The bartender had recognized the picture of Erin on my phone, but he didn't know much about her. On our way out, the band started playing one of my favorite Craig Morgan songs. I paused and sighed.

Marc nudged my elbow. "Come on. Let's dance."

He didn't have to ask me twice. We squeezed through the crowd and found space on the edge of the dance floor.

Marc wrapped his arms around me. Perfect fit. We swayed to the beat of "God Must Really Love Me." He sang along with the words. Soft and smooth.

Chills danced along my spine. What would it be like to dance with Marc anytime I wanted? The band shifted to a faster song, but Marc continued to hold me close. Who cared if others were country swinging or doing the Texas two-step? I was dancing with Marc, and the rest of the world could sail away.

People clapped at the end of the set.

The lead singer lifted his black hat in the air and leaned toward the microphone. "You've been a great audience. We're going to take a break and give you a chance to wet your whistle. Rest while you can 'cause we're going to crank it up in the next set."

More clapping and hoots ensued.

Still in Marc's arms, he said, "I guess it's time to head out."

I wasn't anywhere near ready to leave the dance floor, but Nate depended on me to find answers. "Yeah, it looks like it." I backed out of his arms, but he held my hand all the way to his truck.

In the parking lot, Marc opened my door. "Flamingo Bar and Grill next?"

"Sounds good." I checked their website as Marc drove. "A country band is playing there tonight. Is country your favorite kind of music?"

"Yeah." The lights from the dash flickered on his face.

"Earlier today I couldn't help but notice you've got a nice voice. Were you ever in a band?"

He kept his eyes on the road and remained silent.

"Marc, were you in a band?" He had my full attention.

"I played some in college to help with expenses. It's a quicker way to make money than working on boats, and the hours don't interfere with classes."

Again, he surprised me. "Did you ever consider making a career from it?"

"Nope. Too much uncertainty."

Something was missing. "I feel like there's more to your story."

His hands clenched then unclenched the steering wheel. "A country singer paid me to record one of my songs."

"Marc, that's huge. Who was it?"

"Lincoln Zane. It was a fluke. He's got another one of my songs but hasn't recorded it yet."

"Are you kidding me? Lincoln Zane? He's one of the nicest guys, according to the news."

Marc zipped into the parking lot. "Yeah, he's nice. Ready?"

I laughed. "Looks like you're ending this conversation."

"We're investigating a murder. We can discuss my brief music career another time."

Apparently, end of subject. I glanced around the lot. People scattered around the area, smoking and talking. Marc opened the door where a large group of women clustered around the hostess, pestering her about the wait for their table. The poor hostess had hair falling from her bun, and not in a fashionable way. Her lipstick had worn off, and she looked terrified.

I stepped closer to the young girl. "Can they sit at the bar until a table opens up for them?"

She shook her head. "There's not enough room."

"What about the back patio? It's not too cold tonight."

Her gaze darted to the loudest woman. "We can seat you on the patio."

The women conferred and agreed.

The hostess led them away.

Marc smiled at me. "You can't stop yourself from helping others."

"If I had to deal with those barracudas, I'd want somebody to help me."

The hostess returned, her face flushed. "Thanks. Table for two?"

Marc said, "Can we sit at the bar?"

"Sure. Have a nice evening."

We settled ourselves in the middle of the bar. Two beautiful young women sat at the end closest to the music. Both had straight long blond hair and low-cut tops. Four men circled around them, vying for their attention. Two men were old enough to be sugar daddies, and the other two were decades younger than their competition.

"What can I get you tonight?" A tanned muscular man stood in front of us on the other side of the bar. His name tag read Gerard.

"I'd like a ginger ale. Do you have anything to eat besides pretzels?"

He pulled out a laminated menu and slid it to me.

Marc said, "Coke for me. We're both designated drivers tonight."

Gerard nodded. "Gotta stay safe."

Marc reached for my phone. "For sure. Listen, we're looking for a friend who may be bar-hopping tonight because she got some devastating news this week. Need to make sure she gets home safely tonight. Can I show you her picture?" Marc flashed Erin's photo at him before Gerard had time to reply.

"Yeah, I've seen her before, but not tonight." He squeezed his eyes shut. "She was here Monday buying drinks for some guys who didn't look like they were in her league."

"How's that?" Marc drummed his fingers on the bar. "I'm probably not in her league."

"Your friend's an uptown girl." Gerard shook his head. "The guys she hung with that night wore ratty jeans, faded T-shirts, and hats with a work logo on them. Construction or landscaping."

My head jerked up. "Nate's Landscaping and Designs? Gray shirts and hats with this design?" I found a picture on my phone and showed Gerard.

With his fingers, he circled my wrist and pulled my phone closer to him. "Yeah, that looks about right. Cool."

Not cool, but I bit back the words. "Can we get an order of nachos?"

"Be right back." He disappeared.

"I'm not hungry, but I thought we should spend some money in order to get more answers. What do you think about Erin hanging out with Nate's crew the night before the murder?"

"Interesting, to say the least."

I tapped my nails on the wood countertop. "Nate's men called in sick Tuesday morning. It's why he doesn't have a witness and maybe why he was focused on his work and not his surroundings."

"It's possible Erin bought the guys a lot of drinks on purpose—so they'd be too hungover to show up for work the next morning."

"We need to let David know." Marc looked up. "Gerard's coming back."

The bartender placed our order in front of us. Tortilla chips piled high with meat, cheese, black beans, salsa, jalapenos and sour cream. "Oh, yum."

"The cook doesn't scrimp on toppings." Gerard walked down and refilled drinks for the ladies. All four men pulled out credit cards, offering to pay.

My stomach rolled. "Do men and women really meet their future spouses in bars?"

"It happens all the time." Marc pointed to the others.

"I guess I've lived a sheltered life. Do you think I'd be married by now if I hadn't raised Nate and Lacey Jane?"

He reached for a chip, and cheese trickled off it. "Possibly, but would you have been happy if you'd let others raise your siblings?"

"Probably not."

"Definitely not. You're not the kind of person who thinks of herself first. It would've killed you to let Nate and Lacey Jane live with strangers." His gaze met mine. "You have a huge heart, Andi Grace."

My face warmed, and I popped a chip into my mouth.

His gray eyes twinkled. "You're welcome, by the way."

"Thanks." I ate a few more chips. "We need to ask Nate if Corey knew in advance the landscapers would be working at the plantation Tuesday morning."

Marc pinched his lower lip between his thumb and finger. "Odds are Erin didn't randomly buy drinks for his employees."

I waved to Gerard. "Did our friend always buy drinks for men?"

"Not on my shifts."

"Is she a good tipper?"

"Oh, man, was she. Best tip I ever earned." He wiped a smudge of cheese off the bar and refilled our drinks. "Your friend can come back anytime she wants."

"I'll be sure to let her know."

Gerard pointed to the group of people at the end of the bar. "Now those guys buy drinks for women, expecting something in return. It was different with your friend. When the guys were wasted, she came over and paid her tab. In cash. She also gave me money to make sure they got a ride home. When I saw how much she laid out for a cab, I decided to drive them myself."

I leaned closer. "You drove them home? What'd they say?"

"Bottom line is they were all grateful for the drinks but stumped about why she was so nice to them. They weren't celebrating a birthday, and it was a Monday night. By the next morning, I doubt they were thankful. I imagine they were puking up their guts."

"Why do you think she paid their bar tab?"

He shrugged. "Who knows? Maybe she wanted to relive her glory days and got cold feet at the last minute. She was sober and kept the guys entertained. She laughed at their stories and said things to make them laugh."

Marc handed Gerard his credit card. "You've been very helpful."

I waited for the man to finish the transaction and peeked at the receipt as Marc signed it. He gave Gerard a generous tip and shook his hand.

"See you around." Gerard waved a hand and walked over to a couple who'd arrived.

I held onto Marc's arm as we squeezed through the Saturday night mob. Once we were both in his truck, I breathed easier.

"What do you think?" He started the truck.

"We need to see Nate. Erin must've found out Nate and his men would be working Tuesday morning at the plantation. I don't know if Corey mentioned it or she overheard the men. The less people around, the easier it'd be for Erin to kill her husband."

"True, but it seems like a mighty big coincidence she'd overhear Nate's crew."

"I agree it's more likely Corey told her, but stranger things have happened. I believe Erin killed Corey and framed Nate on purpose. I've got to talk to my brother."

"First, we need to contact the sheriff's department." Marc rested his elbow on the console.

"I doubt he'll believe my theory."

Marc leaned toward me. "I'll contact David, which will give you time to touch base with Nate."

"Deal."

Chapter Twenty-Three

MARC AND I SAT in my family room waiting for David to arrive while
Sunny snoozed on her red-checked dog pillow by the fireplace. Chubb
was in the yard chasing squirrels or shadows, or something active.

I ended my conversation with Nate and plugged my phone into the
charging station on the shabby chic table beside my couch. Kicking off
my wedge sandals, I dropped my head back on the cushion. "Oh, dear."

"What'd Nate say?" Marc still wore his now-wrinkled blue dress
shirt. His light gray jacket lay draped on my yellow wingback chair.

"He informed Corey and Asher he'd be on the property starting
early Tuesday morning until the project was complete. That's one of the
reasons I was meeting him there. He didn't have time, and the B&B was
opening Friday. He brought some mulch for me. We were going to
move what I needed into his old work truck." Did it sound like I was
stealing? "I'd already paid Nate for the load, so it was on the up and up.
I wasn't taking what belonged to the plantation."

"Slow down." He held out a hand. "I wasn't accusing you of anything wrong."

"Really? Because, in hindsight, it seems sketchy. But it's not. There's
a section on the trailer where you can haul dirt or mulch. Then you push
a button and empty it. My mulch had been pre-weighed or measured or
whatever you call it. I even gave Nate a check ahead of time in case
Corey questioned us."

This time Marc held both hands up, palms out. "Andi Grace, I
believe you."

"Oh. Okay." I fanned myself with a magazine.

"Did Nate say why he told the men he'd be there so early?"

"Corey wanted to make sure Nate followed the plan he'd presented
to the board. Nate informed Asher because he didn't trust Corey. He
didn't expect Asher to referee, but he wanted the man to be aware."

"Interesting."

The doorbell rang. Sunny barked and ran to inspect our visitor.

"It's okay, girl. He's a good guy. At least he's supposed to be." I signaled my German shepherd with a hand motion. "Sit."

She sat, and I opened the door.

David stood on my lighted front porch in his uniform. "Andi Grace, Marc said you need to speak to me."

Marc joined us. "Yeah, David. Come on in. We learned something tonight and thought you should be aware."

The three of us settled around the kitchen table, and Sunny sat on a throw rug facing us with her ears propped up and eyes opened wide.

"Do you have one of those Toughbook computers like Wade?"

"Sure do, but I like to take notes on my phone and translate them later. Why don't you tell me what you know?"

I began with our goal to visit local bars to learn more about Erin. "The bartender, Gerard, remembers seeing Erin on Monday."

David paused typing into his phone. "Where was this?"

"Flamingo Bar and Grill. Gerard said Erin began buying drinks for a group of men who work for Nate. As in a lot of drinks for them." I spread out my hands. "Then she paid Gerard to get the men home. He said they were sloshed. David, there's no way they could go to work the next morning, and Erin knew it. She was aware Nate would be alone at Richard Rice Plantation Tuesday morning. It's conceivable she planned to murder Corey and plant evidence to make it look like Nate killed him."

David lowered his phone and his dark eyes pierced me. "That's quite an accusation. What's her motive?"

"Corey was having an affair, and he stole money from Daily Java. Erin hasn't had the best relationship with her parents, but Granny Farris was the one relative she adored."

"Wait, why is their relationship relevant?"

"Granny Farris left Daily Java to Erin. They were so much alike and had a deep connection. We know Erin met with Norris Gilbert at least once, and we believe she wanted a divorce."

"Again, why kill him?" David's left eyebrow rose, causing his forehead to crinkle.

My face grew warm.

"Can't arrest a person because it helps your brother."

I counted to ten in French silently before I answered. "What if she recently learned he was embezzling from her business? It was too much to comprehend. She confronts him, and it spirals out of control. Next thing she knows, Corey is dead. She refuses to lose everything and frames Nate."

He set down his phone and crossed his arms. "Suppose your theory is correct. Why'd she hit Nate with a shovel?"

I froze. Why indeed? Maybe I wasn't equipped to help my brother.

Marc cleared his throat. "Consider this. Erin kills Corey. She hears Nate and runs into the woods. She can't let Nate find the body until she gets away, so she improvises by sneaking through the woods, coming up behind him, and wham. She whacks him in the back of the head. He drops the flowerpots and turns to defend himself. She hits him again, and he's out. This leaves Erin free to plant evidence and escape."

"That's a possible theory." David added to the notes on his phone. "We don't have proof."

"Did y'all find the broken pots my brother was carrying?" I leaned close to hear his answer.

"Yes, but they were under a tree in the woods and not on the path Nate indicated."

I didn't understand. "Which means what?"

"Off the record, it could mean the killer moved the broken pieces, hoping to hide them for some reason."

"How could Erin have cleaned the mess so fast?" It didn't make sense she'd waste her time.

Marc said, "It's possible she planned to return and remove it all. If there was no sign of flowers and broken pots, it might mean Nate lied about being attacked. It'd make him look more guilty."

"Well, what about the lipstick?" I assessed David's expression. The man would make a great poker player. His facial features gave me no clue to his thoughts. "On the handkerchief. Did you run DNA tests on it?"

"Those tests take time, but we're checking it out." David's gaze bounced back and forth between Marc and me. "Just for kicks, who else do you suspect?"

Yes. I was winning him over. "How much time to you have?"

He checked his black watch. "I knew better than to ask. Give me your best ideas."

"Wendy Conn, Ben Davis, Asher Cummings, Erin Lane, and Norris Gilbert." I counted the names off with my fingers. "Five suspects."

"You've got quite a list." David returned to typing notes on his phone.

"I've ruled out Ben and Asher. Have you questioned either of them?"

"That's not the way this works. I can listen to your theories, but to protect my investigation, I can't share much with you."

"Got it." I understood, but I wasn't happy. "Do you know Wendy was having affairs with Corey and Norris?"

David smirked. "You've told me before."

"I've got more." I shared what I'd learned about my suspects. Then I paused, remembering Asher had spotted a bike leaning against a tree the morning of the murder. "Is there any possibility you or one of the other deputies found a bike Tuesday morning?"

"Not that I remember. Why?"

I'd promised Asher to keep his observation a secret. "I have a source who saw a bike propped against a tree the morning Corey was murdered. It makes me wonder if Erin rode a bike through the woods, surprised and killed her husband, and rode away on her bike. Or maybe she rode with Corey and had stashed the bike the day before to make her getaway."

"Who's your source?"

I turned to Marc. "Do I have to tell him?"

"Let's talk in the other room." Marc stood.

David rose, too. "I'll save you the trouble. Andi Grace, if I decide you're obstructing my investigation, I can arrest you."

Yikes. I wanted to do the right thing without ratting out Asher. "I told my source he needed to let you know. Can I talk to him again?"

"Can you convince this person to come to me?"

"It's worth a shot."

"I need the name by Monday morning. Nine o'clock sharp." He walked to the front door, and we followed.

"I promise you'll know by then. If he won't tell you himself, then I will. Thanks, David."

He paused on the porch. "I want justice for Corey. My job is to catch the killer, no matter who it is. I'm not trying to railroad your brother."

My legs grew weak. "I believe you. Good night."

Once he left, I leaned against the door. Weariness washed over me. "That could've gone better."

Marc shook his head. "It also could've gone a lot worse. Be glad you're sleeping in your own bed tonight and not on a cot in jail."

"True, but I'm not ready to give up yet. There's so much more to figure out."

"Like what?" He ran a hand down his face.

"If you were going to buy a bike, where would you go?"

"Locally?"

I nodded. "Yeah."

Seconds ticked by. "I'd go to a box store and pay cash if I didn't want anybody to know me. I'd even go to Georgetown or Mount Pleasant, where I'd have a better chance of not seeing people I know. If I didn't have time to go that far, I'd buy one at HOSE. Still pay cash and hope the cops didn't get wind of my purchase."

"Heyward Outdoor Sports Establishment is better known for kayaks and canoes. If you bought a bicycle there, you'd probably get the attention of the clerk, especially if you paid cash."

"True, but the store is usually not crowded. Odds are the only person who'd see me is the clerk, but I'm sure they have security cameras all over the place. Their stuff is top-of-the-line and expensive."

"One of Asher's businesses deals with security solutions. If they handle security for HOSE, I don't guess he could view the footage." I was hopeful we were on to something.

"Not ethically, and I'd never ask him. However, we can ask him to contact David. Would you like me to reach out to Asher? Set up an appointment to meet with him tomorrow?"

"We can meet in the parking lot after church if he doesn't have much time."

"If he cares about his daughter's political career, he'll make time."

Chapter Twenty-Four

STANDING ON THE beach with my face to the ocean, I hugged my blue jean jacket tighter around my body. Chilly air and sea mist caused me to regret not wearing a heavy coat, but I couldn't leave. Asher had agreed to meet us on the beach, claiming there'd be fewer witnesses. The man knew something was up.

"Cold?" Marc wore a navy blazer, white button-up shirt, and blue jeans.

"That's an understatement, but you're probably freezing." I'd opted to wear slim black slacks, a blue blouse, and an infinity scarf. A purple striped cardigan had been in the back seat of the Suburban for weeks, and I'd slipped it on under my jacket after church for this rendezvous. It'd never occurred to me Asher would want to meet on the beach, where the temperature was at least ten degrees colder.

Marc slid his arms around my shoulders and pulled me close. Warmth from his body seeped into mine. "You worried?"

"A little. What if he stands us up?"

"He's got more to lose than we do. We're offering him the opportunity to confess to David what he knows about Tuesday morning."

A dark cloud drifted out to sea. The sound of ocean waves meeting land usually relaxed me, but waiting for Asher wore on my nerves.

"Don't forget David threatened me about obstructing justice. I might go to jail for my siblings, but I won't for Asher." Two seagulls played tag with the waves drifting on shore.

"You told him you wouldn't lie to the police. This is offering him the chance to do the right thing on his own. If he refuses, that's on him. Not you."

Tires squealed, and we both looked toward the beach access parking lot. The tall, lean man stepped out. He looked both ways before walking to us.

I waved. "Showtime."

"You've got this." Marc stepped away from me, and the cold air hit me full force.

"Don't you mean we've got this?"

The smile that lit his face warmed me. "Yep. It's nice to be included."

"Oh, Marc. I definitely need you. I don't think I can save Nate by myself."

The sparkle in his eyes dimmed. "Don't forget this morning's sermon. God will help you in your quest to clear Nate from the allegations, and you've got me as his defense attorney." He rubbed my shoulder. "God is in control."

"You're right. Thanks for the reminder." God had watched over us after my parents died. I'd trust Him again.

Asher approached us. He was even taller than Marc. With his long legs, it didn't take long for him to reach us. "I don't have much time. We're hosting a luncheon for Hannah. It's a small affair, but if these people back her, it could be huge."

"I'll be brief." I crossed my arms. "You need to tell Deputy Wayne about your visit to Richard Rice Plantation on Tuesday. He never saw the bike, and I think it could be an important piece of evidence."

Asher's nostrils flared. "This isn't a good time."

I lifted my chin. "It's not convenient for Nate either. He's hiding out in his town house, trying to avoid the public as much as possible. Thank goodness it's January and not June because he's losing business. People are canceling jobs they hired him to do. Meanwhile, David insists I tell him who saw the bike. He's demanding an answer before nine o'clock tomorrow morning."

"What have you done?" He clenched his fists.

I scooted out of Asher's personal bubble, but I stood as firm as I could in the sand. "I told Deputy Wayne about the bike. You mentioned it looked new, and I think the killer may have bought it for the murder. Deputy Wayne is interested in my theory and wants to talk to you."

"You gave him my name?" His deep voice vibrated over the sounds of the ocean.

"No, sir. Not yet, but I will if you don't. I told you in the beginning I wouldn't lie to the deputies." My heart pounded against my sternum.

Asher turned around, kicking up sand as he walked away from us.

I glanced at Marc. "Now what?"

He shrugged. "Give it time to play out."

We waited. My attention was fixated on Asher's every move until he stopped. He looked up and stayed in one place. It appeared as if he pinched the bridge of his nose or maybe rubbed his face.

At last he swung around and came back to us. Much slower this time. "Give me until later this afternoon. Then I'll call Deputy Wayne and tell him what I saw."

"Sounds good."

The man's shoulders slumped as he walked away.

I reached for Marc's hand. "He looks older now than he did a few minutes ago. It's a terrible thing when you're in the wrong place at the wrong time."

Marc pulled me into a hug. "You're right. It's terrible, but that's life. Somebody runs a red light and kills another person. One drink too many then deciding to drive can ruin a person's life. Witness a crime, and before you know it, the goons are after you."

"What about you? Both of your parents died in a car accident."

"Exactly. Wrong place. Wrong time. There are consequences, and we must move forward the best we can. I don't see how Asher's presence at Richard Rice Plantation can adversely affect Hannah's run for office." Marc's chest vibrated under my cheek.

I inhaled his woodsy scent with touches of citrus. The last thing I wanted to think about was Corey's murder or Hannah's chances of becoming our next state representative.

"Andi Grace, are you okay?"

I nodded and forced myself to push away. Consequences. This was the wrong time to think romantic thoughts about Marc. "I'm fine."

"Let's get you somewhere warm."

"Sounds good, but let me shoot a text to David and tell him my source should contact him later today." I pulled out my cell phone.

"Send the message to me as well. Ask David to inform you if he doesn't hear from your source. The last thing you need is to get dragged in for questioning."

"Good idea." I sent the message then looked at Marc. "Now what should I do?"

"Have you got any dog appointments this afternoon?" His eyebrows lifted.

"No. It's a slow day. I guess I could help Juliet clean rooms at the B&B."

"Or you can relax and have a little fun."

I laughed. "You may need to teach me how."

He rubbed his hands together. "Let's take my kayak out on the river."

"Brrr. Won't we freeze?"

"Not if you have a wet suit." His eyes sparkled. "What about disk golf?"

"Much better than risk freezing to death in your kayak."

"I wouldn't let you freeze, but we'll play disk golf. Let's go." He reached for my hand.

"Can I bring Sunny?"

A smile stretched across Marc's clean-shaven face, and his dimple appeared. "Absolutely. She and Chubb can run around the property. We'll play in the area between my house and the river."

I'd never played disk golf, but I always enjoyed spending time outside. It'd been a while since I did something fun. Marc's presence would be like the cherry on top of a hot fudge sundae.

Chapter Twenty-Five

MY RELAXING afternoon was interrupted by a call from Juliet while Marc and I played the third hole. "Andi Grace, I need you at the barn." Her panicked tone spurred me to action.

"We're on the way." We rounded up the dogs and drove to Kennady Plantation in my Suburban. I parked behind the main house. "It never seems real."

Marc opened his door but paused before exiting. "What?"

"I own a plantation, at least the main parcel of one." I pointed out the window.

"Hey, I own a parcel of the original Kennady Plantation, too." He exited the vehicle, and both animals followed him.

True, so why was I struggling to adjust? I hopped out of the truck. It didn't take long to catch up with Marc and the dogs, and we joined Nate, Griffin, and Juliet in the dog barn. Marc opened the gate to the play area.

Sunny claimed her spot of authority on top of the slide while Bo and Chubb ran around the perimeter. Juliet held Pinky in her arms. The little thing had a hot pink bow on its head and matching nail polish.

Griffin leaned against the railing separating us from the dogs. "Jules, why'd you call this little get-together?"

Her gaze darted from one to the other of us. "I don't have guests for the next few days, and I thought Andi Grace should update us on Corey's murder."

Nate turned his ball cap around backward. "Stay out of it, Juliet. It's bad enough my sister's sticking her nose into the investigation."

Juliet's eyes narrowed. "Do you think I can't handle myself? Or am I not smart enough to catch a killer?"

Pinky yapped with her gaze trained on Nate.

"I know you're smart enough to realize the cops are trained to catch killers. You and Andi Grace are not." His voice was devoid of emotion.

"If the sheriff suspected me of murder, I'd accept help from anybody who offered." A tear trailed down her cheek. "It's not fair the cops are looking at you."

Nate ignored her crying. Growing up with two sisters probably taught him to stand firm against tears. "I'm sure they have other suspects. The thing is, the real killer is on the loose. What if he comes after you or Andi Grace to stop you from revealing the truth? I'd never forgive myself if something happened to you."

Juliet burst into sobs. "I need to do something."

I reached for Pinky and glared at my brother.

Nate hugged Juliet. "You've got to understand. I don't want you to get hurt."

She cried harder.

I rubbed Pinky's ear. "Marc, why don't you and Griffin go with me to the office? They can join us when they're ready."

Dylan appeared from his apartment. "What's going on?"

"Juliet's upset, but we're okay."

"I'm no good with women, but I can entertain Pinky if you'd like my help." He reached for the puppy.

"Thanks, Dylan. We'll be in my office if you need us."

"Yes, ma'am." He disappeared with Pinky in his arms, and we went to my office. It wasn't as neat as my home workroom, but I often focused more on the animals when I was at the plantation.

Griffin entered last. "Marc, is your offer to crash at your place still open?"

"Sure is."

"Starting tonight?" His eyebrows lifted. "I feel like my sister doesn't need me underfoot."

"Not a problem."

I pulled card table chairs from the corner of my office. "If Juliet and I had the same conversation, there would've been lots more words."

Marc took a chair from me and set it up. "Yet, we worked it out."

"True." I laughed and moved around my desk.

Griffin said, "Is there something going on between Jules and Nate?"

I sat down. "I sometimes wonder if the only people who can't see they're in love is them. Would you give Nate your blessing?"

He held up his hands, palms out. "There's a big difference between proving a friend is innocent of murder and allowing him to date your sister."

I didn't know whether to laugh or punch his arm.

Juliet entered the room with red puffy eyes, but she was smiling.

"We reached a compromise. I'll help think through suspects, but I won't question one by myself."

Griffin squeezed his sister's shoulder. "Sounds reasonable."

Nate followed her in and looked more relaxed. He shot me a wink. "Y'all have a seat."

"Where are we?" Juliet sat between Griffin and Nate.

I pulled my file of suspects from my drawstring bag. "Nate, if you wanted to buy a new bike, where would you go?"

"HOSE."

"Why?"

"They'll let me ride a bike in their parking lot to see how if fits. The place only carries quality bikes and boats. If there's a problem, they can fix it. Customer service is the reason I'd choose them."

"Spoken like a man who owns his own business." I wrote down his answer. "Juliet, you're a woman. Where would you go?"

"Honestly, I'd probably go to a retail store, figuring it'd be more affordable." She glanced at Nate. "Sorry. I never gave it much thought."

"Sis, why are you asking?"

"This can't go any further than us." I met Marc's gaze, and he nodded. "Asher was at Richard Rice Plantation Tuesday morning. He didn't see the murder, but he saw a new bike leaning against a tree. Somehow, it's got to fit into the murder."

Griffin stood. "I know the owner of HOSE. I'll head to town and look for him. See if he remembers selling a bike recently."

I checked my notes. "Asher said it was red. He thought maybe it was a mountain bike."

"Got it." Griffin saluted and left.

Juliet said, "What else?"

I reviewed my notes with them. "Juliet, can you try to call Wendy and convince her to tell you where the apartment is?"

"I can try." She left my office, leaving me with Marc and Nate.

"Andi Grace, I hate for you to spend so much time looking for the killer." Nate removed his hat and ran a hand through his unruly red hair.

Marc said, "You're wasting your breath, Nate."

He sighed. "I never come out ahead of her in any argument."

"Hey. I'm sitting right here." I waved my hands.

Nate played with the bill of his cap. "I may not be able to solve the murder, but I can work on your landscaping. See ya later."

"And then there was one." I gazed at Marc. "Sorry to waste your afternoon."

"Spending time with you is never a waste. Plus, if this meeting leads us to proving Nate's innocence, it'll be well worth it."

Juliet raced into the room, waving her hand with a scrap of paper. "Got the address. Where are the keys she gave you?"

"In my purse." I leapt to my feet and reached for the Coach bag I'd bought deeply discounted because of a scratch near the bottom. The refined brown leather was smooth to the touch, and the bag was big enough to handle all my junk. I fished out the keys. "Here. Who wants to go with me?"

Chapter Twenty-Six

MY HANDS SHOOK as I inserted the key into the white door of the second-story apartment. The gray building accommodated twelve units on three floors. Each was accessed by elevator or concrete stairs. I turned the key, it clicked, and I pushed the door open. "Hello. Anybody home?"

Marc squeezed past me and turned on the lights. The foyer contained generic beach pictures. Suitable if the place wasn't your primary residence.

I shut and locked the door before following Marc. On the left we passed a bathroom, and the kitchen entry was on our right. Straight ahead was a combo living room and dining area separated by a kitchen island. Outdoor living space in the form of a covered patio could be accessed on the other side of the leather couch. Sleek furniture filled the space, giving the apartment a modern vibe. "It's neat, but there's no personality."

"Are you saying messiness means personality?" He elbowed me and chuckled.

"Very funny." I paused at the granite island of the gourmet kitchen. "Life is usually messy. This place could be a hotel room. There's nothing . . . personal."

"Let's check the bedrooms." Marc angled left and disappeared into one of the rooms. "Whoa."

I scooted into the room. Marc's reflection bounced off one mirror after the other. "Ugh. So disgusting." I turned and opened the walk-in closet door and choked. Negligees filled the space. Different colors and styles, but each one was lacy and didn't leave much to the imagination.

"What?"

I backed out and slammed the door. "It's too embarrassing to be in there together. Save yourself."

"Hey, Andi Grace, you did realize we were coming to their secret love nest, right?" His eyebrows dipped down.

I shrugged. "Feel free to laugh, but I didn't really consider what we'd find. Call me naïve, but I still hope we'll find a clue leading us to the killer."

Marc positioned his body to face me, arms at his side and toes pointed in my direction. "If it's too uncomfortable for you, we can leave."

"No. I can do this."

"All right then, let's look through the drawers. Maybe Norris hid something in them."

"Why don't you look there, and I'll tackle the bathroom?" Determined to keep it together and not get embarrassed again, I searched through a linen closet and under the sinks. Drawers opened and closed in the bedroom, and soon Marc appeared. "Any luck?"

"Not yet. Did you find anything?"

"There's an empty suitcase the size of a carryon and a baseball bat under the bed." He studied me. "I'll be in the kitchen rooting through drawers and cabinets."

I returned to the master closet. The space was as big as my home office. A pair of men's running shoes, leather sandals, and loafers were on the floor next to a small stack of duffle bags. I sat on the carpeted floor and opened one after the other. The only things I found were deodorant, black compression shorts, athletic shorts, and a baseball cap in the last bag. Atlanta Braves. The brim was stiff and Norris was bald. Why'd he need a cap to work out? The apartment complex had a state-of-the-art athletic facility. Indoors. Was the cap a clue that he ran outside, or did he use it as a disguise?

Nate always insisted on curving the bill of his hat. I carried it to the kitchen and placed it on the island. "Do you shape the bill when you buy a baseball cap?"

"Always." He stepped out of the pantry. "Why?"

"This visor is flat." I ran my hand along the panels and touched the top button as well as the eyelets. "The sweatband isn't stained. Nate always has sweat stains on his ball caps. I often washed them and he got mad, complaining a clean hat made it look like he wasn't working hard enough."

"I understand. Maybe it's new." He opened a maple cabinet. "Three shelves of glasses. Who needs so many unless you've got a bunch of thirsty kids?"

I ran my fingers along the fabric at the bottom of the hat. Clean and flexible sweatband. No perspiration to make it crackly. I stopped when I hit a hard spot. "Marc, feel this."

In two strides, he stood beside me. "What?"

"Run your fingers along the sweatband area."

"Okay." He began the process of feeling and turning until he stopped at the same place that snagged my attention. "Hold on, there's something here."

"I need a pair of scissors."

"Hold up. There were some in the knife drawer." He reached over and opened it then whipped out a black-handled pair. "Here."

I clipped the threads and unrolled the band. *Plink*. A flash drive dropped onto the counter. Chills popped out on my arms. "This could be big."

"Huge." His voice vibrated.

"Why didn't I bring my laptop?" I met Marc's gaze.

"The memory stick isn't going anywhere. Let's finish our search."

"Good idea. I'll head to the guest room. The drive is in my pocket." I left him in the kitchen. As much as I wanted to stop and examine the jump drive, Marc made sense. He knew me well enough to guess my desire and probably thought I was as flighty as a sanderling.

I crossed the threshold into the second bedroom. It'd been converted into an office. Cherry desk, wingback chairs, file cabinet, and credenza. The wall over the credenza was covered with pictures of Norris with politicians and celebrities. Baseball players, governors, two presidents, our mayor, and Clem Farris, Erin's dad. "Marc, you need to see this."

Hurried footsteps pounded on the floor, and he breezed into the room. "I didn't expect an office."

"Look at this picture. Norris and Erin's dad."

"They look younger." He lifted the frame from the wall and wiggled the backing off.

"What are you doing?"

"In the old days, the date of pictures was printed on the back." He turned it over. "Voila. October two thousand ten."

"Very impressive, Mr. Williams."

He bowed before snapping pictures of the photo with his phone. "Let's see what else we can find. I'll start with the file cabinet."

"I'll search the desk." I sat in the swivel chair. "Too bad Norris doesn't have a laptop here."

"It'd probably be password protected. There's no chance he'll come by this afternoon. Right?"

"Wendy talked like this place was for their trysts, but she could hang out here anytime she wanted. It's hard to picture Norris working in this room while his mistress was here."

"He must have. Otherwise, why'd he convert this to an office?"

"This gets stranger and stranger all the time." I finished my search through the big drawers and reached the skinny one. Pens, rubber bands, paperclips, and another flash drive. I held it up. "Ta-da."

"Two memory sticks? It must be our lucky day. You're sure Wendy gave us permission to be here."

"Definitely. She's scared, and if Norris is guilty, she wants him off the street." I slipped the flash drive into my pocket with the other one.

He slammed shut the bottom drawer. "Nothing obvious in here. Let's roll."

"I'm right behind you."

Marc stopped near the kitchen counter so fast I bumped into him. "Oh."

"Shh." He pointed to the door.

The sound of a key in the lock filled the silence.

Chapter Twenty-Seven

MARC SPUN ON his toe and pushed me toward the patio. I seized the demolished Braves cap before moving to slide open the patio door. We dropped to the teal outdoor rug on the concrete surface. Marc pushed the door most of the way closed.

"Wendy? Are you here?" Norris's voice called out, and the front door slammed. "I thought you were staying with your sister."

Silence.

I studied the patio area for hiding places.

"Wendy?"

No way Marc or I could squeeze under the wicker love seat. I crawled to the other side of the patio and tried to fit between an Adirondack chair and the railing.

"I'm not in the mood for games, honey. Where are you?" Norris stomped through the apartment and returned to the living room.

Marc flattened his body on the far side of the coffee table. The late afternoon sun was setting on the other side of the building, leaving us in shadows.

I managed to see into the apartment through the chair slats.

Norris took his phone off his belt and tapped the screen. "Hello, Wendy?"

Pause.

"I'm at the apartment. Were you here today?" He listened and looked around the space. "The lights are on all over the place. No telling what the next electric bill is going to be. I miss you, baby doll. When are you coming back?"

The man sure asked a lot of questions.

"You've got my credit card. Gas up and meet me here. It shouldn't take more than three hours if you're in Columbia." He walked into the bedroom.

I whispered. "What are we going to do?"

Marc pointed to the rail. "Jump."

"No way."

Norris returned to the living room. "That's it. We're firing the maid. She left the patio door open." He shut the glass door, and the lock clicked into place, preventing us from entering the apartment after he left.

I met Marc's gaze. "At least he didn't see us."

Marc rested his forehead on the back of his hand. "Nice attitude, but we're not home free yet. We can't jump while he's in the main room."

I glanced at the ground. The faded grass looked about fifteen feet away. Maybe less. Could I jump? "What if I scream?"

Norris's shadow floated over the patio.

I held my breath. Seconds ticked by. He continued to talk on the phone, but it was impossible to understand his words clearly. His tone pleaded and cajoled. If he was still speaking to Wendy, she held her own.

At last the call ended, and Norris threw the phone across the room. It hit the mirror in the dining area. Shards fell to the floor. The frown on his face reminded me of the day he caught me at Wendy's house. It'd be so much worse if he found me tonight.

The man stalked to the kitchen and grabbed a liquor bottle from the pantry. From my hiding place, I watched as he stood at the counter and splashed liquid into a whiskey glass and gulped it. He refilled the glass and gulped it again. Then, as calm as you please, he picked his phone off the floor, turned out the lights, and left the apartment.

Marc whispered, "Don't move until we're sure he's not returning."

"Pas de problème."

"What?"

"No problem. I don't know why I try to remember my French classes from high school. I'll never make it to France. Despite years of saving, I only have fifty-eight dollars and some change." My cheeks burned. Shame on me. "Sorry for the pity party. I have no idea why I'm thinking about France at a time like this." I shut my mouth.

"What about Peter's money?"

I shook my head. "It's tied up right now."

"Don't give up your dream, Andi Grace." Marc army-crawled until he faced the apartment's community grounds. "Too bad we're facing the pool and not the parking area."

I inhaled deeply. "Are you ready to jump?"

"Let's wait until it's a little darker before we try. There's less chance we'll be seen."

"I'm going to make sure he locked the patio door."

"Knock yourself out." His sarcastic tone surprised me.

I giggled. "Now who's in a bad mood?"

Marc sighed. "We didn't eat lunch. If we get out of here without injuries, I'm going to take you out to dinner."

"Before we see what's on the flash drive?"

"You bet." His confident tone returned and reassured me.

I crawled to the door and pulled on the handle. It budged a bit then stopped. I slumped. "It's locked."

"I figured as much. May as well get comfortable. It'll be a few more minutes before dark."

I sat in the Adirondack chair and faced Marc, who was seated on the floor with his back against the wicker love seat. "I'm sorry we're in this mess."

"No need to be sorry. I didn't have to come." He straightened his legs and bumped my foot with his. "We had a close call tonight. If Norris had caught us, well, there's no telling what he's capable of. You saw how he threw the phone."

"I've seen his temper before, but I never dreamed he'd appear today."

Lights flickered on around the swimming pool and tennis courts.

Marc stood and held his hand out to help me stand. "I'll jump first. I can catch you if you're scared."

"I'm sure I'll be fine." What a whopper. I was terrified to jump.

"I don't believe you, but we don't have a choice."

I grimaced. "Let's get it over with."

"Okay. Try to relax when you jump, and bend your knees when landing." He swung one long leg over the railing then the next. "I think I weigh too much to hang onto the bottom of this rail, so I'll jump like this."

"What do you want me to do?"

"Climb over, hang onto the rail, squat down and bring your hands with you to the bottom rail. Hold tight and let your legs dangle."

"Do what? Why?" My voice squeaked.

"It'll be a shorter jump, and I might even be able to grab your legs and help you down." He leaned out and jumped. He landed with a soft thud then tucked and rolled before standing. "Your turn."

I gripped the top rail, swung one leg over and froze. I wasn't as athletic or as strong as Marc. Escaping from Wendy's apartment could kill me.

"Come on, you can do it, Andi Grace." In the quiet atmosphere, his voice sounded as loud as whitecaps in a storm.

"Easier said than done."

"Concentrate."

I shifted my weight and twisted my right foot as my left leg completed the transition. My toes pointed at the apartment, and my rear end faced Marc. Lovely. I inched my hands down the metal posts until I was squatting. "Now what?"

"Hold tight with your hands and drop your legs."

Leveraging myself with my elbows, I slid one foot off the concrete balcony edge, then the other, scraping my ribs in the process. My arms stretched straight, and my body swayed.

Marc's arms circled my calves. His nose touched my knees. "I've got you."

I let go and slithered down Marc's body until my feet touched the sandy grass. "I did it."

"Oh, yeah." His voice sounded like a country song. "You were so brave."

The patio lights flashed on at the apartment under Wendy's and a masculine voice rang out. "Who's there? I'm tired of all the shenanigans from you two. I'm going to report you to the HOA."

Marc grabbed my hand. "Run."

Chapter Twenty-Eight

ALMOST AN HOUR passed before we made it to Tony's Pizzeria. My mouth watered at the scent of oregano floating in the air. Eating here would calm my jitters, and I couldn't wait to take my first bite.

"Andi Grace, where you been lately?" The owner's voice boomed across the room. "You not come to see your old friend Tony in weeks. Come have a seat."

I hugged my friend. "I've missed you, but Juliet and Nate bring me your takeout. You're still my favorite restaurant."

"Thatsa good to hear." He led us to a table nestled against the brick wall. Neat stacks of wood filled the space under the counter where customers usually ordered. Mismatched tables and chairs filled the dining space. Every table had a yellow flower in the center. After Hurricane Hugo, Tony had rebuilt his restaurant with the goal of looking like an authentic Italian pizza place, right down to his wood fire oven. "How's this?"

"Perfect. Tony, this is Marc Williams."

"*Piacere*. Nice to meetcha." Tony shook Marc's hand with vigor. "New attorney in town. I hearda you. One of my waitresses wasn't getting child support from her deadbeat ex-husband. You take good care of her. I appreciate that. Grazie."

"Just doing my job, sir."

"She said you didn't charge her much, which tells me you're more interested in people than money. You gave her the dignity of paying you, but not gouge her." He placed his hand on his heart. "I be right back with a snack for you."

Marc's eyes were wide. "I should've figured you didn't have to order at the counter like us mere mortals."

I grinned. "Tony watched out for us after my parents died. Some days he'd call and say he had leftovers and offered them to us."

"Leftovers, my foot. I bet he made extra to share with you."

"He's a nice guy. Same as you." I winked.

Tony returned with a basket of breadsticks, appetizer plates, and two soft drinks. "What can I get you tonight? We got stuffed manicotti, and the pizza of the day is the Deluxe Supreme."

Marc said, "Pizza sounds good to me. Want to split one?"

"Sure." I reached for a parmesan crusted breadstick and swirled it through marinara dipping sauce.

Tony eyed us. "I bring you a salad, too. You both look hungry to me."

I laughed. "You've got a good eye, Tony. We're starved."

"Trust me to take care of you."

When he disappeared, I bit into my breadstick.

Marc reached for one. "I've got a feeling we're not going to leave hungry."

"More like stuffed." The marinara begged me to double dip. I reached toward the sauce then pulled my hand back. It'd be rude to do dip twice with Marc.

He took one of the small plates and poured some of the sauce on it then passed me the bowl of marinara. "The rest is yours."

"A move like this will get you hero points."

Marc laughed. "Giving you the largest portion of sauce makes me a hero? It seems like catching you when you jumped from the balcony would make me heroic."

I swiped the other half of my breadstick in the marinara. "Definitely a noble act, but I don't want you to get a big head."

Tony appeared with two Caesar salads. "*Buon appetito.*"

"I can't believe we're sitting here like nothing happened an hour ago. I was terrified Norris would catch us and either kill us or call the cops." I stabbed lettuce with my fork.

"Calling the authorities might not have been in his best interest. The police report is public information, and he doesn't want his wife to discover the affair. No good divorce attorney wants that."

"What do you think he'd have done to us? Kill us? Rough us up? Threaten to spread rumors about us?"

Tony reappeared. "Too much talking. Not enough eating. Who is this man you are discussing?"

I leaned closer to my Italian friend. "Norris Gilbert."

Tony pulled a chair over to our table and sat on the side between us. "He's a bad one. Unfaithful to his wife, rude to my staff, and some kind of wise guy."

I dropped my fork and leaned close. "How do you know he's unfaithful?"

"His favorite pizza is deep dish with coconut, shrimp, cilantro, and extra garlic. Mr. Gilbert is offensivo. Nobody wanted to wait on him. Finally, one day, I tell him no more. He not welcome at Tony's any longer." He pounded his fist on our table, and a couple at a nearby table glanced at us.

"Okay, but how did you figure out he was having an affair?"

He tossed his hands in the air. "Thatsa odd pizza combination, no?"

"Very weird." I kept my gaze fastened on Tony.

"So one day, the hair lady, Wendy, she comes in and orders the same pizza. Curiosity got the best of me, and I asked why she ordered her pizza thata way. She say a friend introduced her to it. Then she ordered a salad with no dressing. You know this Wendy?"

"Oh, yes. She's something else."

"Precisely. I know the salad is for her because thatsa what she always orders. Pizza is for Mr. two-timing-on-his-wife Gilbert." He tapped his temple with a finger. "I asked her if she still worked at the beauty shop. Maybe is possible she started working for the man. She say yes. Still at beauty shop, and she owns it now. Have you noticed it hasn't been open the last few days?"

I stirred my straw in the Coke. "Wendy left town to visit her sister."

Tony nodded. "Very good. Maybe Mr. Gilbert can pay attention to his wife now."

With both forearms on the table, Marc bent close to him. "Tony, if you ever want to work as a detective, I might have a job for you."

Tony stood and patted his belly. "I'm a pizza man. Let me check on your food."

The restaurant was less than half-full, and I checked my watch. "It's only seven. I hate the shorter days in January. The darkness makes it feel so much later."

"Yeah. I'm ready for spring." He reached over and squeezed my hand. "How do you feel after our adventure?"

"I don't know if it's the food or the normalcy of eating at Tony's, but my nerves are settling down." I smiled at Marc.

"It might be the man himself. I already like your friend."

A young girl carried out a pizza stand and an extra-large Deluxe Supreme and placed them in the middle of the table. "Would you like fresh parmesan?"

Marc released my hand and sat straighter. "You bet."

She grabbed a cheese grater and shredded cheese over the pizza. "I'll be back soon and refill your drinks. Coke?"

"Yes, thanks." I picked up the stainless steel pizza server as a group of men entered the building. The sight of Wade, David, and Deputy Hanks almost took my appetite away. "Marc, look who walked in."

He glanced toward the counter, where most customers placed their order. "Oh, boy. And here we sit with possible evidence to Corey's murder."

"Maybe they won't see us." I hunched my shoulders.

"Or maybe we should greet them. Try not to act guilty."

My face grew hot. "Easier said than done."

David paid for his order and walked to the drink machine a few feet from where we sat. He filled his glass with ice and Coke.

I waved. "Hi, David."

He took a sip of his drink and strolled toward us. He wore his khaki pants and dark brown polo with a circular star emblem on the left. His belt was loaded down with a gun and who knew what else. "Andi Grace. Marc."

I wiped my damp palms on my jeans. "Did my source call you today?"

"Asher reached out to me. Thanks. Anything new I need to know about?"

"Do you have time to meet us tomorrow?"

His eyes narrowed. "Why wait?"

"I need to mull something over."

He held one hand up. "Two words. Obstructing. Justice." He ticked off each word with a finger. "What do those words mean to you, Andi Grace?"

My shoulders dropped with my sigh. "Don't interfere in your investigation."

"Exactly. I'm gonna let you two eat your dinner. Stop by my table on your way out."

Marc's hand covered his forehead, and he massaged his temples. "What are you going to do now?"

"I'm going to dig into our pizza. I usually think better on a full stomach, and you do, too. Dig in." I used the server to place a piece on each of our plates.

Pepperoni, sausage, mushrooms, green and red peppers, and black olives peeked out of bubbly mozzarella cheese. It'd cooled enough to bite into it and not burn my mouth. It was so delicious, and I took a second bite before I finished chewing the first one.

Marc bit into his piece.

Tony walked over to the deputies and patted Wade and David on their shoulders. He said something to them, and the men laughed.

"He's amazing."

Marc stopped shoving pizza into his mouth. "Walking past him, you wouldn't look twice. A sixty-something-year-old man wearing a pizzeria T-shirt, long shorts, and Birkenstock sandals. In here, he's in charge, and he wants to make sure you have a good experience."

"This is where he's comfortable, but he always wants what's best for the other guy. He's got a big heart."

"Yes, he does." He stuffed the rest of the piece in his mouth and wiped his mouth with a napkin, leaving a smear of red sauce.

I pointed to his face. "You've got a little sauce on your cheek."

He wiped it with the white paper napkin. "Thanks."

I stared at his napkin. "That reminds me of the handkerchief at the crime scene. Did it belong to Corey? The lipstick was more of a smear, not like when a woman blots her lips."

"Why do women blot their lipstick?"

"To keep it from getting on our teeth. You usually apply lipstick first. Place a tissue between your lips and gently tap them together. Like this." I demonstrated with my napkin. "It leaves an image of your mouth."

"Can you show me again?" His eyes twinkled.

I laughed. "You've already proven how smart you are, so one demonstration is all you get."

"Okay, so no smear."

"Right." I leaned back in my seat. "I'm stuffed."

"I feel like I've got room for one more piece."

"Will I be in trouble if I see what's on the flash drive before giving it to David?"

"He was clear. You're going to have to talk to him when we leave."

"No wiggle room?"

His gray eyes pierced mine. "Andi Grace, this is serious. You can't disobey a direct order from David."

I let Marc finish eating, with only the sound of Michael Bublé singing in the background.

Tony joined us. "How wassa the pizza?"

I smiled. "Delicious, like always."

He beamed. "Did you save room for tiramisu?"

"I'm afraid not. Maybe next time."

"What do ya mean next time? I'll send a piece home with each of you."

A squawk came from the table where the men from the sheriff's department sat. A woman's voice spoke in code, and all three men raced out of the restaurant.

This was my opportunity to leave without reporting to David. "Tony, we've got to go. Can we get a box for the leftovers? We also need our bill."

"Tonight, your money's no good here." He patted his apron. "You come back soon."

"You bet I will."

He shuffled to the back and returned with an empty pizza box and a brown paper bag. "For the road."

"Thanks so much." I hugged him, and we hurried out before David returned.

Chapter Twenty-Nine

WHEN WE GOT to my house, we headed to my office after putting away the food Tony sent home with us. Marc pulled an extra chair around, and we sat at my desk, looking through the files on the flash drive. I printed off Norris's calendar. "I need time to study his schedule."

"Let's hope he doesn't have two calendars. One for work and the other for his social life."

I opened the next folder on the list. "Another divorce case."

"It's what he does. The only divorce file I'm interested in seeing is Erin's. Can you search for her name?" Marc's nearness both excited and calmed me.

"Sure." I moved the mouse to the search box and typed in Erin's name. "Bingo."

"If Erin hired Norris, I lean toward them only having a business relationship."

"I agree. Let's give her the benefit of believing she was a loyal wife to Corey." I opened the designated file. "Here we go, and before you tell me not to, I'm going to print a copy for myself." I tapped the button, and my printer spit out one sheet at a time.

Marc sighed and crossed his arms. "It won't be the end of the world if I lose my license to practice law, but I can accomplish a lot of good as an attorney."

"I know. Why don't you hang out with Sunny? Take her for a walk or something. If you don't know what I'm doing, you can't be disbarred."

Marc stood before I finished talking. "Sunny, come on, girl. Let's go out." He disappeared with my German shepherd.

I came across a folder of photographs and opened it. Quite a few of the pictures were of the Gilberts at various parties and social functions, and many times they posed with Erin's parents. Concerts, charity events, auctions, boat rides, golf tournaments, and 5Ks in the Low Country, raising money for cancer research. If word of his affair got out, he risked losing not only his wife but also his friends and network of potential clients. "No wonder he kept a secret apartment."

I jumped at the sound of my voice in the empty house. This place was way too quiet, or else my guilty conscious pricked me. Either way I refused to stop.

I scanned the other folders, removed the drive, and inserted the one I'd found in the desk. Hairstyles, recipes, and workout videos were the only folders listed. Why did Wendy keep the disk in the apartment's office?

I removed it and organized the papers I'd printed.

The information on Erin's divorce verified she knew about Corey's affair. The documentation was proof positive Norris knew Wendy was seeing somebody besides him.

The front door opened and closed. "We're back."

I jumped up and joined Marc in the living room. "I'd like to hire you as my attorney."

"Why?" He removed the leash, and Sunny trotted to her water bowl. "I'm already representing Nate."

"I need to talk to you and invoke client and attorney privilege."

"Attorney-client privilege. Do you have a dollar to hire me?"

"Hold on." My purse lay on the wood chair where I usually dropped it. I dug deep into my leather tote and pulled out four quarters floating around the bottom. "Here you go. One dollar."

He slid the money into the front pocket of his jeans. "What do you need to discuss?"

I waved to the couch. "Have a seat."

He took one end and crossed an ankle over his knee. "Go ahead."

I dropped onto the middle cushion. "Erin definitely knew about the affair between Corey and Wendy, and she told Norris. She was mad. She was also aware Corey was stealing from Daily Java weeks ago."

"A woman scorned."

I snapped my fingers. "Exactly. I doubt Norris revealed his affair with Wendy, otherwise Erin would've hired another lawyer. She told Norris to remove Corey from the will."

"Makes sense to me."

"My head is spinning. There were pictures of Norris and Ivey with Erin's parents. I mean a ton of photos. They're friends."

"Do you think Norris told Clem Farris that Corey was cheating on Erin?" Marc quirked an eyebrow.

"If Clem knew, he wouldn't be the first dad to protect his daughter." My dad had been an honorable man who watched out for us.

"True. Norris displays signs of a narcissist. He needs praise and admiration. He displays a sense of entitlement and lives in a fantasy world. He thinks he can be with two women and get away with it. He's also a bully with a bad temper."

"The day of my confrontation with Norris at Wendy's house, I felt like he wanted to hurt me. Norris was clear with his threat. Leave Erin alone, or else."

"I remember." His foot bounced.

"He must really be horrible if sweet Tony told him not to return to the pizzeria."

Marc chuckled. "I imagine it takes a lot to anger Tony. He was protecting his staff, though."

"He put manicotti and tiramisu in the bag he gave us, as well as a small loaf of bread."

"You don't have to tell me again how nice Tony is. I'm a believer."

"Why do you think Norris decided to have an affair with Wendy? Because of his wife's cancer?"

Marc straightened, placing both feet on the floor. "We don't know the affair started when his wife was diagnosed with cancer. My opinion is he feels like he deserves to have two women. One who is acceptable in high society, and one willing to do whatever he wants and hide it."

"Seeing the file of photos, one would assume Norris and Ivey were happily married. Smiling and schmoozing with the Low Country rich and famous."

"Don't forget the pictures in his office. He also knows celebrities, athletes, and politicians."

I clicked my pen open and closed. "Unless Norris is connected to the murder, I need to quit worrying about his sick ways."

"How would you imagine he's tied to the murder?"

"He killed Corey in a jealous rage. He told Wendy to end her affair with Corey, or he'd do something to punish her. Or maybe he told Erin's dad about the affair so Clem would hurt Corey or convince him to end things with Wendy."

"All of those possibilities lead to Norris getting Corey out of the picture. The only thing he had to lose by Corey's murder was one less divorce case." Marc stood. "We need to find David, give him the memory sticks, and share your theory."

"It can't wait until tomorrow?"

"No. We're lucky the deputies were called away. Otherwise, we wouldn't have as much information as we do now. Let's get this over with."

"If he arrests me, you'll still be my attorney? I only gave you a dollar."

"Andi Grace, you can always count on me. I've got your back." He touched my shoulder and sent delightful chills up my spine.

"Give me five minutes to freshen up, and I'll be ready to go with you to the sheriff's office."

He reached for my hair and pulled out a blade of brown grass. "How'd you get grass in your hair if I caught you?"

"No idea. Why'd you let me be seen in public if I had grass in my hair?"

He shrugged. "I didn't see it until now. I'll play with Sunny until you're ready."

I ended up taking fifteen minutes. As much as I dreaded facing David, Marc was right. Obeying the deputy was the smart move to make.

Chapter Thirty

WE SAT ACROSS from David at the scarred oak desk in his office. His Toughbook lay in front of him, and his hands were posed over the keyboard. "Thanks for coming in."

"I guess you want to hear what happened to me today." My pulse thudded in my neck, and I lifted my hand to calm it.

"If it's related to the case, yes."

I glanced at Marc in the chair beside me and took a deep breath before meeting David's gaze. "Wendy gave us the address of her apartment. It's near Market Commons, and she gave us permission to enter and go through it. The place is in her name, but Norris Gilbert pays the bills."

"What's the exact address."

I rattled off the information as well as the directions.

David's jaw twitched. "How'd you get inside?"

"We had a key."

"You saw Wendy today?" His focus on me was intense.

I never wanted to be a suspect questioned by him. "No, she gave the key to Juliet and me a few days ago before she left town. I showed it to you the day you found us inside Wendy's house Problem was, we didn't know where the apartment was then."

"Were you by yourself?"

"No. Marc went with me."

David glared at Marc. "Have you lost your mind?"

"I'm Nate's defense attorney, and I had permission to be there."

David closed his eyes and shook his head. "Did you two find anything?"

I slid the flash drives across the desk and told him about our search for answers. "Before you ask, I looked at them. Alone. Marc can't get into trouble for what I did by myself."

"I'm not going to argue with you over that right now."

"There are files on divorce cases Norris is handling. I only opened folders relating to Erin, and I looked at his pictures."

"Why?"

"Until we entered the second bedroom-turned-office in the apartment, I didn't realize Norris and Erin's dad were good friends. There are lots of pictures of Norris and Ivey with Clem and Gina Farris. Were you aware of the relationship?"

"Can't say I was." He typed more. "Why do you think this is relevant?"

"It's possible Norris told Clem about the affair so he'd take some kind of action against Corey. Erin was preparing to divorce her husband, but a divorce wouldn't force Corey to end his affair with Wendy."

David's eyes grew wide. "You're not seriously insinuating a respected attorney leaked protected information hoping Clem would murder his son-in-law."

"With Corey out of the picture, Norris didn't have to share Wendy. He's an evil man."

"I'm struggling to believe your theory."

I picked up the devices. "When you look at the flash drives, you won't think I'm so crazy."

"Is there anything else I need to know, Andi Grace?" His eyebrows lifted.

I laid each of the drives back on the desk and crossed my legs, afraid of David's reaction. "Norris showed up before we left."

David lurched out of his seat. "I'm surprised he didn't have you arrested."

"He never actually saw us." I scooted my chair back, giving me a bit more distance from the deputy.

Marc said, "The apartment includes a patio. We were about to leave when Norris unlocked the door. We were walking past the kitchen when we heard the key. There weren't many options. We darted across the living room and hid on the patio. The sliding glass door remained open by less than an inch."

"It's amazing he didn't catch you."

"It was close." Marc told him about the phone call, Norris locking us out, and our escape.

"Andi Grace, each time you pull one of these stunts, you shave years off my life. I don't need another dead body to deal with." He plunked onto the edge of his seat.

"I'm sorry, but I've got to watch out for my brother's best interests."

David ran a hand over his face. "If I told you Nate's no longer a suspect, would you quit?"

I leaned forward. "Is this a trick question, or have you ruled out Nate?"

"Look, I grew up with Nate. I don't want it to be him, but I can't let my personal feelings obstruct justice. It's a slippery slope when friends get entangled with a crime."

"Then it's a good thing I'm helping, because I know he's innocent and don't have to follow procedures to remain unbiased. Do you need anything else from me?"

David looked at Marc. "Can you help me here?"

Marc held out his hands palms up. "I've learned it's easier to go along with her. It's amazing how often she's right."

He dropped his head into his hands, speaking through his fingers. "Y'all are free to go."

We headed out and paused at the doorway. "David, Norris told me I can't go to the funeral. In fact, he threatened me. Will you go?"

"Why?"

"You might hear something useful. Wear real clothes, and people might relax and open up to you. I think one reason I hear so much gossip is because I dress casual, usually have a dog nearby, and I'm approachable."

"You want me to wear a suit?" He chuckled.

"Shirt and tie. No jacket. Don't use product on your hair."

"A suit jacket will hide my gun and holster."

I opened my mouth.

David held out a hand. "Please, stop. I don't need fashion advice from you. I'd already planned to attend the funeral. But before you ask, no. I won't report back to you. Yes, I'll keep an eye on Norris. He shouldn't have threatened you."

"Thanks." Disappointing, but it was the most I could ask for. Marc and I walked down the wide hall with tile flooring.

Our drive back to my cottage was quiet. After Marc pulled up to the house, he zipped around the truck and opened my door.

"Lots of guys don't open doors for women." His politeness touched my heart.

"Bobby Joe taught me to be a gentleman. He said women's lib was fine—women deserve equal pay for equal work and all, but I should always show them respect."

"Very nice." We walked to the front porch.

At the door Marc paused. "Are you going to keep investigating?"

"I can't stop."

"I figured as much. What's your plan for tomorrow?"

I shrugged. "Besides walking dogs, I'm not exactly sure. Any suggestions?"

"Read over your notes. Maybe something will hit you."

"Thanks for hanging out with me today."

"Spending time with you is better than most cardio workouts. My heart went into overdrive more than once."

I laughed. "Mine, too. I don't know if I was more scared when Norris entered the apartment or when I climbed over the porch rail to drop to the ground."

"Don't forget, I caught you."

"Yes, you did. Thanks, Marc." I got onto my tiptoes and kissed his cheek. "Good night."

"Night." He whistled a country love song as he walked to his truck.

I closed the door and leaned against it. Marc had suggested I review my notes. I let Sunny out the back door, brewed herbal tea, and soon settled into bed with Sunny lying beside me.

I added Clem Farris to my list. If he was guilty, Norris had manipulated him. The main thing I remembered about Erin's dad was how much he loved his girls. It broke his heart when Erin married Corey, and he'd distanced himself from her. But I didn't see him as a killer. He was a gentle soul. I drew a line through his name.

Norris was nasty and more believable as a killer. I yawned and laid my notes on the bedside table. My eyes grew heavy. Sleep would help me think more clearly, and it'd take all my faculties to solve Corey's murder.

Chapter Thirty-One

FLUFFY WHITE clouds floated in the blue sky. I munched on a pecan granola bar in my Suburban on my way to Heyward Outdoors Sports Establishment. Griffin hadn't located the owner, which left me trying to find the man on a beautiful Monday morning.

From an insulated travel mug, I sipped my cup of wake-me-up. Sunny snoozed in the back seat. We'd already walked two rambunctious puppies who belonged to a woman who'd left town in the middle of the night because her daughter went into labor in Asheville. She'd called me early, and I had her house key from previous times of walking her dogs. When she requested I watch her fur babies, I didn't hesitate to agree. The dogs were fun and needed plenty of attention.

I signaled and turned into the empty parking lot of the outdoor equipment store. Not another vehicle in sight. "Perfect. You want to go inside with me?"

Sunny breathed heavy.

"You can stay here." I rubbed her head and darted into the shop. Kayaks, canoes, paddle boards, and bikes filled the concrete-block building.

A forty-something man greeted me from behind the counter. "Howdy, how can I help ya?"

"I'm Andi Grace Scott. I own Kennady Bed and Breakfast."

He rubbed his scraggly beard that matched his frizzy ponytail. "Peter Roth's old place."

"Yes. I thought this spring visitors might like to ride bikes on some of the trails at my place."

"You know there are rental places around." White stitching on his khaki shirt spelled out Joshua.

"Yeah, but I thought if I already had them on the property, it could be a perk. Don't tell anybody else, though. I hope it will give me an edge on the competition."

"Cool. May as well buy kayaks and canoes as well since you're on the river."

"Your idea might be a little ambitious for this year. We're a new business, but maybe next fall I can squeeze your suggestion into my budget." I moved to the bicycles. "Do you give discounts if I buy more than one?"

"I've never considered it, but yeah. I can do that." He left his spot at the counter and joined me.

"Great. Can I call you Joshua?"

"No need to get formal. I'm Josh Tecco, the owner of this fine establishment."

He offered his hand, and I shook it. "A friend of mine recently bought a red mountain bike, and she loves it."

He squeezed the tire on a bike built for speed. "You must mean Erin."

My plan had worked easier than I ever dreamed. "Yes. We've known each other for years."

"Too bad about her husband." He checked more tires and avoided eye contact.

"Yeah. Poor thing. Do you know Erin very well?"

"Erin's a class act. When she gets over the grieving process, I might ask her out. I'd sure treat her better than her husband did."

"Really? He always seemed nice." I listened intently.

He crossed his arms. "Trust me, it was an act."

"What do you mean?"

"You might see them out in restaurants or at Daily Java acting crazy about each other."

"But?" I stepped closer.

He frowned. "But if you frequented bars late at night, Corey would be there flirting with other women. Erin always went to bed early so she could get up in the middle of the night and bake fresh pastries for the coffee shop."

"So y'all were close friends?" He'd finally answered my earlier question.

His nostrils flared. "Friends. Period. Nothing fishy. We met at a meeting for business people in the Heyward Beach area. It's called HEBB."

"Sounds familiar. What does it stand for?"

"Heyward Beach Businesses. Most of the members own small businesses in the area. You should join us."

"Sounds like a good idea. You and Erin both attend the meetings?"

"Yeah. We're on the free-spirited side of the group. If you come, sit with us."

"Thanks, Josh. Did you learn about Erin's work schedule at those meetings?"

"Sure did. When there are meetings, I close the store for a couple of hours. Erin has to schedule more help to work in order to attend." Josh pointed to one of the bikes. "This is the one Erin purchased. Do you want to take it for a spin? There's plenty of space behind the store."

"I'll take a picture and talk to my friend who runs the B&B for me."

The front door swooshed open, letting in a fresh breeze.

"Knock yourself out. I need to check on this customer just as soon as I grab my coffee." He turned on the toe of his water shoes, making a slight squeak in the process.

"Thanks." I suppressed a grin and snapped pictures with my phone.

"Ahem."

Chills shot up my spine, and I turned.

"Andi Grace, what are you doing here?" David wore his uniform and stood with his feet planted shoulder-width apart. Did he use that same pose for all the people getting on his nerves or just me?

"I'm about to ride a bike?"

"Are you telling me or asking?" His frown deepened. "Either way, I don't believe you."

"I thought you were going to attend the funeral."

Josh returned and lifted his insulated mug. "Corey's funeral is at one."

My mouth dried faster than bread in a toaster. "I better scoot. Josh, I'll think about the bikes."

"Don't you want to ride one first?"

"Next time. Can you come up with a quote for four bikes?"

"No problem. Catch you later."

"Bye, Josh." I steered my way out of the store, staying as far from David as possible.

"No parting word for me?" David's frown lifted.

"Bye, David."

"Stay out of trouble," he called after me as I dashed out the door.

I hustled to the Suburban and took off. "Sunny, you missed all the excitement. If David had hauled me to jail, my one call would've been to find somebody to take care of you." I ruffled her fur.

David's presence in HOSE couldn't be a coincidence. He was there to get information about the red bike. That was a positive sign. I U-turned and drove straight to Marc's office. His truck wasn't in the parking lot, but I stopped anyway.

Once inside, Rylee greeted me. "Hello, dear. What brings you our way?" Her thick red hair waved around her face in a becoming style for a woman her age. The seafoam cardigan emphasized the color of her captivating green eyes.

"Hi, Rylee. Is Marc around?"

"I'm sorry, but he's in court this morning." She checked her computer screen. "He's slammed all day."

Disappointment smacked me in the chest. "I wonder why he didn't ask me to help with Chubb?"

"We had a couple of last-minute emergencies." She used her fingers to make quotations when she said *emergencies*. "So now his day is packed."

"Any chance Lacey Jane is around?"

"No, hon. Your sister has classes today. Can I help you with something?"

Arg. I knew that. "Right, it's Monday. Rylee, will you give Marc a message?"

"Sure." She reached for a pen and lime green sticky pad. "Shoot."

"If he'd like me to check on Chubb, y'all let me know." I shifted from one foot to the other, feeling like I stood in front of the school principal.

"What about a key?" She gave me a tight smile.

"I have keys for all of my clients." I stopped moving like a school kid and lifted my chin like a successful business woman.

"Smart."

"I also need to discuss a bike with him."

"Alrighty. I'll make sure he gets your messages." She lined the sticky note on her computer monitor under about a dozen other messages.

"See you later." I left and drove to Kennady Plantation, parking near the dog barn. "Come, Sunny."

Griffin stood in front of the old kitchen holding a sketchpad. "Hey, Andi Grace. You got a minute?"

"For you, I've got two. What's on your mind?"

"Follow me." We walked to the fence around the dog playground, and I opened the gate for Sunny. She trotted in with her tail high.

Griffin said, "Last night Marc and I discussed you and this renovation."

My heartbeat picked up its tempo. "Okay."

"From what Marc said, it sounds like you'd rather stay in your place on Heyward Beach."

"I love my home, but does it make sense to stay there when I own a plantation?"

"Hear me out. I drew some rough sketches for different options of how you can use this building. Let's sit at the picnic table."

With heavy feet, I trudged to the table near the dog play area and sat. Was he about to reveal a plan I'd be crazy to reject, forcing me to move to the plantation? "Show me what you've got."

He spread the papers on the table. "Option A is a honeymoon suite. B is a place for your employees to live. I mean, like Juliet could live here and still run the B&B, or Dylan could live here."

"He's in the little apartment."

Griffin met my gaze. "For now he is, but what if he gets married? He'll want, no, he'll need more space."

"True, but what if it never happens?" So far nothing he had said struck a chord with me.

"That's where plan C comes in. If you make Kennady Plantation the place to get married, it would be perfect to host the bridal party."

I studied his drawings, and one appealed to me most. "I need an estimate on turning this into a home for Juliet. I worry she's going to burn out if she doesn't have a space to call her own."

"My sister is happier running the B&B than I ever saw her as a hairdresser."

"I'm glad, but I'd still love to do this for her." I pointed to the bathroom in the sketch. "We need to include a tub, because she loves to take baths."

He wrote the word at the bottom of the page. "I'll get to work on pricing this out for you."

"Thanks, Griffin. Please don't tell Juliet yet. I don't want to get her hopes up if I can't afford it." Inheriting the plantation both blessed and scared me. Affording the upkeep mystified me. I'd never been comfortable with the accounting end. Equity, accounts receivable, spreadsheets, accrued, and many other basic words often confused me, but I knew enough to proceed with caution.

"My lips are sealed. I'll be in touch." He strode toward the back door of the house.

I headed to my office. The flutter in my stomach affirmed my desire to continue living in my beach cottage on the island. Most people would consider my inheritance a blessing, but I was a simple woman. The only part I enjoyed was the dog area. The rest stressed me out.

Some place in the Bible said God wanted us to prosper. He didn't want to mistreat me. He wanted to give me hope and a future.

Hope. Juliet loved the house and the opportunity to run it as a bed and breakfast. The place stirred her creativity, and I was thrilled for her.

What did I want to happen? I'd given up my youthful dream of a career in investigative journalism, but the hunger to solve mysteries stirred my soul. I loved Sunny and enjoyed taking care of other animals, but was it enough to satisfy me for the rest of my life? Or was there a way to combine my investigative instincts with my love of animals? Over ten years of my life had been devoted to caring for other peoples' pets. It'd be easy to continue, but would I be content? What would I do if I changed careers?

A dog yipped, and I went to the play area.

Dylan worked with Pinky on simple commands. Down. Stay. Heel. Sit. He never rushed her or showed frustration with the amount of time it took.

My phone vibrated, and I slipped outside in order not to interrupt the obedience lesson before answering.

Marc's voice drifted over the line. "Hey, I got your messages. First off, I'd love for you to check on Chubb. What's the message about a bike?"

The sound of his voice lessened my stress. "I went to HOSE and learned Erin bought a bike recently."

"Good detective work."

"Maybe not. David caught me." I held my breath, expecting a lecture.

Marc's laugh astonished me. "You must not be in jail since you were able to answer your phone."

"No, but he was ticked."

"Not surprised." His voice trailed off.

"It sounds like you're busy. I'll take care of Chubb this afternoon."

"Thanks. I'm juggling a lot of fire batons. Talk to you later." He disconnected before I could say bye. I hopped into the Suburban and drove to his house.

Marc's return to practicing law energized him. He and Juliet both were working jobs that fit their personalities. Could part of my problem be I'd never completely formed a personality? I always took the next step needed to survive and never had a chance to think about what made me happy. Had I missed the window of opportunity to pursue my dreams? Was I allowing fear to hold me back from something better?

My inheritance had turned from being a true gift to an albatross weighing me down. I refused to sink under the pressure. No. I'd appreciate the plantation no matter where I chose to live. The decision could wait. I parked in front of Marc's house and walked with determination to the front door. I'd walk Chubb and return to my list of suspects. Doubts and fear caused trouble, and I didn't have time for them.

I had a killer to catch.

Chapter Thirty-Two

EARLY THAT AFTERNOON, I sat in the waiting room of the sheriff's office as the receptionist directed. Wade entered the building while I behaved like a model citizen, waiting to speak to David. The sheriff stopped in his tracks when he spotted me.

"Hi, Wade." I flipped my hair back and stood.

"Andi Grace, why are you here?" His dark eyebrows rose, and he sounded curious. "Nate's still a free man."

"Great, but I'm here because I have information for David about the murder. The lady at the desk told me to wait until David returns."

Wade checked his watch. "I know he attended the funeral, because I stopped in for the visitation beforehand. He should be back soon."

"I'll wait." I held up my folder. "I can study my notes on the murder."

He jingled the change in his tan slacks pocket. "Come on back. I'll buy you a Coke. It beats the coffee around this place any day of the week."

I followed him to the break room. "Is David keeping you informed about his case?"

Wade inserted the coins, pushed the button for a Coke, and handed a bottle to me. He repeated the process for himself. "David has more than one active case, and he updates me daily. Trust him to do a good job."

"I believe in David which is why I came here to share what I know." I unscrewed the cap from the plastic bottle and took a swig. Tiny chunks of ice tickled my throat. "I love when it's icy."

"Me, too. It's why I set the temperature colder than necessary."

"For South Carolina, it's necessary all year round." I took another swallow.

Wade smiled and shook his head. "You're not here to tell David he's doing a good job. What's on your mind?"

I huffed. "It's almost been a week since Corey was murdered."

My indignation did nothing to ruffle Wade's feathers. "Investigations take time. We want a case that will stick when it goes to trial. David is a professional with a good track record of cracking tough cases."

"I trust David, but he's not as easy to work with as you were." I gripped my drink.

One side of Wade's mouth shot up. "It's not his job to work with you. He's getting paid to solve the case."

"You also thought I was a nuisance, but I helped catch Peter's killer. I can help David, if he'd only give me the chance."

"Hey, now." David entered the room wearing a black suit, crisp white shirt, and sky-blue tie. His black dress shoes shone. "I listened to plenty of your ideas. Sometimes I asked you to share your thoughts, and other times I couldn't shut you up. Still, you've had your say."

Wade made a T-formation with his hands. "Time out. David, I invited Andi Grace back here. She didn't come to complain about you. I'm sure you're aware, you can't speak to her these days without her mentioning the murder. There's nothing to worry about. It's her way." He lifted one shoulder.

David loosened his tie. "If you say so, sir."

"Good attitude." He inserted more change into the machine, retrieved another Coke, and handed the cold bottle to his deputy. "However, she's here to talk to you about the case."

"Shoulda known. Andi Grace, why don't you come to my office?" He motioned with his hand for me to follow him.

Deputy Hanks jogged into the break room before any of us left. "Sheriff, a man just walked in and confessed to killing Corey Lane."

My skin tingled. "A man? Not Erin? What in the world?"

David's eyes narrowed. "This is none of your business."

"I need to see who it is." I'd convinced myself Erin had murdered her husband.

He pointed at me. "You need to leave. I'll call you when I'm free to discuss your news."

Deputy Hanks threw up his hands. "We've got a man confessing to a murder, and we're gabbing in the commissary."

"Lead us to him." Wade's voice rasped like he was holding back a burp, and he thumped his chest with his fist.

David and Wade followed the bald deputy to the waiting area, and I was fast on their heels. How could I have been so wrong? Erin had the motive, and she'd bought the bike. Who was turning themselves in for the murder?

In case I was arrested for butting into David's case, I texted the news to Marc while hustling down the hall. They couldn't prevent me from at least getting a glimpse of the alleged killer.

Chapter Thirty-Three

CLEM FARRIS STOOD at the front desk with his shoulders slumped. Gray complexion and puffy eyes aged him at least a decade. He wore a black suit, black shirt, and black tie. None of his apparel improved his haggard appearance.

His gaze landed on each man one by one. "I killed Corey Lane. He was a no-good wastrel. Erin never should've married him, and she'd come to her senses recently. She wanted to divorce Corey but feared he'd take Daily Java. He'd been unfaithful and stolen from her business. It was too much for me to handle. I tried to pay him to disappear. When he refused, I killed him."

From my vantage point in the doorway between the reception area and hall, I pressed my lips together. Clem? His story sounded rehearsed. He was a doting father, and he didn't have the killer instinct.

David Mirandized Clem and asked him to empty his pockets. "Let's discuss this where we can have a little more privacy."

Wade pulled me into a small side room. "Looks like your brother is free and clear."

"Yeah." I twisted the Coke cap back and forth.

"You don't sound too happy." He propped a hip on a small wood table.

"I don't believe Clem's story. He's more likely to kill a person with kindness. Besides, I thought he was out of the country last Tuesday. David needs to investigate his whereabouts."

Wade groaned. "Explain to me why Mr. Farris would confess if he didn't do it?"

My heart leapt. "To protect Erin. He's given his daughters pretty much anything they wanted. The family was super close until Erin and Corey started dating."

"You beat all, Andi Grace. Let's go back to my office. I need to take notes on what you're saying." He spun around and departed.

I followed Wade to his office worrying about poor Mr. Farris. Desperation must have driven him to declare his guilt.

The sheriff pointed to a chair. "Take a seat. I'll be right back."

I sank into the seat and texted Marc about Clem.

A reply message from Marc beeped. Left a conference call and should be there in two minutes.

I drank my cold soft drink. No more ice, but it hit the spot. Sometimes a girl just needed Coke. It comforted me in a weird way. Maybe because my dad sometimes took me out on a coffee date, except I always got a Coke.

By the time I finished my drink, Wade, David, and Marc entered the office.

Marc claimed the leather office chair nearest me and gave my hand a quick squeeze. Wade took his seat behind the desk, and David pulled a chair to the side.

Wade made eye contact with of us before speaking. "Andi Grace doesn't believe Mr. Farris is the killer. She thinks he's protecting Erin." He typed on his Toughbook.

David huffed. "He's confessing to the murder. I didn't pressure him. He came to us on his own."

I leaned forward. "He's also lying. Clem would do anything to keep his family safe, even if it meant he'd go to prison for a murder he didn't commit."

David tapped his thumb on his thigh. "You're the one who told me about the connection between Farris and Norris Gilbert. That much of the story is true."

"Don't you see? If you weave truth with untruths, it seems like you're being honest." I crossed one leg over the other and swung my foot.

Wade drummed two fingers on his desk. "David, what about Norris Gilbert and Wendy Conn?"

His ears turned red, and he sat straight. "Sure, I brought them up as possibilities, but we've got a man confessing. I'll investigate his story, but I won't release him until I'm confident he didn't kill Corey. Why is this so hard to understand?"

"I actually came over with new information to share with you. Ask Clem about the red bike." I rubbed my stiff neck.

"I'm aware Erin bought a red bike." David's nostrils flared.

"I think it could be the same one Asher saw the morning Corey was killed. How does it fit into the puzzle? Also question him about his vacation to Europe. I brought it up to Wade earlier. There's no way he could have killed his son-in-law if he was still out of the country."

"Why don't I just let you question my suspect?" He staccato-like articulation of each word clued me in to his unmistakable sarcasm.

Marc touched my arm. "Let's go and allow David and Wade to perform their jobs. If Clem is innocent, they'll unravel the truth."

"Fine. I only stopped by to tell y'all about Josh and the bike."

David sighed. "I questioned Josh earlier, Andi Grace. Give us some credit. Please."

My arms circled my stomach. "I'm sorry, David."

"Are we free to go?" Marc's relaxed posture in the chair contrasted with my stress. How did he remain so calm?

The deputy and sheriff made eye contact with each other.

David stood with drooped shoulders and waved us toward the door. "You're free to leave, but don't spread Clem's confession all over town."

"Do you think Erin realizes her dad is turning himself in? If so, she must be devastated."

David crossed his arms and frowned. "Do *not* walk out of here and find Erin. This isn't any of your concern."

I opened my mouth to argue, but he had a point. If the deputy focused on Clem as the killer, then proving Nate's innocence wasn't necessary. "You're right."

David's eyes widened.

Marc stood before the officers spoke. "Let's go."

Wade dashed after us. "Andi Grace, can you check on Duke later this afternoon? I feel like it's going to be a long day."

"No problem. Should I take him home with me?"

"I don't think it's necessary, but thanks for the offer."

"Let me know if you change your mind. You're still my friend, and I'd never neglect Duke." Wade nodded and turned toward his office. Marc and I walked to the parking lot and stopped at my Suburban.

I said, "What do you think?"

"Tell me more about the red bike." He loosened his tie.

I zipped up my puffer coat and told him everything that'd happened at the outdoor shop. "After my conversation with Josh, I became even more convinced Erin killed Corey. The bike confuses me. When did Erin ride it to the plantation? According to Asher, it wasn't in the tourist area."

"Off the beaten path." Marc tilted his head to the side.

"Yes." I gave him time to process.

"A safe place to leave it. Less likely to get stolen and taken to lost and found."

"Exactly. Suppose Erin left it there on Monday. She could've gone to the plantation with Corey in his fancy car for some reason on Tuesday. Killed him and ridden away on the bike. Or did she ride the bike over Tuesday morning and surprise Corey?"

Marc leaned against my SUV. "You're not going to drop this, are you?"

"How can I? Erin's dad never hunted and rarely fished. When he did go fishing, he always threw back what he caught. Catch and release, I think it's called."

"You need to know how to catch and release properly, or the fish die anyway. So what's your point?"

"The point is, he's a soft-hearted man." I crossed my arms.

"He could also be a father protecting his daughter the best way he knows how." Marc lifted his face to the sky full of clouds. "Heyward Beach is Erin's home turf. Corey married her and made his place here."

"Don't forget he was in financial trouble because of gambling. He took bribes from contractors without getting caught. He embezzled from Daily Java, and Asher had questions about donations given to Richard Rice Plantation. He thinks Corey dipped into their money." I glanced around the parking lot. "Where's your truck?"

"I decided to walk over in case the parking lot was full. I thought it'd be faster."

"Hop in. I'll give you a ride back."

Once we were settled, I fired up the Suburban. "How about a cup of coffee?"

His head swiveled to me, eyes wide. "You can't be thinking of Daily Java. David was clear in his warning."

I grew warm and wiggled out of my jacket. "Donut Dreaming has good coffee."

He reclined his seat. "Sounds good."

I headed to the donut shop. "Do you believe Clem?"

Marc ran a hand through his wavy blond hair. "I mean it's possible he's guilty. The red bike could be a coincidence."

I picked up my phone from the console's cupholder and placed my finger on the screen to unlock it. "Look in my pictures app. Josh let me snap photos of a bike exactly like the one Erin bought."

"All right, but I never saw the mystery bike at Richard Rice Plantation." He swiped through my photos. "Can I text these to my phone?"

"Sure. You're right about Asher. He's the only one we know who saw it. I need to show him the pictures." I tapped the brakes for a four-way stop.

Marc checked his phone. "I've got an appointment in twenty minutes. We'd better skip the coffee. Drop me at the office and go see Asher."

I glanced at him. "You don't mind?"

"Not at all. I know you're dying to find out more."

I turned at the stop sign and drove to his office. "By the way, Chubb's at the dog barn playing with Sunny."

"Thanks. I'll swing by later and pick him up."

"You inspired me to name my doggie day care Stay and Play." I parallel parked by his office so we could end our conversation without a car honking at me to get out of the way.

"I don't remember suggesting the name."

"You said it was good to bring Chubb over to stay and play. It rang a bell and stuck with me. So Juliet will run Kennady Plantation Bed and Breakfast and I'll handle Stay and Play. Two separate businesses on one property. What do you think?"

"It sounds incredible to me." He opened the door and stepped out. "Thanks for the ride."

"I enjoyed a few minutes alone with you." I waved and drove away. It didn't take me long to reach Cummings Security Company. The receptionist led me to Asher's office and closed the door when she left.

"Andi Grace, what brings you by?" Asher stood and motioned for me to sit in an upholstered wingback. "I already talked to Deputy Wayne."

I settled into the comfortable seat and opened the photos on my phone. "I heard, but I'm here to ask if this looks like the red bike you spotted Tuesday morning."

Phone in hand, he reached for his reading glasses and sat down. "The bike was in the shade, so I can't be one-hundred-percent positive, but it looks the same. I remember the handle bars stuck up like that. It made me think a tall person would be comfortable on it. It also had red spokes like your picture."

I fanned myself with one hand but quit when I realized it didn't cool me down. "Sensational. Now to find the bike."

"Can you please keep me out of this while you conduct your search?" He removed the reading glasses and laid them on the mahogany desk.

"I'll do my best." I rubbed my hands over the soft material on the chair arms. "You should know, Clem Farris confessed to killing Corey."

Asher rubbed his chin. "I don't see it, and I bet you don't either. Otherwise, you wouldn't be here questioning me about the bike."

"You're right. I don't believe the confession, and I told David my feelings." I gripped the arms of the chair.

Asher's eyebrows rose. "How'd he react?"

"He told me to stay out of the investigation. Again." I blew out a puff of air.

"Something tells me you're not going to drop the issue." He handed the phone to me.

I took my cell from him. "How can I can drop it when deep in my soul I know he's innocent?"

"Same way you believed in your brother?" A small smile appeared.

"Kinda, but I would've staked my life on Nate's innocence. Please, don't tell David I came to see you about the bike. He's already on my case." I stood.

"You don't have to worry about me. The less I get involved, the better it is for Hannah." He walked me out of the office. "Juliet reached out to Hannah, and I know we made the right decision booking her announcement at your place."

"Thanks, Asher. We won't let you down." I left his office and drove to my afternoon clients. The two puppies were first on my list. Their mommy had called and told me she'd be back in the evening. Her daughter was safe and had delivered a healthy baby boy. My client wanted to pack for an extended stay and thought this would be the perfect time to return home.

After spending longer than normal with the puppies, I headed to Wade's house. Was he really too busy to leave the office? Or did he know I'd pass by Erin's house while walking Duke? Was this his secret way of telling me to keep investigating, or wishful thinking on my part?

Either way, I planned to go by Erin's house.

Chapter Thirty-Four

PER WADE'S REQUEST, I walked Duke around the neighborhood. We slowed our approach to Erin's house. Corey's shiny blue Audi, Erin's white Prius, and two SUVs filled the driveway.

Other vehicles parked along the street. More SUVs and pickup trucks than anything else, although pickup trucks were the unofficial vehicle of Heyward Beach so it wasn't a big surprise.

I'd never wanted Erin to be guilty of killing her husband. She must be exhausted from the constant stream of visitors, and now she'd be forced to deal with her dad's confession. It didn't matter if he was the true killer or if he was covering for Erin. The stress of his action might push her past the breaking point.

Before Corey died, Erin had always been nice to me. Not so much now.

I paused when Duke hiked a leg near a mailbox.

A white Range Rover slid into a space between two black pickup trucks. I glanced toward the driver and looked again. Of all the bad luck. The last thing I needed was another confrontation with Norris.

"Let's go, Duke." I gently tugged the leash, and he followed my lead.

Ivey stepped out of the passenger side of the expensive vehicle and waved to me. Norris had his attention fixed on the phone in his hands.

I waved to Ivey and shuffled in the opposite direction with Wade's black and white mutt, which I predicted was part collie and part beagle. Duke sniffed one spot after the next, making it a slow trek.

When we reached Wade's place, he sat on the swing at the end of the porch. "Andi Grace."

"Wade, I thought you wanted me to walk Duke."

"I did, but I got away earlier than expected. Did you encounter anything interesting on your stroll?"

My stomach flipped. "I'm not sure what you want me to say."

Duke pulled me toward Wade, and I let go of the leash.

The dog hopped onto the swing, and Wade loved on his pet. "Did you go to Erin's?"

"We were on the street where she lives, but I didn't go to her house. Norris and Ivey arrived while we were there." I sat in a white wicker chair that needed a fresh coat of spray paint.

"Be careful around Norris. David told me you had a close call this weekend." He lifted his chin, and Duke licked his neck.

"Too close for comfort, but it wasn't my first encounter with the man. He threatened me last week when I was at Wendy's house. He even put a tracker on my car."

"He what?" Wade roared, and Duke barked.

"Didn't David tell you? Norris showed up out of the clear blue sky when I was at Wendy's. I was shocked he found me there. I mean, what were the odds?"

Wade unclasped the dog's leash and stood. "How'd you discover the tracker?"

Duke made his way to a water bowl near the front door.

"Marc found it, and we reported it to David. He knows about the incident. Although, to be fair, we don't have proof Norris is guilty of putting it on my SUV. But it makes the most sense."

"Did Norris speak to you today?" He propped a hip on the white porch railing.

"No, but maybe it's because his wife was with him."

"Could be."

I glanced toward the street and didn't spot a soul. "Wade, I didn't go to the funeral because Norris threatened me. When you were at visitation, how did Erin appear?"

"Strained."

"She wasn't crying?" Pretend crying would've been better than nothing if she didn't want to look guilty. Then again, if she was innocent and trying to keep her emotions under control, it might never have occurred to her to fake grief.

"Nope. She twisted a handkerchief, but she never sobbed while I was there." His booted foot swung back and forth.

"A white hanky? Like the one at the crime scene?"

Wade tilted his head and stared at me. "It's possible, but I was more focused on Erin than what she held or wore. I'll go over the evidence we've collected."

"Since you brought up evidence, I spoke to Asher about the red bike." I showed Wade the pictures on my phone. "See the red spikes and funky handlebars?"

"Yep. Where are you going with this?"

"Asher saw a bike like this last Tuesday." My heel tapped on the wood planked porch floor. When I realized the nervous habit, I pressed down on my knees and stopped.

"Interesting." His flat tone didn't reveal what he was thinking.

"I think it's evidence. Can you search Erin's garage for the bike?"

"Not without a subpoena, and neither can you." The rasp in his voice alerted me to be careful.

My throat constricted, and I didn't respond.

Wade stood. "I mean it, Andi Grace. Don't search her garage or house."

I nodded. "I won't interfere with David's investigation. I really do want the real killer put away."

"I know you do." He stuffed his hands in his pockets.

"Does Erin know about her dad's confession?" I searched his face.

He met my gaze. "I'm not sure. Clem used his one call to contact his attorney."

"Norris?" I rose to my feet.

"Doubtful. Clem needs a homicide attorney. If he hires anybody else, it tells me he doesn't want to get free."

"Interesting. He confessed earlier. If he hires the wrong kind of attorney, he'll get convicted. Erin will be free to live her life, and Clem will have saved his daughter."

Duke whined.

Wade stepped past me and opened the front door, allowing Duke to enter the house. "Thanks for taking care of him."

"Anytime. He's a good boy."

Wade pulled out his wallet.

"It's on the house today." I jogged away before he could argue.

Our conversation confirmed Wade didn't believe Clem murdered his son-in-law. I slid into the Suburban with one pressing question. How could I find proof to help Wade and David without interfering in their investigation?

Chapter Thirty-Five

I LEFT WADE'S place and drove past Erin's house. A little flash of black darted in front of me. I slammed on the brakes and skidded to a halt.

Yip.

The bundle of fur raced to Erin's side of the street.

A car coming from the other direction screeched to a stop.

Another yip. The puppy made it to the front yard two doors down from Erin. I parked and jumped out of the Suburban.

The elderly man in the other vehicle lowered his window. "I never saw him."

"I understand. You okay?"

"Fine, but I can't run after a puppy. Bum knees." A blue-and-white handicap placard hung from his rearview mirror. "I'll wait here for you. We may need to take him to the vet."

"I'll do my best to catch him." I raced after the dog, who'd scampered into the backyard of Erin's neighbor.

Tricycles and bikes with training wheels were on the back patio of the white brick house that looked like it could use some fixing up. I checked behind the bushes before moving to the swing set in the middle of the yard.

The little rascal ran out from under the slide and darted to the yard next door.

"Hey, whatcha doing, lady?" A freckle-faced boy with two missing front teeth jumped rope on the patio of the adjacent house.

"Can you help me catch the puppy?"

"I'm not supposed to talk to strangers." He frowned. "Mom, there's a stranger!"

My face grew hot. "Go get your mother, sweetie. I've got to reach the puppy before he hurts himself."

The child ran inside.

A French gothic paneled fence around four feet high enclosed Erin's backyard. Brown steel patio furniture with thick beige cushions had been placed on a deck, along with a grill and a red bicycle.

Goose bumps popped up along my arms. A red bike. No way. The evidence had materialized right before my eyes.

The puppy barked.

Ignoring the potential evidence that could get Erin arrested, I returned my focus to the puppy.

The little dog halted at a clump of white pampas grass and sniffed.

I tiptoed close, while his attention was diverted from me. I knelt on the ground. "Here, puppy. I won't hurt you." I pulled a treat out of my pocket and held out my hand. "Here, baby. Come to me. You don't want that nasty stuff. I've got a yummy treat."

He turned on three limbs and cocked his head.

"Poor baby. You're missing a leg." I blinked back tears. "Please, let me help you."

He hobbled toward me with amazing speed and ate the dog biscuit.

I snatched him with my free hand. "Got ya."

"What are you doing in my yard?" A woman's voice verged on hysteria.

I shot her my best smile. "Do you know who owns this puppy? He ran across the street in front of me and another car. It's a blessing neither one of us hit him."

Her gaze never left mine. She didn't even look at the sweet little furball. "I've never seen him before. You need to leave."

"Aw, Mom. She's saving a dog. See how cute he is?" The little boy took a step forward, but his mother grabbed his shoulders and pulled him back so hard her braid flung forward.

The woman's eyes narrowed. "I don't care how adorable he is. We don't talk to strangers. Especially when they're in our yard."

I said, "I never would've come onto your property or spoken to your son if the puppy didn't need to be rescued."

"I understand, but I'd appreciate it if you'd leave now."

"Yes, ma'am. My name is Andi Grace Scott, and I'm going to take this little one to Doc Hewitt's office, if you want to check me out. I'm sorry for trespassing and upsetting you." I crossed the yard toward Erin's side and hoped to find a way to get a picture of the red bike.

The little boy said, "Lady, you did a good thing. God will be real happy with you."

I glanced back to the child. "Thank you. I needed a kind word today. God will be really happy with you, too."

I left before his mother called the cops. With the puppy secure in my arms, I turned my attention to Erin's deck. The red bike had disappeared.

Chapter Thirty-Six

AFTER GETTING THE little pup a clean bill of health from Doc Hewitt, I drove to my plantation with the adorable puppy in a travel crate. She was a mongrel with some black lab in her DNA.

We parked under the Spanish moss-draped oak tree near the dog barn.

Griffin appeared and opened the door for me. "I've got some plans to show you."

I smiled. "Great timing. I've got a surprise for you. Come on."

"What's up?" He followed me to the back of the Suburban. "Uh, Andi Grace, you've got dirt on your knees and shoulder."

"Not surprised. Now close your eyes."

"I'm not five." He shook his head.

"You're slowing me down."

He huffed but shut his eyes.

I removed the puppy from the dog carrier and gave her another biscuit. "You can open them now."

Griffin laughed long and loud.

The puppy whimpered, and I cradled her close. "Shh, you're going to scare her."

"No way. I don't have time for a dog. Plus, I'm living with Marc, who incidentally warned me you'd match me up with a dog."

"Look at this sweet thing. I'll help with training, but she needs an owner. I think you should name her Grace or Favor." I held the bundle of fur out to him.

He took her in his big hands. "What kind of names are those?"

I explained how she'd almost gotten run over. "It's a blessing she's alive."

The puppy nuzzled Griffin under the chin, and he laughed. "If you convince me to adopt her, Grace won't work. She's black as coal but soft as silk."

"You can't name her Coal."

"Midnight. Inky. Ash. Shadow."

She barked when he said Shadow. "I think you've got a winner. Put her on the ground."

With amazing gentleness, Griffin placed her in the grass.

"Now call to her."

He scooted a few steps back and knelt. "Shadow, come here girl."

The three-legged dog lunged for him.

He laughed and reached for the cute mongrel. "I don't know the first thing about dogs, and I for sure can't take care of a handicapped puppy."

"PCP."

"Say what?" His head was bent, and Shadow licked his chin.

"Physically challenged puppy. It's possible she was born with three legs and doesn't know what it'd be like to run with four."

"I'm not sure." He kept his eyes on the fluffy pup.

"What if Marc agrees?"

"There's still the issue of time."

"That's where I come into the picture. Each morning when you come to work, drop Shadow off at Stay and Play. We'll take care of her."

His focus was on the puppy. "Let me talk to Marc before I commit."

"No problemo." Matching the puppy with her new owner gave me joy. "You mentioned you had plans?"

"Boy, do I."

"Let's go to my office, and I'll find a crate where Shadow can rest."

"You're going to leave her alone? Won't she be scared?" Griffin held the puppy to his chest.

"She probably needs a good nap after everything she's experienced today." I headed to the dog barn with Griffin trailing behind. Once inside, I took Shadow from my friend. "Give me a minute."

He hesitated before handing the puppy to me. "You sure she'll be okay?"

"Yes. Trust me." It didn't take long to settle Shadow into her space with a dog pillow and a chew toy. "Sweet dreams, little one."

In my office, Griffin had laid out his sketches on my desk. "I hope you don't mind that I came in without you."

"I keep it unlocked so you, Dylan, and Juliet can come in when you need. I figure by being in the barn, it's protected, and I don't keep cash in here, so why not leave it open?"

He nodded. "Great, so here's what I'm thinking now. The old kitchen is a moneymaker. There are four points of entry, allowing us to turn it into four guest suites. They won't be huge, but it can work. Juliet's content in the main house for now."

"I'd love to turn a profit, but is it really possible after paying you to convert it?"

"I'll crunch the numbers again tonight, but at first glance, there's great potential. For starters, you've got good bones to work with." He tapped his sketches.

"Explain to me what I'm looking at."

"The main floor of the building can be divided easily into two suites, where you can accommodate guests. One will have a fireplace, and the other won't. The upstairs can be converted into two small guest rooms, but if we do two, they'll need to share a bathroom."

"What if we make the space one big room?"

"Perfect for families. There will be two bedrooms. The landing at the top of the stairs can be a sitting area with a small kitchenette, and the bathroom will be for the family."

"Marketing the upstairs as one rentable unit sounds more appealing to me. I know if I stay at a B&B, I want a private bathroom." I paused. "Did you hear me look at this from a business perspective? I might get the hang of being a business woman yet."

"Way to go." He scribbled notes on a fresh sheet of paper. "You had mentioned wanting a place for your doggie day care employees to sleep."

"Stay and Play, but go on." I studied his sketches closer.

"You know the old kitchen has been remodeled from time to time. The back porch has a firm foundation and is huge. There's also an outdoor shower. I think we can frame walls and create an en suite bedroom. It'll be small, like a New York City loft apartment, except no kitchen."

"As long as there's a bathroom, I think we should go for it."

"It'll have the essentials. Shower, sink, toilet. Like I said, the space will be tight." He sketched out his plan. "This is rough, but you get the idea."

"It's great. I imagine there are young single people who'd like to work with the animals and have free rent."

"It's a great perk. If you don't have any takers, I'll pay you to live here." He laughed. "I'm not out to waste your money."

"I like all of your ideas."

"Okay. I'll get a bid to you in the next day or so."

A dog barked in the background.

"Griffin, you're hired, but I'd like Nate to landscape the area."

The grim set of his mouth relaxed. "For real? You're not accepting other bids?"

I shrugged. "We've been friends forever. I trust you, and I know you'll do an amazing job on the renovation. If you give me an estimate, and I can't afford it, we'll come up with another plan."

"Thanks, Andi Grace. I won't let you down."

"I know. If you don't need me for anything else, I'm going to check on the dogs." I left him standing at my desk and made haste before I cried. After my parents died, many people had been kind to me. It did my heart good to be in a position to help Griffin.

Sunny, Chubb, Pinky, and Shadow needed attention before I checked on Juliet. Despite their different sizes, all of the dogs were still in the puppy phase of life, except for Sunny.

Shadow. Asher had seen a red bike in the tree shadows the morning Corey was murdered. I saw the bike while trying to rescue Shadow. Erin had moved the bike when I'd been distracted with the black lab mix.

Did she realize I'd already seen it?

I released the big dogs to the outside play area and leashed Pinky and Shadow. We strolled to the rice fields and back, which gave each puppy time to relieve themselves. I let the little ones play inside and watched from the fence.

I tried to call David, but it rolled to voice mail, and I hung up. Marc would eventually arrive to take Chubb home, so I decided not to disturb him.

Butterflies filled my belly.

Erin's next-door neighbors and I hadn't been quiet. Had Erin heard us and watched from the shadows of her yard? If she'd moved the bike, where had she taken it? Behind some bushes? It would've been too obvious to take it inside with a house full of guests.

Pinky and Shadow lay beside the dog teeter-totter next to each other.

I headed outside to check on the big dogs before going to find Juliet. If the B&B was going to survive, I needed to think about more than Corey's murder.

Chapter Thirty-Seven

JULIET AND I HAD dusted everything in the plantation house, and the kitchen was spotless by late Tuesday. Some of the work needed to be done after the weekend guests, and some of our cleaning burned off nervous energy. The political announcement was a great opportunity for good publicity for us as well as Hannah.

Plans were in place. If the weather cooperated, Hannah's announcement would be on the front lawn. Refreshments would be served inside afterwards where friends and the press could gather to get to know Hannah better.

Juliet and I arranged the furniture in the living and dining rooms for the large gathering. The doorbell rang.

"I'll get it." I left Juliet debating where to serve refreshments.

I opened the door and my heart fluttered. Marc had changed from his suit to jeans, a T-shirt, and a bright blue hoodie with up-and-down lines like a heart monitor and a white sailboat in the middle.

"I tried to call earlier."

"Really? Come inside." I pulled out my phone with a blank display screen. "Looks like it died. That could explain why I didn't hear from David."

"Whoa, what happened in here?" He stopped in the center of the living room and turned around.

"We're getting ready for Hannah's announcement. Where'd Juliet disappear to?" I spun in a circle. My friend seemed to be making a habit of leaving so I could spend a few minutes alone with Marc.

"Do you want to use my phone to call David?"

"Hey, he might answer if he thinks you're the one calling." My gaze connected with his, and it became hard to breathe. "Is it warm in here?"

"Feels good to me, but you've been moving furniture."

"Come back to the kitchen. I'll charge my phone and get a glass of water." I led him through the dining room and into the bright kitchen. "Are you thirsty?"

"No. Why do you need to talk to David?"

I plugged in my phone and launched into my story of finding Shadow and the red bike.

Marc leaned against the island. "You just happened to be driving down Erin's street?"

"I'd been in the area to walk Wade's dog and drove past her house when I left." I filled a glass with ice and water. "I'm worried Clem is going to go to prison for a crime his daughter committed."

"Not just any crime. Murder." He sighed. "Did you learn anything?"

I finished my water and put the glass in the dishwasher. "It can't be a coincidence Erin moved the bike while I was next door. Do you think she saw me?"

"It's a distinct possibility."

"What am I going to do?"

Marc placed his hands on my shoulders, bent his knees, and looked me in the eyes. "You're going to be more careful than ever. If Erin killed Corey, she could've shot you this afternoon. I don't want you to be her next victim."

My knees shook. "I'm not sure what my next move should be."

"David and Wade will find the real killer. Trust them." He wrapped his arms around me, and I clung to his strength. I'd been brave earlier. It couldn't hurt to lean into Marc's strength for a few minutes.

The back door squeaked open.

I pulled away from Marc as Juliet and Griffin entered. My best friend's eyes rounded, and she gave me a thumbs-up.

Griffin said, "Marc, you were right. Andi Grace rescued a pup today and is trying to convince me to adopt her."

Marc laughed. "You can always count on Andi Grace to take care of others. When we adopt her dogs, it's like she's taking care of us and the animal."

How did Marc know me so well? His words touched my heart because I never wanted an animal or person to go unloved.

Juliet tugged on her brother's arm. "Come on, guys. I need help setting up outside."

I dodged them and headed to the bathroom, where I splashed cold water on my face. The icy liquid removed the sting from my face and squelched the desire to cry.

Smitten. Worse than smitten. I'd fallen in love with Marc and couldn't deny it any longer. No matter how much time I spent working and staying busy, my heart longed for Marc. The man had been hurt time after time in foster care, and the father figure who'd shown him love had died before Marc finished high school. Even if he couldn't offer more than friendship, I still loved him.

There was a gentle knock on the bathroom door. "Andi Grace, are you okay?"

I exited and faced Juliet. "I needed a moment to compose myself."

"Do you need to talk?" Her gentle tone inspired me to share.

"Marc gets me, you know? It's like he can read my soul." I paused. "If I say more, I'll be a blubbery mess."

My friend hugged me. "Okay, but I'm here for you, too."

I squeezed and pulled back. "Thanks, but let's discuss the old kitchen. Did Griffin tell you our plans?"

Juliet hooked her arm through mine, and we traipsed across the main house. "He seems excited but wants to work out the finances with you before showing me his drawings."

"Are you comfortable in the main house?"

"Yeah, why?"

"One day I'll figure out a place for you to live with more space, but right now it seems like turning the old kitchen into guest rooms is the best financial decision."

"Don't worry about me. I love living in the main house."

"I'm glad, but if you need time away, don't hesitate to let me know." I opened the front door.

"We're good friends, and I'll always be honest."

There was no sign of the guys or the porch furniture.

Juliet started sweeping the porch. "They loaded their trucks and took everything to the old barn."

"How do you see the announcement happening?"

Juliet stopped her movements and gestured. "Hannah will stand on the third step. I think it'll make her tall enough to be seen but not so far up as to seem too good for regular people."

"She'll appear more approachable. You're brilliant."

"Thanks. The press will stand on this side of Hannah. Invited guests and family stand, or sit, over there. I haven't bought white chairs for weddings, so I'm renting a few chairs in case it's hard for people to stand. Hannah will make her announcement and answer questions, then we'll go inside for refreshments. The press can come inside, but no big video cameras. There's simply not enough space."

"Is Hannah okay with that?"

"Yeah. I was upfront about what we could reasonably do to accommodate her."

Headlights swept over the grass and trees. Marc and Griffin parked, and soon we all stood on the porch. Marc grabbed the broom and swiped at a spiderweb, where a column met the porch ceiling. "Got it."

"Yuck, thanks." Our hands touched as I took the broom from Marc. I shivered and blamed it on the cool breeze drifting up from the river. Yeah, right.

Juliet said, "Who's hungry?"

Griffin slapped his belly. "I'm starved." Griffin and his sister left us standing alone on the shadowy porch.

Marc backed away. "I've got a case needing my attention. A single mom lost everything when she hired a man to build her a modest home. He took advantage and disappeared with her money and more liens than I ever imagined possible."

"I'll get Chubb for you, unless you need me to keep him overnight."

"He needs to come home with me before he forgets where he lives, but thanks."

"Sure."

We walked to the dog barn in silence. A twig snapped and echoed in the quiet night. My heart lurched. "Did you hear that?"

"Yep. Feels like déjà vu when we were trying to find Peter's killer. Let's get in the barn."

We broke into a run.

Boom.

Frantic barking.

Marc wrapped his arm around my shoulders, forcing me to run faster.

Boom. Fizz. Whap. Sandy dust exploded on the ground in front of us.

"What is that?" I knew, but I didn't want to believe it.

"Somebody's shooting at us!"

Chapter Thirty-Eight

WE CRAWLED THROUGH the dog barn. "Do you have your phone? Mine's still charging in the kitchen."

"Keep your head down. We'll call after we find a safe place. Where's Dylan?"

"He went to visit his dad." Shallow breathing made me dizzy.

"Good. Any hiding places around here?"

On hands and knees, I reached up and pulled four leashes off a nail on the far wall. "Not that I know of. Let's take the dogs to my office. We can barricade ourselves in there with the file cabinet."

Marc said, "I'll get the big dogs and meet you in the office."

I attached the leashes, just in case, but I duck-walked, carrying the puppies to my office. Marc, Sunny, and Chubb entered right behind us, and I slammed the door before turning on the light. One advantage of a windowless office was the shooter couldn't take aim at us from outside.

"Marc, there haven't been any more shots."

"Either the shooter gave up, or he's coming in here to take care of us."

"Or she. It could be Erin."

"True."

I took turns stroking each dog. All of them panted, and somebody needed their teeth brushed. Shadow chewed on the hem of my jeans. "No, girl." I picked her up.

"Listen, I hear a siren."

I strained so hard it made my head ache. At last I heard the wail. "I guess Juliet and Griffin called for help."

Marc sat on the floor beside me. "This must be Shadow."

I nodded. "Poor little thing only has three legs, but the missing limb doesn't seem to slow her down one bit."

Marc lifted the puppy. "Hey, there."

Chubb climbed all over Marc's legs and licked his chin.

"You may have some sibling rivalry at your place if you allow Griffin to adopt Shadow."

Marc loved on Chubb. "Griffin already named this little girl, and you matched the two of them together. Of course Shadow's going to live at my house until Griffin gets a place of his own."

"You sometimes act gruff, but you're a big old softy." My voice wobbled with uncontrollable emotion. I couldn't prevent it, because Marc's kindness knew no limits.

He threw his hands up and grinned. "Hey, now. Don't be spreading vicious rumors."

The sirens grew louder then blipped. Car doors slammed and footsteps crunched the gravel. "Andi Grace? Marc? Are y'all in here?"

I inched open the door. "David, we're in my office. Be careful. Somebody was shooting at us."

The deputy appeared. "We've got men scouring the area. Let's move into the house. Juliet's worried sick. She said you left your phone in the kitchen, and she didn't know how to reach you."

"Sorry, it died earlier." Lesson learned. I needed to keep my phone charged or I needed to buy an external phone charger. "Is it safe to come out?"

"Wade's here and will help me protect you." He pressed his lips together and glanced back and forth.

We hurried to the entrance of the barn, where Wade stood with his gun out. David spoke to him in hushed tones, and before I knew it, we were all in the main house hugging each other. The dogs wound around our legs and barked.

Wade said, "There's a deputy posted on the front porch. Let's talk in the entry hall. It should be safe there."

Juliet sniffed and handed me a packet of tissues. "I was so afraid you'd been shot. How could we survive if anything happened to you?"

"I'm safe." I hugged my friend again. "Take care of Pinky. She's pretty anxious. Griffin, you need to comfort Shadow." I probably sounded like a bossy older sister, but the animals needed some love, too. It took a few moments for us to calm the dogs enough to carry on a conversation.

Wade patrolled the long front hall. He glanced into each of the rooms. His revolver was in the holster, but he remained vigilant, even when he paused to speak to us. "We received multiple reports of gunfire. Juliet's call was the most specific, and it made sense to come here."

Marc said, "There were two shots. One hit the ground in front of us near the dog barn. The other may have lodged in the barn."

David took notes on his phone. "We'll see what we can find. What direction did the bullets come from?"

"My right." Marc rubbed the bridge of his nose. "So north. The shooter was in the woods. I never suspected a thing."

David faced me. "Did anything related to the murder happen today? I saw you tried to call."

"Yeah, I didn't want to leave a message. It's too complicated."

He motioned with his hand for me to keep talking.

"I drove down Erin's street today, and a stray puppy ran into the road. The little black one with three legs. Anyhow, another car and I almost hit her. But she's okay, and Griffin is going to adopt her."

David huffed. "Andi Grace, can you speed this along? We've got a shooter on the loose."

"Right." I rubbed Sunny's head. "I hopped out of my Suburban and chased after the puppy to save her. She scampered into the yard next door to Erin. You'll find this interesting. There was a red bike on the back patio."

"Yes, but we already knew she bought a bike from HOSE."

"True, but it gets weirder. By the time I caught Shadow and left, the bike was gone."

"Meaning?"

"I think Erin saw me in the yard, and she hid the bike. She doesn't know I've been asking around. She may not even be aware Asher spotted a red bike. But she's smart enough not to take any chances, so while I was focused on saving the precious puppy, she hid the bike."

David continued typing notes. "We'll swing by and question her tonight. Did any of you see the shooter or a strange vehicle around here in the last few hours?"

Chubb walked from one of us to the next. Marc tightened his hold on Chubb's leash. "Sit."

I passed Marc a treat. "I'm sorry, David. The shooter caught me by surprise."

Marc rubbed Chubb's head before giving him the treat. "Good boy."

Griffin said, "Marc and I were driving around the plantation moving the outdoor furniture to one of the barns about an hour ago. I didn't see anything unusual."

"Me, either." Marc's relaxed stance reassured me.

I shook my head. "I've been so focused on an event we're hosting that I never considered watching for danger."

David said, "Juliet, what about you?"

"Sorry. I never dreamed we'd have a shooter on the property. Do we need to install a security system?"

Wade paused from his pacing. "It couldn't hurt. Get one of my men to offer suggestions where to place outdoor cameras."

Another expense. Fantastic. Little by little my inheritance covered various expenses. Would I be smart enough to make the plantation a success before I spent all of Peter's money?

Marc gave my shoulder a reassuring squeeze. "Is Juliet safe here tonight? What about Andi Grace? Can she go home?"

David said, "I'll leave two deputies here, but we're a small force. Andi Grace, can you stay here tonight?"

"Yeah." I removed my phone from my pocket. "I'll also ask Nate to come out and spend the night." I texted him.

"Perfect. We'll have patrols go by your place on the island, but you'll be safer here tonight."

My phone vibrated in my hand. **On the way.**

"Nate's coming over. Will you let your deputies know to expect him? He should be driving a white pickup with his landscaping logo on the sides of his truck."

"Done."

"David, we've got an event tomorrow morning. Will it be safe, or should we reschedule?" I needed the money Hannah's announcement would bring, but I didn't want to put anybody at risk.

He scratched the back of his head. "You're the target. Not Hannah Cummings."

Juliet's jaw dropped. "How'd you know?"

David laughed. "You'd be amazed at the secrets I carry. I'm heading to Erin's now unless there's anything else I should know."

"Can we take the dogs outside real quick like?" Quick wasn't possible with my shakiness. David was right. If there was a target tomorrow, it'd be me. Not Hannah.

"Sure, but there'll be two men on watch all night. If you scream, they'll come running."

The six of us walked out the kitchen door. While the dogs did their thing, David and Wade drove off with a spray of dirt and sand. Deputy Hanks escorted us inside, where we waited for Nate's arrival.

I sat on a chair with Sunny at my feet. "Marc, I know you have an important case to work on. Why don't you leave?"

"I'll wait for Nate." His stomach growled.

Juliet said, "That's my cue to fix dinner. I forgot about it once the shooting started. How about grilled cheese and tomato soup?"

I smiled. "My comfort food."

Griffin opened the refrigerator. "I'll help."

Marc sat beside me and took my hand. "We had a close call tonight. I don't like getting shot at, and I really don't like you being the target."

"I'm sorry."

His thumb ran along my knuckles. "It's not your fault, but the seriousness of this case escalated tonight. You shouldn't be alone. If I had my way, I'd lock you up in your house and not let you out until the real killer is caught."

I pulled my hand from his and tapped the table. "You're right. Clem's in jail, so there's no way he shot at us."

Marc held up his hand. "True, but it doesn't mean he's innocent of Corey's death."

"I never believed it was him, and you know this wasn't a random attack on us."

"I agree. It's related to Corey's murder."

"But? What's bothering you?"

Marc frowned. "Did the shooter mean to scare us or kill us?"

Chapter Thirty-Nine

I LAY IN A GUEST bed at the plantation's main house, tossing and turning.

After our light dinner, Marc and Griffin took off together with their dogs, and promised to check on us the next morning. In a few more hours, I'd see Marc again.

Nate had thanked the guys for their help before fussing at me for not calling him sooner. My brother had arrived with a supply of baseball bats and three containers of pepper spray he'd intended to give us for Valentine's Day. He'd also told us to scream bloody murder if necessary. He promised not to tease us if it was a false alarm.

Lacey Jane was spending the night with friends in Conway. They were studying for a big exam, and we didn't want to scare our sister. After the test would be soon enough to tell her.

Nate had elected to sleep on the longest couch we'd pushed to the side of the living room, and Juliet was in her bedroom with Pinky. Sunny and Bo slept downstairs with Nate.

I punched the pillow and glanced at my watch. It was already Wednesday.

Had the police questioned Erin? Had she denied shooting at us? Did they ask for her alibi at the time of Corey's murder? The days since his death had flown by, and I'd narrowed my suspect list. Despite Clem's confession, I continued believing Erin was guilty.

Indiscernible voices drifted through the stillness of the night. My heart leapt to my throat. Was it Juliet, or had somebody entered the house with sinister intentions?

Wearing an old T-shirt and shorts, I tiptoed downstairs toward the kitchen. Lights shone, and I peeked into the room.

With a wooden spoon, Nate stirred something in a large bowl. Juliet filled a muffin pan, and the dogs lay at the back door. So much for me thinking they were resting.

I backed away, not wanting to intrude. The floor squeaked.

"Who's there?" Nate's menacing deep voice would've scared me if I'd been an intruder.

"Just me." My voice squeaked.

Nate turned on the dining room light and faced me with an iron skillet. "What are you doing snooping around?"

Juliet joined us. "You liked to have scared me to death."

"Sorry, y'all. I thought I heard something and decided to investigate. Why are you up at this hour?"

Juliet shrugged. "I couldn't sleep. Baking calms my nerves, and I decided to make blueberry muffins. Come into the kitchen with us."

I followed them into the warm and homey space. "Nate, what's your story?"

"Couldn't sleep. When I heard Jules, I decided to help her."

"May as well put me to work since I can't sleep either." I reached for an apron with the B&B logo on it.

Nate chuckled. "You're going to help?"

"Shame on you, Nate." Juliet nudged his arm. "Andi Grace, can you wash and slice the lemons? Put them in one bowl then do the same to the limes. Next, the kiwis need to be peeled and sliced for a fruit salad. And if you really want to get adventurous, I'll give you the pomegranate to tackle for healthy parfaits."

"Ugh, they always stain my hands and clothes." I started with the lemons, while they worked on muffins. "I haven't heard from David. It's hard to believe somebody shot at me. Erin and I were friends growing up, and it's really hard to imagine she'd deliberately shoot me."

Juliet removed a pan of muffins from the oven and inserted the next batch. "Yet, you believe she murdered Corey."

"Well, yeah. He cheated on her, gambled, and stole money from Daily Java. A woman can only handle so much. Nate, you're a guy. What do you think?"

My brother set the mixing bowl on the counter by the sink. "If Erin tried to frame me for killing her husband, it stinks. If she's guilty of murdering Corey, it seems like she'd go to great lengths to keep the secret. If it means offing you to protect herself, it's possible. You're the one stirring the pot. You helped David find clues." He filled the sink with a squirt of dish detergent and hot water.

I wanted the killer to be Norris Gilbert or even Wendy. "I need to look at motive again. Who had the most to gain from Corey's death, and who wants me out of the way?"

Nate washed the mixing utensils and glanced over his shoulder toward me. "Clem confessed, so why come after you now?"

I tapped my mouth. Why indeed? "Suppose Erin learned her dad confessed to Corey's murder. If she blames me for the lie, it gives her more motive to come after me."

"Exactamundo." Nate washed measuring cups with a sponge. "Her anger turned to fury over her dad's confession, and she blames you. If she can kill you, it'll prove her dad's innocence and stop you from solving the murder. Two for one."

"How does my death prove Mr. Farris is innocent?"

Nate rolled his eyes. "He can't kill you from jail which means the killer is still free."

"Oh, okay." It didn't take long to finish the lemons and limes, and I rinsed my hands. There weren't enough words to describe how much I didn't want to deal with the pomegranate. Kiwis weren't so bad, especially if I used Juliet's fancy little kiwi slicer once I peeled off the brown fuzz.

I retold the story of rescuing Shadow. "Norris and Ivey were at Erin's today. If Erin killed Corey, the press will want to know why. Then Corey's affair with Wendy will become public. The press will learn more about Wendy, and a good reporter will discover she also had an affair with Norris. He can't let that happen. It'll damage his reputation and his marriage."

Nate said, "I landscaped the Gilberts' pool area last spring. I think Ivey had been to a chemo treatment, and a friend brought her home. The windows were open, and I overheard part of their conversation."

Juliet and I stopped working and stared at Nate.

He dried his hands on a towel.

My pulse pounded at my temple. "Don't keep us in suspense."

Nate winked at me. "One of the women said she'd made her husband sign a pre-nuptial. She came from old Southern money. If the marriage didn't work, she didn't want to lose the family fortune. The way she spoke, I felt like it was Ivey."

"Why?" I stepped closer, in order not to miss a word.

"She told the other woman she'd changed her will. Her husband had cheated but claimed the affair was over. She didn't know if she believed him, but fighting cancer took all of her strength. There was no energy left over for a divorce, but in case she died, the new will would protect her family."

I pulled a notepad and pen from the junk drawer. "Norris told Ivey he wasn't seeing Wendy any longer, but we know the affair hadn't ended.

Norris needs to be super careful to keep his secret. Hence, the secret apartment."

The oven beeped, and Juliet removed another batch of blueberry muffins. "I may as well start a pot of coffee. At this rate, none of us will get any sleep tonight. Andi Grace, continue."

I wrote my thoughts in bullet points. The nutty aroma of coffee helped me think more clearly. "One way to prevent Erin from getting arrested is to find a schmuck to confess. Enter Clem."

Juliet set three cups and two travel mugs on the counter. "Poor Clem."

Nate shook his head. "Who better to convince than a loving father?"

"Right. Norris confides to Clem he's concerned the sheriff suspects Erin. The only way to protect her is if the real killer confesses. Norris must have laid it on thick, because right after the funeral, Clem turned himself in."

Nate pulled creamer from the refrigerator, and Juliet placed a sugar bowl next to the cups.

"Norris is the most despicable man I know. How could he treat his best friend so horribly?"

Juliet poured coffee. "Don't forget lying to his wife about the affair with Wendy."

I pointed to the travel mugs. "What are those for?"

"I thought the deputies might be cold." She dropped sugar packets and creamer tubs into a plastic sandwich bag along with stirring sticks then trotted outside.

I grabbed Nate's arm, preventing him from pouring creamer. "What are you waiting for?"

His eyes widened. "Say what?"

"Have you told Juliet you care about her?" I kept my voice low.

"It'll never work." He looked at the floor.

"Why not?" I didn't lessen my grip.

Nate glared at me. "I don't have enough money to court a woman like Juliet. Plus, she's too good for me. She's a Christian and always doing nice things for others. I mean, who thinks about the cold deputies outside? I'm not worthy of her."

"I've got news for you, little brother. She's crazy about you. Get your act together and ask her out." I didn't know whether to hug him or shake him.

"How do I get the courage to date a person as wonderful as Jules?"

"The same way Juliet handles situations. Pray about it."

Juliet breezed into the kitchen. "Did I miss something?"

I let go of Nate. "I'm going to take my coffee upstairs. Some doctor on the news claims if you drink coffee before a nap, you'll wake up refreshed and ready for anything."

"That's a lot to ask of one cup of coffee." Juliet giggled.

I grinned at her then shook my finger at Nate. "You two need to talk without my interference."

Juliet tugged on her ear. "What?"

Nate closed his eyes. "Go to bed, sis."

Sunny followed me to the bedroom.

I patted the empty side of the bed. "Come on, girl. I know dogs aren't allowed in the upstairs rooms, but it's officially my house."

Owning the inn was a privilege, just like owning Daily Java. Erin must have been infuriated when she discovered Corey's embezzlement. Plus, his affair. Which cruel act did she discover first? Had she confided in anybody besides Norris?

I opened the duffle bag I always kept in the Suburban for possible work emergencies. More than once an untrained dog had surprised me by pulling on the leash, causing me to fall and get dirty. Other times I'd had to chase dogs and gotten sweaty. Inside were three extra T-shirts, a change of underwear, shorts, extra socks, and a pair of flip-flops. I slipped on the biggest shirt and jumped into bed.

Sunny snored beside me while I sipped my coffee.

Corey had a habit of alienating others. Erin had been popular in high school, but who were her current friends? Did she see herself as a failure? Had Corey spun some kind of tale to make her doubt her abilities? I'd assumed running a business had consumed Erin's free time, but maybe her husband had isolated her when she wasn't at Daily Java. It could explain why she'd spent so much time at the coffee shop. Poor Erin.

Still, even if Corey had been a terrible husband and stolen the inheritance she'd received from her grandmother, it didn't give Erin the right to kill him.

As soon as we finished with Hannah and the press conference, I'd find a way to prove Erin was guilty.

Chapter Forty

I RACED INTO THE kitchen with Sunny on my heels. "Juliet, I need a hot cup of good-morning-sleepyhead."

"You might want to finish buttoning your blouse because we have company." She nodded to the table where Nate, Griffin, and Marc sat.

I squealed and ran out of the room and upstairs. Of all the mornings to oversleep and cavort around the plantation house without being fully presentable. I finished buttoning the light pink silk blouse Juliet had loaned me and zipped her slim black skirt. Her black pumps pinched my little toes, but there wasn't time for me to drive to town and change into my own things. Besides which, my clothes weren't as nice as Juliet's. Dogs didn't care what I wore as long as I showed up. A political announcement deserved better attire than jeans and a shirt.

"Oh, no." I checked my phone calendar. Had I forgotten anybody? No appointments until the afternoon. I texted Dylan who'd gone to visit his dad. **When do you get home?**

In no time he replied. Home? Cool. You're the sister I never had. I'm driving now and texting with my voice. Eyes on the road.

Be safe and check in with me when you get back. Thanks. Aw, he thought of me like family. I loved how he made sure I knew he wasn't driving and texting.

I studied my reflection in the mirror. Clothes perfect. Hair a disaster. Leaning over, I brushed it and righted myself. "Messy bun it is." After a few adjustments, I walked as fast as possible in heels without killing myself. I'd take cross trainers any day.

Marc stood at the island when I returned to the kitchen. "Coffee? Or what'd you call it earlier? A cup of good morning?"

I smiled. "You left off sleepyhead. Where's everybody?"

Marc poured coffee into a mug, allowing enough room for me to add cream and sugar. "Juliet took coffee and muffins to the deputies. Nate and Griffin are taking care of all the dogs."

I doctored my coffee and sniffed it before taking the first sip. "Ah, wonderful."

"You look pretty this morning."

I flushed. "This all belongs to Juliet. Even the shoes. You know me, I wear practical clothes."

"I didn't say the outfit was pretty. You are." He propped a hip against the counter.

Nobody else was in the kitchen, so he had to be talking to me. "Thanks."

"I heard y'all had a late night."

"No kidding." I took another sip and closed my eyes.

Marc chuckled. "Are you going to fall asleep drinking your coffee?"

I smiled and met his gaze. "I'm savoring the moment. Were you able to work on your case last night?"

"I pulled an all-nighter, but I'm ready to go."

"Stupid shooter. I'm so sorry."

"I'm glad I was here." He lifted a mug to his perfect lips.

I caught myself staring and averted my eyes to the vintage blue-and-white pedestal dish holding mini muffins. "Do you have a busy day?"

"I cleared this morning so I could be here for Hannah's announcement. Put me to work if you need help." His early morning rasp could grow on me.

I met his gaze. "It's supposed to be a beautiful day, so we'll start in front of the house and move inside for refreshments afterward. I think we've got it handled."

"I'm sure you do, but I'd also like to hear what Hannah stands for." His gray eyes sparkled, flabbergasting me. Was I missing a subliminal message?

I lifted my chin, pretending I wasn't clueless. "If you're going to be here this morning, why don't you board Chubb for the afternoon?"

"Thanks. I hate for him to get lonely." He refilled his cup. "But I don't want to take advantage of your kindness."

"Marc, you can bring Chubb over every single day if you want. No charge." Taking care of a dog I'd persuaded him to adopt was no big deal.

"Su-weet." He reached for my hand. "Andi Grace, we need to talk."

My mouth grew dry. Good or bad talk? "Okay. Now?"

"After work because I don't want to be rushed. Do you have time tonight?"

"Sure." The word came out breathy, like Marilyn Monroe, which was *très embarrassant.*

Juliet opened the back door and breezed in, carrying two travel mugs. "The air is brisk, but the sun is shining. Yay."

Marc grinned. "Definitely tonight so we won't get interrupted."

"Tonight it is." I sipped my coffee.

Juliet left the mugs in the sink and stood in front of us. "The first van is here from the press. Can you text Hannah? I'm sure she wanted to arrive before the reporters."

"On it." I texted Hannah.

My friend pointed to Marc. "Will you help Griffin set up chairs?"

"Yes, ma'am." He saluted and disappeared.

Nate entered the kitchen. "Ladies, the dogs had a walk, breakfast, and another walk. No wonder you're so fit, Andi Grace. They're comfortable in the barn, and I'm ready to pitch in. What next?"

My phone vibrated with a text. "Hannah's on River Road and will be here soon."

Juliet said, "Nate, will you direct people where to park? Not too close to the house."

"Sure." He disappeared, and the front door slammed a few seconds later.

I slurped the last of my coffee and filled the dishwasher. "We can hand wash these later, but out of sight makes us look more professsional."

"When Hannah gets here, take her upstairs to freshen up. Whatever she needs, handle it." Juliet's head jerked up. "Please."

"You can count on me." I waited on the front porch until Asher dropped Hannah at the bottom of the stairs.

She joined me, carrying a bag and feminine briefcase. "I can't believe two TV stations are already here. I've still got thirty minutes."

"Don't worry. Juliet can handle the press. We've got a room where you can dress, breathe, pray, or whatever. Do you need anything to drink?"

"No thanks. I drank water on the way here."

"Follow me." I took her to a guest room with a queen-sized walnut cannonball bed. "There's an attached bathroom. What can I do for you?"

Hannah patted her cloth duffle bag. "I'm good."

"I'll wait for you on the landing. Do you want us to introduce you?"

"Dad will handle the introductions." She placed her hand over her stomach. "I've got butterflies."

"You're going to be great. I'll be right here in the hall." I closed the door and sat on an antique wood chair with steel blue fabric on the seat. My eyes drifted shut.

Hannah said, "I'm ready. Dad's going to meet us at the front door."

I jerked and felt my face for drool. Nice and dry, thank goodness. "Awesome."

"I was surprised how many sheriff's vehicles were here when we arrived. I never considered security."

"You can't be too safe these days." Telling Hannah about the shooter wouldn't help her nerves, but I'd be honest as soon as the event ended. If she was angry, I'd refund her money.

Asher stood in the foyer with his hands behind his back.

Did we have enough law enforcement on site? Presidents Garfield, Lincoln, Kennedy, and Senator Robert F. Kennedy had all been assassinated. Over a dozen other presidents had attempts made on their lives. They were the bigwigs, though. Was it crazy to be afraid a person might try to kill Hannah? This early in the game, nobody knew what she stood for.

"You look beautiful, darling. You're going to kill it." Asher beamed at his daughter.

I shivered at his choice of words.

"Thanks, Daddy." Hannah swept past me and moved outside with her dad.

I joined Marc standing along the fringe of supporters in the grass. "Nice crowd."

"Asher is well-known and respected. I'm sure he's pleased with the turnout." Marc kept his voice soft.

I tried to smile, but my facial muscles felt stiff.

"What's wrong?"

"I'm not sure. Where are the deputies?"

Marc surveyed the area. "I see one near the camera crew. The other officer is bound to be nearby. Relax. Everything is running smoothly."

"Yeah, maybe you're right."

"Are you still spooked by last night's shooting?"

"It's possible." The vehicles parked behind us mostly consisted of TV station vans, pricey sedans, and SUVs. A metallic-colored Lexus was parked in back. "Is Norris here?"

"Not that I'm aware of. I haven't seen him or his wife. Why?"

"I'm sure it's a coincidence. He can't be the only person who drives a Lexus."

"Rylee drives a black one."

"Your office manager?" My voice squeaked, and a man turned to stare at me.

Marc placed a finger in front of his mouth. "Shh. Yes."

Asher held out a hand to Hannah. "Ladies and gentlemen, may I present Hannah Cummings."

People clapped and cheered.

Marc slipped his arm around my shoulders.

Hannah had parted her shoulder-length brown hair down the center. Subtle highlights accentuated her flawless complexion. She smiled, and a hush spread over the crowd. "I appreciate y'all coming out today. As my father told you, I'm running for the office of state representative. I love South Carolina, and I love you. I will protect the coast of Heyward Beach by voting no for off-shore drilling. I will find ways to bring more tourists to the area, providing jobs for our people. The children are our future. I'll vote to increase school funding and work with law enforcement to stop drug abuse."

The crowd cheered for a moment then grew quiet, allowing Hannah to continue.

I watched individuals for frowns and guns. People smiled and nodded, making me feel ridiculous for considering an assassination attempt against Hannah. Her personality was warm and down to earth. There wouldn't be a shooting at my plantation today. I blamed my jitters on lack of sleep.

I relaxed against Marc and focused on Hannah's words until she invited everybody into the house for refreshments.

Juliet stood beside Asher and raised her hands, attracting the attention of our visitors. "Because we're an old plantation, we have lots of antiques in the main house. The press is welcome to come inside and visit with future Representative Hannah Cummings, but there's not room for your equipment. Only small cameras are allowed. I hope you understand."

Despite mild grumbling from the press, the announcement didn't stop them from entering the house. The cameramen strode to their respective vans and stowed their big equipment.

I smiled at Marc. "I could use some help with the food. Can you stay, or do you need to get to work?"

"I'm here for the morning."

"Nice. Mingle a bit. I'll let you know when I need your help." I circled the yard to the back door and entered the quiet kitchen.

Juliet emerged from the dining room entrance. "I've filled the coffee urns, and the trays are loaded. Can you keep an eye on the punch while I brew another pot of coffee?"

"Sure."

In the dining room, guests filled their plates with muffins and fruit. Griffin ladled punch into glass cups, and Nate manned the coffee station. Across the room, Marc was in conversation with a couple I'd never met. It was always easy to spot him because he stood over six feet tall. His hair was darker now than it'd been in the summer, but I suspected the sun would lighten it again when the weather warmed.

Marc turned and caught me watching him. My heart careened against my ribs at his nod and smile. Ooh, la, la. The man was *très beau.*

I smiled back. He was always kind to me, but how did he feel? No matter how innocent his touches were, they never failed to produce a chemical reaction on my part.

Marc claimed he wanted to have a conversation, but what about? Did he sense I cared more for him than he did me? That would be the ultimate humiliation. Years earlier, the entire population of Heyward Beach knew my mortification of being dumped by my long-time boyfriend after my parents died. Heartbreak upon heartbreak. I'd practically been a kid then. It might be best to avoid relationships altogether.

Me and my dogs. Instead of an old maid cat lady, I'd be a spinster dog woman who would never knit. I'd watch TV mysteries while drinking ice cold Cokes or flavored coffee and walk my dogs on the beach between shows.

"Andi Grace, what are you doing?" Juliet hissed.

"I, uh—" Daydreaming wouldn't be a good answer. "I'm going to get more punch for Griffin. They sure are thirsty this morning." I hurried to the kitchen before I got on Juliet's last nerve. In the refrigerator were large pitchers of punch, and I pulled one out. After stirring it with a wooden spoon, I carried it to the crowded dining room.

It seemed as if close to a hundred people had squeezed into the small space.

"Andi Grace, I thought I spotted you." Frank Hoffman blocked my path to Griffin. "This is quite the shindig you got going."

"Thanks. This is our first event since we started the bed and breakfast." I relaxed and smiled at the older man.

Somebody jostled me from behind.

"Excuse me, Frank. I need to get this over to the punch bowl."

"The muffins were delicious. I think you gals will be a big hit."

Wasn't he just the nicest man? "If you have time to stick around, I'd love to show you the dog barn."

"I got nothing but time." His answer confirmed my suspicion. Frank was lonely and not ready to call it quits.

"Wonderful. I'll look for you after the crowd dies down." I wiggled through the people, getting jostled each step of the way.

A few feet before I reached Griffin, a man backed toward me. I dodged right to avoid a collision. The guy, wearing a white polo shirt, pointed his phone toward Hannah and kept backing my way.

"No." I gripped the pitcher full of punch tight. "Stop."

"What?" The phone guy jerked around with his arm still straight out, and slammed into the pitcher. Red liquid drenched my pink blouse. Er, Juliet's blouse. I wanted to disappear. Hannah was supposed to be the center of attention. Not me looking like a doused doggie.

Chapter Forty-One

ICY LIQUID CHILLED my skin. I yelped. Griffin lunged for the pitcher and snatched it from my hands. I teetered in the high heels and fell on my rear end into a puddle of party punch. If I hadn't been cold before, this sealed the deal.

The room grew silent. All eyes were on me.

Marc appeared with an outstretched hand. "You okay?"

"Just dandy." I stood in what remained of the puddle of punch.

Juliet's eyes had never been so wide, and her mouth hung open.

Marc said, "Folks, let's move this to the other room. The front porch is also available if you don't mind the cool air."

People moved away from the disaster, leaving us alone in the dining room to assess the damage.

The man who'd plowed into me shrugged. "Sorry about that. You know the story always comes first." A local TV station logo was stitched on the front of the solid polo of the middle-age man with yellow teeth and a beer belly.

"Make sure I'm not the story." I glanced at the mess. Blouse, skirt, and shoes were all probably ruined. The worst part was I'd borrowed the clothes from my best friend.

Juliet, Nate, and Griffin joined Marc and me.

I avoided eye contact with Juliet. "I need to get out of these sticky, wet clothes. Can you guys move the tables to the living room or front hall? I'll run upstairs and change then come back to help."

They agreed and moved away, leaving me to stand alone in the punch puddle. I slipped out of the shoes and tiptoed upstairs to my room from the previous evening. I surveyed myself in the bathroom mirror. "What a disaster." Even my hair was damp from the punch, which left me with no choice other than to take a quick shower and dress in my regular clothes.

I studied my reflection once more. Who was I kidding? I didn't belong on the plantation. Wearing fancy clothes wasn't my style. There'd be no more seesawing back and forth on making a wise decision. Peter left his estate to me as a gift. Not a burden. No more worrying about the money I'd lose by not selling my cottage.

Whatever estimate Griffin gave me to renovate the old detached kitchen, I'd find a way to make it work. Griffin needed a job in Heyward Beach, and I could help him get started. Juliet longed to have her brother around, and I had a way to make it happen. But I'd be smart. There had to be a way for all of us to be happy.

Please, God, help me make this happen. I can't do it without you.

I was a sea-loving beach girl. I'd live on Heyward Beach and work at Stay and Play. An unexplainable peace settled over me. I carried my duffle bag into the bathroom and turned the valve in the shower to hot. Before long, steam appeared and I hopped in. My worries swirled down the drain, along with the sticky punch.

After the shower, I dressed in my extra dog walking clothes and braided my hair. Presentable for cleaning up the party mess.

I hurried to the kitchen. Bags of garbage and recycling sat by the back door. Unwilling to embarrass myself further by returning to the party, I carried the bags outside to the shed Dylan had built. One bin for recycling and one for trash. I disposed of the bags in the proper containers.

A dog howled, then the others barked. Deep sounds mixed with higher pitched yelps. Not happy barks. It made sense the puppies might bark incessantly, but Sunny's deep woof was unmistakable. I'd heard of a fox in a henhouse, and with all the commotion coming from the dog barn, there had to be something invading their space.

Dealing with wild critters wasn't my area of expertise, but the dogs needed me to protect them. I strode across the grassy area until I reached the entrance. I stopped dead in my tracks. The barn door stood wide open. Chills raced up my spine.

The cacophony continued.

Nothing was going to hurt them on my watch. I crept through the opening toward the dog kennels. Unsure what awaited me, I grabbed the long-handled pooper scooper hanging on the wall. The serrated edges might scare a stray animal or rat.

I entered the kennel room.

"Andi Grace, so nice of you to join us." Wendy stood in the middle of the sparse room, holding Pinky and Shadow in her arms.

The puppies panted and struggled to escape.

Sunny's nonstop power barking should've scared the snot out of Wendy. If the kennel door had been open, there was no doubt my

German shepherd would attack.

"Wendy, put the puppies down."

She laughed. "Or what? You'll come after me with your plastic scoop thingy?"

It might be feeble, but it was better than nothing. "Please, let them go."

"Call off your German shepherd, and I'll consider it."

"Sunny. Quiet." My voice shook when I uttered the command.

My dog settled down, but Bo and Chubb continued barking.

I said, "If you let me give them chewy treats, they might calm down."

"Go ahead, but don't try anything sneaky."

Unsure how to handle the crisis, I slipped braided chews into each kennel and uttered soothing words to the dogs. With Wendy at my shoulder, it was impossible to unlatch the door on Sunny's kennel. "You said you'd let go of the pups."

"You never make life easy." She adjusted her grip on the puppies instead of releasing them.

"Why are you here, Wendy?"

"You've become a royal pain in my backside. A complication I never expected."

"You killed Corey."

"That's right, and I'll kill your precious dogs if you don't do exactly as I say."

"Fine, but tell me why." I gripped the ergonomic padded handle of the pooper scooper. No wonder she laughed. It wouldn't be much protection, but there weren't many options if I couldn't release Sunny.

"He rejected me, and you know what they say about a woman scorned."

"Fury. Got it, but now what?" I was desperate to get her away from the animals.

"You're going to disappear." Her toothy smile chilled me to the marrow.

"Why me?" I held my hands together and hoped she wouldn't spot my shakiness.

"Despite everything I did to make it look like Erin murdered her husband, the cops wouldn't arrest her, and you kept digging." Wendy's eyes narrowed. "It was only a matter of time before you figured it out."

The woman gave me more credit than I deserved. How did the red bike fit in to the murder? Clem had confessed to protect his daughter. "What about Norris? Does he know you're the killer?"

Wendy snorted. "I thought you were smart. Norris is like the conductor to an orchestra or the drum major to a marching band. Only he's more devious. You don't even realize he's pulling your strings."

"Is Norris here today?" I needed to keep her talking while I formed a plan of escape.

"No." Wendy moved to the dog food bin. "Open this up and dump the food out."

I followed her demand.

She dropped the puppies inside, and the poor little things yelped.

"Oh, you hurt them." My jaw tightened.

"I'll do worse than that if you don't back away." She yanked the lid out of my hand and sealed the container.

"No, they'll suffocate." I reached for the bin to peel the top off.

Wendy pulled a gun out from under her denim jacket. "Step back, Andi Grace."

"Did you shoot at me last night?" I only lifted one corner of the container before she pushed the gun against my ribs.

"If it weren't for my stupid allergies, I would've hit you. Watery eyes threw off my aim."

My legs trembled. "Yeah. You were close."

"You're not going to be so lucky today."

"If you shoot me now, all of those people at the main house will hear. You might think the dogs went crazy when you had the puppies, but if you shoot your gun, their reaction will deafen you."

"That's why you're coming with me."

Rule number one to survive being kidnapped was not to get in a car with your abductor. It stood to reason the same theory applied to my situation. "There's no way I'm leaving with you."

"Wrong. There's one thing I know about you, Andi Grace. You love dogs. All the years you came into the salon, you were always concerned about somebody's pet." She came closer to me.

What did animals have to do with Corey's murder? "I don't understand."

She aimed the gun at Sunny and placed her finger on the trigger. "I'm going to shoot your dog first and continue down the line until you agree."

"Stop. I'll go with you." Never had my heart beat so hard.

Wendy lowered the weapon mere inches but still pointed it at me. "I thought as much. Let's go."

I exited the room and paused at the play area. "If I'm going to die, will you at least tell me why you killed Corey?"

"I didn't go to Richard Rice Plantation with the intention of killing him. I'd planned to tell him I was pregnant and ask him to marry me." Her steps slowed.

"You're pregnant?" I turned to face Wendy.

She nodded.

"How do you know Corey's the father? What about Norris?"

"Norris had a vasectomy years ago, which leaves Corey. I was finally happy." Her face morphed into a dreamy expression.

"What happened?" Besides being curious, I still hadn't come up with a way to escape.

"I planned to surprise him with coffee and share the news. He was on the phone in the parking lot when I arrived. Corey hung up and told me he was meeting Asher and didn't have time to talk to me. I blurted out the truth about the baby." Her eyes narrowed.

"What'd he say?"

Wendy kicked the play area fence. "He said he couldn't afford to leave Erin. He'd lose everything if he divorced her, then he demanded I get an abortion. I'd never been so mad in my entire life. I told him Norris would take care of me and my baby, and Corey laughed. He said Norris would never leave Ivey for the likes of me."

"How cruel. I'm so sorry."

"I don't need your pity. I'm used to taking care of myself."

"Is that when you decided to kill Corey?" My eyes landed on the leashes. If I could reach them, it'd be possible to fight.

"It wasn't an actual decision. I just reacted. Your brother's truck was close, and I grabbed a shovel from the bed. Corey charged toward me when he heard the racket. He said something ugly, and I swung the shovel at him. You should've seen his eyes when he realized I was going to clobber him."

"I bet he was terrified. Why did you stab him?" I inched my way toward the wall with the leashes.

"Corey fell to the ground when I hit him, but he was still alive. I was so sorry, and I knelt down beside him. I told him I loved him and begged his forgiveness. Do you know what the big jerk said to me?"

"What?"

"He said I swing like a girl. And he laughed. Laughed!" She screeched.

"Then what?"

"I grabbed a pair of hand shears from Nate's truck and attacked

Corey. I didn't realize I'd started stabbing him until it was too late."

"Then you buried him in the mulch?"

"I needed to buy myself some time. With a strength I never dreamed I possessed, I pulled him a short distance to the flower area and covered him with the wood chips."

"Why'd you attack Nate?"

"I was afraid he'd see me and know I'd killed Corey. When I hit your brother, nobody complained about me swinging like a girl. The second hit knocked Nate out, and I ran."

"And almost crashed into Juliet and me."

Wendy aimed the gun at me. "Speaking of Juliet, we need to get out of here before she starts looking for you."

I raised my hands like I'd seen people do in the movies when a gun was pointed at them. "Where to?"

"I drove Norris's Lexus."

"Smart. It blends in better than your cute Bug." My heart surged. I was near the leashes. I lunged forward and pulled them off the nail. With a flick of my wrist, I threw one of the leather leashes forward and snapped it back like a cowboy with a whip.

It slashed across Wendy's arm, and she dropped the gun. It skidded across the floor.

I ran for her weapon. She was half a step behind me. I fell to the floor and grabbed the gun.

Wendy tackled me and dug her knee into my back.

Air whooshed out of me, but I didn't drop the weapon. Instead, I rolled over and kicked her shin.

She moaned but elbowed my face.

I pushed against her and scrambled to my feet, pointing the gun at her. My hands quaked so hard, it was doubtful I could shoot, but at least she couldn't fire at me. "Don't move an inch."

"You're too nice to hurt me, Andi Grace." Her critical tone didn't affect me negatively.

Calmness washed over me. "Wendy, you crossed a line when you messed with my dogs. Niceness left the building, and I dare you to try and escape."

Footsteps thudded behind me, and Marc appeared. "Whoa, what's happening?"

"Call David. Wendy murdered Corey and scared the dogs." The words left me breathless.

Marc pulled his phone out of his dressy black slacks and tapped on the screen before raising it to his ear. "Hey, David. Can you come to the dog barn? Andi Grace caught Corey's killer."

My legs wobbled like all get out, and my jaw throbbed.

Wendy held out her hands. "Listen, guys. You've got it all wrong. Andi Grace is confused. I didn't kill Corey. Erin did."

Marc said, "Save your breath for somebody who might actually believe you."

David appeared with his gun drawn. "Andi Grace, put your weapon down."

"Gladly." I squatted and placed it oh-so-gently on the floor, as Wade and Deputy Hanks arrived. Once Wendy was handcuffed and read her Miranda rights, they left the barn.

"Oh, no. The puppies." I tried to hurry to the kennel room, but every muscle in my body ached. Like a nightmare when you try to escape the villain, the faster I tried to go the slower I moved. "Marc, can you get them? She stuffed Pinky and Shadow in the food bin." I sat on the floor before I fell.

Marc left and reappeared with Pinky and Shadow. "Here you go."

"My hero." I kissed the puppies.

"Wait, if I'm the hero, why are you kissing the puppies?" He sat next to me and bumped my shoulder with his.

I turned my head and kissed his cheek. "How'd you know to look for me?"

"I thought you were taking a long time cleaning up from the punch spill. Mr. Hoffman asked me if I'd seen you because you were going to bring him out here."

"Yeah. I thought he might like to volunteer playing with the dogs." I massaged the puppies' ears.

"Always thinking of others." Marc took them to the little dog play area and gently set them down.

"Thanks for coming to find me." I stood and faced him.

"We need to have a discussion about your sleuthing talent, but right now I only want to hold you close." He moved close enough for me to breathe in his woodsy scent.

I slipped my arms around him. Regardless of the pain Wendy had inflicted on me, my heart sang. I was alive and with Marc.

"Andi Grace, I don't know what I would've done if Wendy hurt you." The scratchy, lower pitch of Marc's voice captured my attention.

Was I emotionally ready for this conversation after surviving Wendy? "She did hurt me. I'm going to have bruises all over my body. Some visible and others not, but at least the dogs are safe."

"Shh. I'm glad you're alive." He kissed the top of my head.

Tears sprang to my eyes. Yes, I was ready. "Is it too early to have our talk?"

More footsteps alerted us to the fact we weren't alone.

"Andi Grace, I declare. You liked to have scared us to death." Juliet elbowed Marc out of the way and embraced me.

Nate, Griffin, and even Frank Hoffman took turns hugging me.

"Nate, will you check on the big dogs? Wendy scared them all."

"Sure thing, Sis." He stepped back. "Griffin, you want to help?"

"Yeah, man. I need to see how Shadow's doing, too." He disappeared with Nate.

I looked at Frank. "I'm sorry for all the commotion. Can we reschedule for another day? I'm worried the dogs won't react well to a stranger after all this."

"Don't you worry a bit. I'll give you a call."

My gaze met Marc's. I was sinking, but they were all so happy.

"Time out, everybody." Marc formed a T with his hands. "Let's get Andi Grace up to the house. After her scuffle with Wendy, she needs to sit down before she crashes."

Juliet patted my back. "Of course. Let's find a comfortable spot for you, sweetie."

After three steps, my knees buckled. Before I hit the ground, Marc scooped me into his strong arms. "I've got you."

I closed my eyes, and the next thing I remembered was waking up in one of the bedrooms of the main house with Juliet and my doctor.

Juliet fiddled with the bedspread. "We all thought it'd be a good idea for you to get checked out before David grilled you on what happened this morning."

"What about the dogs?"

"We've got them taken care of. Relax."

Exhaustion and pain left me no choice.

Chapter Forty-Two

THURSDAY MORNING, I woke up in my own bed with the quilt pulled up to my chin. Sunny snoozed on the floor until I moved. She hopped up and licked my hand before trotting out of the room.

"Are you decent?" Marc called out from the hall.

I wore a T-shirt and yoga pants. "Come in."

Marc carried a tray with a small vase of daisies, a bagel and cream cheese, and an insulated pot of coffee. "I thought you might be hungry."

Sunny followed Marc back into my bedroom.

"I am, but I need coffee first." The sight of him took my breath away. I didn't deserve his kindness, but I enjoyed every moment with Marc I could get.

"I expected you'd say that." He placed the tray beside me and poured coffee into a pretty, delicate china cup sitting on a saucer.

I pushed myself up and fluffed my pillows then pointed to the tray. "Why so fancy?"

"After this past week, somebody needs to pamper you." He added cream and raw cane sugar to the coffee, stirred it, and passed it to me. "I'll be right back."

"Where are you going?" He'd just gotten here. I didn't want him to leave.

"Sunny, come with me. Chubb wants to play in the yard with you." He patted his leg and the two walked out of my room.

I leaned against the pillows and took the first sip. Bliss. Two sips later, Marc returned. "Why do you have on jeans? Why aren't you at work?"

"One of the reasons I opened my own practice was to help others. Juliet spent the night with you, and I've got the day shift." He poured himself a cup of coffee. "And before you ask, Nate and Dylan are caring for your clients today."

Chills crawled up my neck to my scalp. "Why? Is there something wrong with me?"

"Your doctor said you might be in pain after your fight with

Wendy." Marc pulled a wicker chair close to the bed and sat by me. "You were very brave."

"Yesterday is a bit fuzzy." I sipped my coffee. "The last thing I remember is Dr. Jaggers coming to see me. Oh dear, what will a house call cost?"

Marc chuckled. "Andi Grace, you have no idea how much people love you. She's not going to charge you anything for yesterday's visit."

"Wow." I finished my coffee and passed the cup to Marc. "I think I'm ready for the bagel. Tell me what I missed."

He passed the plate to me. "You might be fuzzy because Dr. Jaggers gave you a prescription for a muscle relaxer. You were loose as a goose."

I laughed. "Let me guess, another expression you learned from Bobby Joe."

He lifted his hands. "Guilty."

Pain zipped across my face when I bit into the bagel. "Ow."

He ran the back of his finger over my cheek. "You're going to be tender for a few days. I'll find something softer for you to eat."

"I hate to be a bother."

"How about cinnamon toast?"

"I adore cinnamon toast and haven't had any in forever, but first tell me what happened after I fainted." I fastened my gaze to his.

"Wendy was arrested, and Clem was released."

"The way you say it sounds rather anti-climactic." I sipped my coffee. "I still have questions."

"No doubt." He moved the plate to the tray.

"What about your important case?" I reached for his hand.

"I helped Juliet get you here and then I ran to the pharmacy to get your prescription. After I brought it by, I went to my office and met with the other attorney. It all worked out for the best."

"I'm so glad."

He disappeared and returned in a few minutes with two pieces of cinnamon toast. "This should be easy to eat."

We chatted about the weather, a new movie, and college basketball until I couldn't eat anymore. "Thanks, Marc. You don't have to babysit me."

"I want to spend the day with you. Case closed."

My heart warmed. "Okay. I'm going to get dressed."

Marc moved the tray to my dresser.

I stood, and a wave of dizziness struck me. "Whoa."

In a flash, Marc took my arm and steadied me. "Maybe you should get back in bed."

My vision cleared. "I'm good now."

Skepticism etched his face, but he released me. "I'll be back in ten minutes to check on you."

"Make it fifteen." I shuffled into the bathroom. My reflection in the mirror almost made me want to dive back into bed and hide under the covers.

Lands sake. Half of my face was purple, blue, and red.

Twenty minutes later, I sat in my family room with a blazing fire and a sitcom on TV. I'd taken a quick shower, dressed in jeans and a decent sweater, and pulled my damp hair into a ponytail. Marc sat next to me on the couch and rubbed my feet. Despite the aches and pains, I couldn't remember the last time I'd felt so relaxed. "Is there any coffee left?"

"Yep. Be right back." He covered me with an afghan and disappeared into the kitchen.

I closed my eyes while listening to canned laughter on the show. The doorbell rang.

"I've got it." Marc set a mug on the coffee table and answered the door. "Erin, I didn't expect to see you."

I froze. Why would she be at my door? My ears tingled as I listened.

"I came to apologize and at the same time thank Andi Grace. May I come inside?"

Marc looked over to me before answering.

My couch was positioned in front of the window on the same wall as the front door, making it impossible for Erin to see me unless she barged into my house. I nodded. "It's okay, Marc."

Erin walked over and perched on the edge of the slipcovered yellow chair, putting her less than a foot from me. Marc sat beside me, and an uncomfortable silence filled the room.

I stared at the fire. Erin had come here. It was up to her to get the ball rolling.

At last she ran a hand over her black silk slacks. "I'm sorry for getting so mad at you. I understand now that you only wanted to catch the real killer."

"I'm sorry Corey was a horrible husband, but he didn't deserve to be murdered. At first, I only wanted to prove Nate's innocence. But there are two things I never understood."

Erin's fists rested on her thighs. "The red bike?"

"Yes."

Her face grew pale. "I rode it to the plantation in order to spy on Corey. It was unusual for him to leave earlier than me, and I suspected he was going to meet Wendy."

"How'd you know where he went?"

"Phone tracker, and he'd mentioned meeting Asher at Richard Rice Plantation. Corey lied as often as he told the truth, making it hard to catch him stealing my money or having his affair. I felt confident he'd be at the plantation, so I headed there with my camera. I needed proof of his infidelity and planned to take pictures of him with Wendy."

I reached for my coffee. "Did Norris suggest you get pictures of them?"

Erin met my gaze. "Yeah, how'd you know?"

"He was also having an affair with Wendy." I explained what I knew. "What happened when you got to the plantation?"

"I hid my bike and hiked through the woods, trying to find Corey and Wendy." She wrung her hands and sighed. "When Wendy drove away, I thought I'd missed my opportunity."

"Do you know anything about the lipstick-smeared handkerchief?"

"It belonged to Corey. I found it and took it with me to confront him about their relationship. It must have fallen out of my pocket." She looked at the floor for the longest time. "What was your second question?"

"Why'd you buy drinks for Nate's crew last Tuesday night?"

She shrugged. "It's hard on your self-esteem when your husband is unfaithful. One of the guys flirted with me, and I felt good about myself. Pretty even. I didn't want it to end, so I bought them drinks."

"Erin, you're beautiful." How could she doubt her loveliness?

She stared at the wall and blinked a few times. "A cheating husband steals your confidence." She sighed. "I'm not proud of my actions. I think I went a little crazy, and I'm truly sorry for how I treated you and Nate. Can you forgive me?"

I placed my cup on the coffee table and patted her hand. "Fear can make us do crazy things. You're forgiven."

"I'd also like to thank you for defending my dad and catching Wendy. I owe you a lot."

"You don't owe me a thing. I'm just relieved Wendy's in jail, and I'm sorry for your loss."

Erin stood. "I'll be back at Daily Java tomorrow morning. Stop by anytime."

"Absolutely. See you later."

Marc walked Erin to the door, and I pulled the afghan up to my chin. He returned and sat beside me. "Are you up to a discussion?"

The timing of his question unsettled me. I crisscrossed my legs and faced him. "Is this going to be a lecture?"

"No lecture." He held both of my hands. "If you're going to continue tracking down killers, maybe you should become an officer of the law or a private detective."

His words shocked me. "But I'm building my business taking care of dogs."

"Does it make you happy?"

"I love the animals. So yeah. It makes me happy. I'm even thinking about how to officially match dogs with owners."

"Will you give up solving murders?" He released my hands and leaned closer toward me.

My face grew warm. "It wasn't my intention to get involved either time. It just kinda happened. I can't promise I won't do it again if a friend gets in trouble."

"I figured as much." He placed his arm across the back of the couch and played with my ponytail. "Will you agree to communicate better with me?"

"Sure."

"Promise?" His eyebrows lifted.

"Yes." My heart raced. "What are you suggesting?"

"How do you feel about me, Andi Grace?"

"I'm glad you're in my life, and I enjoy spending time with you." I avoided declaring my love for him. "How do you feel about me?"

"I may be in a different place than you."

The room grew hot, and I threw off the afghan. "Okay. I understand. You know, you can leave. I'm much better now."

Marc reached for my trembling hand. "You don't understand."

"You say I need to do a better job communicating with you. It goes both ways, Marc. I have no idea what you mean."

He stood, bumped his shin on the coffee table, and muttered, "I can speak in a courtroom because I've rehearsed what I want to say. It's different with you. I want to be open and able to tell you how I feel, but I freeze up and fumble my words."

It made sense his years in foster care would make him leery of opening up. I pushed from the sofa and gave myself a second to get stable, then stood beside him and placed my hands on his face. "You communicate in lots of ways besides words. Like this morning. The lovely breakfast amazed me. You've supported me in so many different ways. It's okay if you can't put your feelings into words, but I don't want to assume you feel one way when you don't."

"I care about you, Andi Grace." His hands went to the sides of my head, and he dipped his head.

Our lips touched, and fireworks exploded across my heart and soul. I reached up on my tiptoes, and the kiss deepened.

Much too soon, Marc lifted his face. "How's that for communication?"

I smiled. "Message received."

"I want more than friendship."

There was a knock at the door, and before we could move away from each other, Nate entered the room with Juliet. Nate held a cardboard tray of drinks, and Juliet carried a bag of takeout from Tony's Pizzeria. They stopped, with eyes opened wide.

Marc and I drew apart.

"Hi, guys." My face was warm.

"Should we come back later?" Nate stepped back.

Marc laughed. "No, come on in."

Nate and Juliet beelined it to the kitchen.

Marc gave me a gentle kiss. "Do I need to tell you how much I'd like to date you? As in consistently. I'm not interested in seeing anybody but you."

"Oh, Marc, I feel the same way." Hand in hand, we entered the kitchen.

I was at home in my beach cottage with family and friends. I'd found a direction for my career, and my future with Marc looked brighter than ever. Life was good.

The End

Acknowledgements:

My family has supported my dream for years. Nobody ever told me to give up. Thanks to Tim, Bill, Amanda, Scott, Kelli, Brooke, Allie and Cameron for your support. Thanks also to Dawn Dowdle, my amazing agent who took a chance on me. I also appreciate Debra Dixon and Alexandra Christle for believing in *Dog-Gone Dead* and helping me make it a better story. I can't forget Tina Russo Radcliffe who has supported me from the beginning. She's an awesome mentor, and I'm blessed to have her in my life.

I also appreciate you, the reader, for investing your time reading *Dog-Gone Dead*. Thank you so much!

About the Author

JACKIE LAYTON spent most of her life in Kentucky working as a pharmacist and raising her family. But she always dreamed of living on a beach and writing full-time. When she and her husband finally moved to coastal South Carolina, a change of jobs allowed Jackie more time to write. She loves her life in the Low Country. Walks on the beach and collecting shells are a few of her new hobbies she enjoys when not writing.

Dog-Gone Dead is the second book in Jackie's new Low Country Dog Walker Mystery series. Jackie also enjoys hearing from readers. Be sure to follow her on Facebook and her website:

jackielaytoncozyauthor.com